IT WAS SET TO BLOW, LOUD AND HOT

"Well, Agent Lemmon, I guess there's not much left to say except I can't recall the last time I saw a G-man walking around in rubber-soled combat boots. I didn't know government issues, the official kind, trooped around with compact submachine guns in special swivel rigging beneath oversize windbreakers. To answer your questions, yes, I have a major deal in the works that could change the entire destiny of the world. My employees were just chess pieces, pawns to take the fall while I rode off into the sunset. You know what my problem is—"

"I'm not your shrink, Colonel," Lyons interjected.

The Able Team leader was already searching for cover, aware that he and Blancanales were in a cross fire. It was something in Lake's eyes, a look, that warned Lyons to make a scramble to save his skin.

He was in the air, flying over a couch as the Uzi appeared, like some sorcerer's trick in both hands.

D0805241

DON PENDLETON'S

STONY

AMERICA'S ULTRA-COVERT INTELLIGENCE AGENCY

MAN®

RAMROD
INTERCEPT

A GOLD EAGLE BOOK FROM

WORLDWIDE®

TORONTO • NEW YORK • LONDON
AMSTERDAM • PARIS • SYDNEY • HAMBURG
STOCKHOLM • ATHENS • TOKYO • MILAN
MADRID • WARSAW • BUDAPEST • AUCKLAND

First edition April 2004

ISBN 0-373-61954-5

RAMROD INTERCEPT

Special thanks and acknowledgment to
Dan Schmidt for his contribution to this work.

Printed in U.S.A.

RAMROD
INTERCEPT

PROLOGUE

They knew.

He couldn't nail down, of course, the when and where he suspected he'd been found out, but Reza Nahru sensed the angry heat of a killing mood in the barracks as soon as he was roused from sleep.

"Get up! On your feet! The general wishes to speak with us!"

There was real menace, he thought, in the way his brother Iranians glanced at him, then turned away, a few of them wrinkling noses as if they were in a hurry to clear a bad stench. He was on his feet, reaching for his assault rifle when Bahruz Fhalid growled, "Leave it."

And then he knew he was a dead man, beyond any scintilla of a doubt.

Time seemed suspended, and he found it strange to the point of some peaceful, easy feeling how he could so calmly accept the inevitable, go and face down his own death. At least, he told himself, he wouldn't die alone, since he heard both men were likewise told to leave their AK-47s where they were leaned up against respective edges of their cots.

Small comfort. Dead was dead.

A moment stolen to look at Tabriz and al-Hammud, rising now from their cots under the dark scowls and black eyes of AK-47s, and he still couldn't help but wonder how his treachery had been uncovered.

It had to have been his CIA contact in Port Sudan or perhaps Khartoum. The secret meetings, accepting the envelopes of cash from the CIA's contract agent in Sudan, had been spied out somehow, by someone. Sudan, he knew, was crawling with Iranian agents, all manner of former SAVAK thugs, and he could have cursed himself for not being more careful in watching his back. Too late to kick himself now—clearly word of his deceit and betrayal had trailed him all the way down to Madagascar.

The sweeping courtyard was just beyond the door. The massive stone walls of the garrison, once home to French soldiers, would be smeared with his blood when he was marched out there to be shot.

Death at the hands of his own. Shot down like a mad dog in the street. A sorry testament, he decided, to a bad life.

A fitting end.

"A moment to pray?" he asked Fhalid.

"Be quick about it."

He slumped to his knees, shut his eyes, clasped his hands. As a Muslim, once devoted to God and his will, committed to prayer and to his faith, he had somehow, somewhere lost that faith, his belief in right and wrong, stripping himself of any sense of humanity. No, he wasn't one hundred percent certain on exactly where and when he had stopped believing in God, but supposed it had begun when he had left—abandoned—his wife and three children in Tehran, right after the way with the Iraqis. From there, a pit stop in Beirut, beefing up on weapons and intel. There, rallying an elite corps of freedom fighters, mapping out strategy against the infidels. Then on the Gaza Strip, where he'd recruited the poor, the angry and the desperate out of Palestinian refugee camps to blow themselves up in Tel Aviv, martyrs for God. There was also an American diplomatic entourage wiped out in Pakistan not long ago that he had played no small role in arranging. At least twenty of the men gathered in the barracks had also been part of creating slaughterhouses in six different countries.

And it was his knowledge of these incidents that had brought the CIA to his doorstep in Port Sudan, dark shadow men picking his brain, putting the ultimatum to him. Play ball or else.

They wanted names and whereabouts of his fellow brothers in jihad. They wanted to know from where recent shipments of high-tech weapons were coming from, to find their way into the hands of his fellow Iranians.

So be it. A change was long since coming anyway.

Sometimes, he thought, conversion of the soul just came to a man, a virgin bride eager to marry the one she loved, or sometimes the man actively and with passion he had never before known sought out the inner cleansing. Who could say?

But for some time Nahru had questioned the morality of the so-called holy way against the Great Satan. He asked himself if God was the creator of all men, why, then, would he want the blood of the innocent on his divine hands?

Silently Nahru asked God to have mercy on his wretched soul.

"Up!"

"We had a deal!"

Rising, eyes wide open, Nahru nearly laughed out loud when the moment of truth was revealed. The old Nahru would have unleashed a torrent of vicious cursing on al-Hammud. The new man simply felt a sense of curious relief sweeping over him. If nothing else, his own Judas would die beside him.

Al-Hammud began blubbering for his life to be spared. "You told me—"

Fhalid stung the man's face with a backhand that slapped flesh with the sound of a pistol shot. "Get these jackals out of my face!"

Nahru allowed himself to be shoved and manhandled through the door. He winced into the beam of white light striking him in the face as he stumbled into the courtyard. He was thinking to be shot couldn't be such a bad way to go. Quick, clean, fairly painless. One well-placed bullet through the heart…

The stench nearly knocked him off his feet. He heard al-Hammud scream out his terror next when he was pushed toward the trio of Madagascan soldiers. It was all he could do to keep the vomit from spewing out. The cattle carcass was still being gutted, long strands of intestines dug out by the soldiers with machetes ripping away, the dripping gore getting smeared up and down the long thin stakes.

Greasing the way.

Nahru felt knees buckle, his limbs turning to boneless mass when Fhalid bellowed the order to strip them down. The blows pummeled his head next, bringing on the stars and the white-hot pain. He was falling hard and fast, then became aware he was on the ground, face plastered in the red earth, hands like claws shredding his clothes.

Reza Nahru offered up one last silent prayer. He asked God to avenge the obscenity of his coming death.

GENERAL FATEH ARAKKHAN was a man without a country. It angered him to no end, this knowledge he was unwelcomed, unwanted in his homeland, not to mention he was a soldier being hunted for alleged war crimes. The rumor floating his way from Khartoum went that his own people, in their greed and hunger to become a prominent oil-developing and -exporting country, were ready and willing to hand his head over to the infidels.

The Arab-controlled north Sudan might be his home

of birth, but a few circumstances had recently dictated he find comfortable lodging someplace far away from Khartoum. One, the military and intelligence bastards and whores of the evil Western empires, he thought, had proclaimed him the Butcher of Southern Sudan, and before the United Nations for five years running. Second, a number of upper-echelon two-faced thieves in the intelligence arm of the National Islamic Front were more than irked that he had helped himself to what they claimed was more than his rightful share of Red Cross and UN planeloads of food and medicine, shipped to southern Sudan under some shaky international-relief agreement.

Yes, it was true enough he had strongarmed enough supplies, reselling them to Somalia—not to mention helping himself to a vast pool of oil money—and mounted a fat numbered back account in Switzerland. But how could a leader, he reasoned, ever hope to lead unless he could feed, clothe, arm and pay his own men properly? A soldier with an empty belly, with no money in his pocket to throw around on R and R... Well, a soldier stirred up with bitter malcontent meant mass mutiny could be as close as tomorrow's kneel to Mecca.

But the former number-two man of the National Salvation Revolutionary Council was working on his comeback. Someday soon he would return to Khartoum in triumph, and more than a few backstabbing colleagues would find themselves gored and suspended high in the air for all of Khartoum to gaze upon, the masses out there meant only to shimmy and shake in fear at the very mention of his name.

Just like the three treacherous Iranian jackals shrieking below, the future was in his mind's eye, and it was looking bright.

The general mounted the parapet, reveled in the screams of traitors. He was short, slightly built, but he felt like a giant right then, the center of grim and undivided attention, decked out in full uniform, epaulets, with ribbons and medals weighing down his tunic. He savored this victory, a vision of tomorrow, as they were raised and the bloody ends of the stakes were buried deep into the ground. Of course, the ankles required rope, fastened to stakes to keep them in the air while gravity did its gruesome work.

As in most countries where Europeans once trod, there was a language barrier. Madagascar was no different. He addressed the Iranians in English, aware most of the Madagascan soldiers had a working knowledge of the universal language. "Behold the fate of all those who give themselves over to the Great Satan like common whores. I am General Fateh Arakkhan, but you already know that. What I am to you is your ayatollah—or sign of God. Treason is unacceptable. Submission to my will is acceptable. You have been brought to this island to serve in what will soon become the mother of all holy wars. Yes, I know you have your own agendas, regarding your islands in the Strait of Hormuz."

The screams faded to bitter weeping as shock set in

and their limbs hung limply by their sides. "We must plan our futures together if we are to succeed in defeating our enemies. These three men were fools, with weak wills and deceit in their hearts. You can clearly see I still have friends in important places in Sudan, watching, waiting for my return." He glossed over the fact it never hurt to spread the wealth around, whether Khartoum or here in Madagascar, where he had the president tucked in his pocket, along with ranking Madagascan officers and about one-third of the People's National Assembly. "I am issuing the fatwa. Anyone who is not with us is against us. It cannot be much more clear and simple. Gaze now upon the fate of our enemies. That is all."

A moan of agony rose up from the courtyard as he moved down the parapet. He would need a few minutes at some point with Fhalid to discuss where it all went from there. For now he would simply let his actions speak the truth, revealing the future of his enemies for all to behold.

RYAN COLLINS HAD a lifestyle to maintain, and figured a measly quarter-million a year wasn't cutting it. There was the beachfront home in Malibu to consider. There were bimonthly trips to Hawaii, three sports cars to think about. There were two ex-wives with their hands clawed deep in his pockets, and their lawyers planted square up his butt. There was a mistress who had a coke habit....

Girls, girls, girls.

All things about the opposite sex considered, he felt right at home as he claimed a table in the far corner, eyes lighting up at the blond vision shaking and baking on stage. He caught a glimpse of himself in the mirror, the coiffed dark hair, the rugged movie-star good looks, couldn't resist a smile.

Feeling good.

He saw she was already cutting a beeline his way, all smiles, ready to rock, waving off the come-ons from the wanna-be lady-killers. He was one of the privileged elite clientele who had access to the back rooms. And why not, he figured, the kind of money he threw away in the place, a fringe benefit or two should always be on the menu. He was in a stressful line of work, after all, needed relief, and things weren't getting any less tense around the office.

Los Angeles was a party town, around the clock, and Collins was looking for some way to keep the good times rolling. He believed he had found the answer, only he was concerned where he might go with his information and who should get it.

And for what price.

Still, he was disturbed about recent events he couldn't explain, but his ticket to paradise was stashed away in the aluminum briefcase by his side.

And there were shadows following him. He couldn't see them, but three of his colleagues had gone AWOL. The past month or so had seen a few grim-faced robots—Terminators, he thought—lumbering around the DYSAT office in Century City. These days, he felt he was always being watched, since he was a top-ranking

executive with access to sensitive information to classified high-tech weapons, microchip processors....

Well, he had stumbled across the order manifests
and they didn't jibe with production output. Not only
that, but the end users—purchasers—were logged as...

He shuddered to even consider whom DYSAT had
fallen into bed with. Okay, he figured he could talk to
the president of the company, a former Air Force
colonel, and put the screws to him. It might cost him his
job, but if he made some noise about going to the Feds
unless there was ample cash compensation...

"Hey, cutie. I've been waiting for you."

Was it his imagination, or did Cyndy look especially
pleased to see him?

"Likewise."

"You want a drink first?"

"After."

She took his hand, leading the way. Paradise.

"You sound real horny tonight."

"Tough day at the office."

She seemed too eager to please, not even bothering
to relieve him of two hundred bucks first, but he figured
she was just hot to get it on. He trailed her through the
rear door, into a narrow, murky hall. He was grateful the
back rooms were nearly soundproof, blotting out the
thunder of heavy metal and the roar of hyenas in heat.
The only kind of noise he wanted to hear was her mewing for more. Down the hall to the last room, and she
opened the door. He was moving inside, looking from

the soft light burning on the nightstand, adjusting his eyes to the deeper gloom, when he spotted the shadow.

"What the...?"

"Mr. Collins. Nice of you to show up."

Collins felt his blood pressure rise like a war drum in his ears, heart pulsing with fear and anger. "What is this? I've seen you before."

"I left your envelope with the bartender."

Collins nearly bellowed with outrage as the whore simply nodded, not even looking at him as she left the room, the door snicking shut.

The Terminator rose, and Collins heard the dialogue leaping to mind, aware he had been set up, screwed. He was about to say, "I can explain," when the behemoth in a buzz cut pulled out a pistol and attached a sound suppressor.

"Your services are no longer required by DYSAT."

"Listen! No, I can—"

A chug, then the lights were punched out.

CHAPTER ONE

"You look like the messenger with bad news—and 'very' bad news."

Hal Brognola was fondling an unlit cigar as he rolled into the War Room at Stony Man Farm. The director of the Justice Department's Sensitive Operations Group swept on, past Aaron "the Bear" Kurtzman, the chief cyber sorcerer who was confined for life to his wheelchair, thanks to a bullet, and grunted at Bear's remark.

"Well?" Kurtzman pressed. "Did the Man give us the green light?"

The Man, of course, was the President of the United States, and half of Brognola's twin-bill duty was playing a critical role as the Farm's liaison to the chief executive. "We're sitting in limbo—still."

No thumbs-up from the Oval Office, and Barbara Price, the Farm's mission controller, groaned. "Unbelievable. Does he have any clue how hard we pushed, maneuvering all the logistical chess pieces, to get it at the doorstep of…this eleventh hour?"

The Justice man knew all too well how many hours— belay that—days the Farm team had racked up, the number of strings tugged, contacts cajoled, markers raked in from the Pentagon to Langley. It galled him alone to think Stony Man's elite commandos were poised on three separate thresholds, combat ready, chomping on prebattle nerves.

Waiting for the phone to ring.

The big Fed poured a large foam cup of Kurtzman's infamous coffee, then dumped enough sugar in the black swill to make it go down a little easier. "Five days, as a matter of fact, since we put this one on the drawing board. I don't mind saying I'm feeling the strain myself, people, and all the way to the hair on my toes," Brognola told the key players, grabbing his seat, dumping himself down at the head of the table. "The Man's as clued in like I was the burning bush to his Moses, all right, but he's firmly stated his concerns about what could become a whopping and ugly international mess."

"Welcome to the Oval Office," Kurtzman groused.

"I damn near said that. At any rate, it's why I've been at my office all day, waiting by the phone, lighting a few more fires around Wonderland." He glowered at the red phone on the table within arm's reach. "Looks like we're all still going to have to wait—if and when—for the tough choice to get made."

The chopper ride from his office at the Justice Department to the Farm in Virginia was roughly ninety minutes. But with only a catnap on the office couch, here and there during the past few days Brognola felt as if he'd just crossed three time zones, jet lag and ten years older. Tired as King Solomon perhaps over the folly and insanity of humans chasing the wind, on edge admittedly, and leaning a little to the mean side.

Brognola worked on the coffee, chomping his stogie, then said, "Okay, sitreps. I know we've run it down before, but maybe we missed something. A to Z. The basics and the particulars. Let's start with Phoenix Force. Barbara?"

The honey-haired blonde, who could have just walked off the pages of a fashion magazine and into the War Room, took up a remote-control box and snapped on one of the large monitors built into the wall. An enlarged grid map of Madagascar and the Indian Ocean to the east flared to life. "The hunter-killer submarine Seawolf *SSN 21* is submerged and still holding its position, forty kilometers and change from where Phoenix will be inserted on the eastern central shore of Madagascar. Sat imagery shows it's a remote area, with only two villages and a scattering of rice terraces, a solitary Catholic church along the march. It will be your basic grunt march—move fast and silent and avoid contact with the locals. According to our and the Seawolf's depth gauges and X-ray sat imagery of the water, the inlet's bottom is smooth enough, slanting evenly up to shore, no crags, no snags, to receive the unarmed torpedo that will carry their gear and weapons onto the beach. Something like an underwater surfboard, special delivery riding right up on the sand. Ready and waiting for them to finish out their swim."

Brognola grunted. "For some reason, I get damn nervous over the idea of inserting them by sea. I see twenty things going wrong all at once. Aren't those shark-infested waters? As in great white?"

"Actually," Kurtzman said, "the eastern coastline of Madagascar is called Whale Highway. Most of the marine life traffic is made up primarily of the larger animals, at least, namely migrating humpback whales."

"I hear primarily and actually and namely, I don't exactly get a warm fuzzy feeling, Bear. I'm not sure, but I don't think they teach wanna-be SEALs in BUDs what the hell to do—other than pray—when they see a sixteen-foot torpedo-like shadow coming at them out of the murk with bared teeth the size of a butcher's knife."

"Your white shark population sticks farther to the south, off the coastline of South Africa where there's an abundant seal menu."

"Why couldn't it have been an air drop instead of going out the hatch of a submersible?"

"A minisub," Price said. "Riding piggyback on the escape hatch of the Seawolf. A submersible requires a surface support vehicle at all times, often needs to be hooked by cable to the mother ship. The state-of-the-art Titan was designed by aerodynamic engineers for the specific intent of inserting soldiers by sea. It's not a

deep research vessel by any stretch. It's built for speed
and deployment of combat troops."

"I stand corrected. If I sounded like a grumpy old
man, Barbara…"

"I understand perfectly. Okay, Aaron and I ran down
the logistics, worked out the timetable from start to finish. Jack Grimaldi and a blacksuit crew are parked on
a military base, courtesy of our own State Department's
clout with a few government officials in Tanzania. Once
Phoenix hits the beach, Jack will be contacted by us,
hooked up on a three-way sat uplink with the ground
troops. The AC-130 Spectre gunship will take off from
Dar es Salaam, fly east by southeast, then due south,
move in, westward, once it hits their insertion point. Sat
imagery lines up the old French garrison, due west, approximately ten kilometers west of where they will
come ashore."

"And if Jack gets there first?"

"He'll fly a holding pattern, and hope. However, we
have this timed down to the minute, Hal."

"There was never any doubt."

"To answer your question," Price said, "about an air
insertion, we know the garrison has state-of-the-art
radar, sold to the government in Antananarivo—or Tana
for short—by France. We've picked up machine-gun
nests, but no antiaircraft batteries and no fighter jets.
However, if one of the terrorists is running around with
a Stinger when this goes down, the Spectre would be
history if it's wielded by even semicapable hands. Be-

sides," she added, a trace of sarcasm in her tone, "the former French colony has been attempting to go democratic for about ten years."

"How? By giving safe haven to a small army of international murderers?"

Price shrugged. "What can I say? All of us know graft and corruption don't care about the difference between communism, iron-handed dictatorship or fledgling democracy."

"I hear you."

Brognola heaved a breath, told himself to drop it down a notch, aware his jacked-up mood was affecting and stretching taut nerves all around.

Price rode out a moment of silence, then said, "The way I figured it, since Madagascar is an island four hundred kilometers from the east coast of Africa by the Mozambique Channel, and with what we have planned, an air drop sounded too risky. Too much open sea, to get them from point A to B. And the Seawolf was available. Going in by cover of the vast Indian Ocean, and at night, was the lesser of two evils. Once the dust settles and the smoke clears, an airfield about two hundred meters west of the garrison can accommodate Jack and company for a landing. Evacuation for our troops. And we assume, there will be some of the more notable terrorists left standing to be brought back to the States to stand trial for what we know is their involvement in just about every major terrorist attack around the world in the past ten years or more."

"We're assuming an awful lot, all of us," Kurtzman said. "We all know the President's position on this. He wants a few live ones to hold up to the cameras. Whipping boys or trophies, I have to wonder."

"I told him up front and in no uncertain terms I wasn't about to make that promise," Brognola said. "Could be why I'm getting the silent treatment. No way in hell am I putting Phoenix into the fire, working under the assumption these fanatics are just going to throw their hands up and let our guys read them their Miranda rights, recite Geneva Convention nonsense, chapter and verse and all that crazy shit. Besides, I have to agree with the Man to some extent on one point. A few songbird fanatics could have the mother lode of intelligence. Give me a numbers crunch on bad guys."

"Bear?" Price said.

"Two full squads of Madagascan soldiers. Thirty-four, now thirty-one Iranian fanatics."

Brognola raised a curious eyebrow over the smoke at the grim tone in Kurtzman's voice. "I get the feeling you want to tell me something?"

"I'll do better. I'll show you, live and in color." Kurtzman palmed his own remote and flashed on a sat image that made Brognola freeze as the steaming brew was being raised to his lips. "We have an ONI-1 satellite, courtesy of the DIA, parked in space over Madagascar."

Kurtzman muttered a curse. "There's our Butcher of Southern Sudan, hard at work, showing off the kind of talent he used on black Christians and the Sudan People's Liberation Army for some five years. Bloody animal. The UN puts his slaughter of mostly innocent women and children in the tens of thousands."

"A real charming piece of work," Price added. "Mr. Sunshine."

"So, who got to know Vlad the Impaler's loving feeling?"

"One of them was Reza Nahru," Kurtzman informed.

"That name sounds familiar."

"It should. He was tried and convicted by the Israelis in absentia for three separate terrorist attacks that claimed forty-three lives," Kurtzman said. "One was a busload of little else but women and children in Tel Aviv. We have also picked up from ONI-1 four other faces belonging to Iranians linked to bin Laden who were likewise convicted in absentia but by the Jordanians. Death warrants issued for these butchers."

"Which leads us to the task at hand, as far as the Madagascar and Sudan situations are concerned," Brognola said. "This General Arakkhan is no small fish. He still carries heavy weight among a loyal military faction in Khartoum who want to see his return to…well, the Vlad the Impaler glory days. The problem is the CIA contract agents who got us this far are disappearing all over Sudan."

"They were working on getting the Company a lead-in," Price said, "to where the shipment of high-tech weapons is located, or being shipped, which is rumored to be an Iranian-occupied island in the Strait of Hormuz.

Now, the rumbling I caught from Langley was that Nahru had jumped to the other side of the tracks, looking to deal or double deal. Who can say now? Obviously word got back to Arakkhan the impaler. Three less fanatics on the loose now, if nothing else. And with what we know about the situation in Los Angeles we can at least surmise the smuggling operation has its origins there."

"DYSAT," Brognola growled. "What do we know about them, other than three of their executives who went to the FBI have been abducted by the DYSAT mother ship?"

Kurtzman filled in the blanks. "Apparently they do classified work, chemical lasers, microchip processors for high-energy X-ray lasers. It took some digging and a few phone calls over to the Pentagon, but that's about as far as we got. Their only office is in Century City, Tinsel Town, which I find sort of strange, planting classified military think tanks in the heart of where all the movie execs and agents do their trolling and scamming."

"Go figure," Brognola said. "I read smoke screen, hiding out in the open. And by classified, I'm hearing you mean to say they are a black project."

"It certainly reads that way," Kurtzman went on. "Since the files I hacked into over at the Department of Defense are full of blacked-out words and whole deleted sentences about the pasts of the head honchos. The top dogs are former Air Force air commandos, nothing, however, untoward that would indicate they would be part of some conspiracy. The workforce is primarily civilian, Harvard, UCLA, MIT grads, pretty-boy types. We did find out DYSAT's production and research facility is located in Idaho."

"I don't mean to get sidetracked here, but can someone explain to me just what a chemical laser is?"

"Akira and Hunt," Kurtzman said, referring to Akira Tokaido and Huntington Wethers, two more vital cogs in the cyber machinery at the Farm, "could probably explain better than I could."

"Give it a shot."

"Well, since the genesis of laser technology some three decades ago, it would appear the research is on the verge of crossing the Rubicon. The brass ring of future high-tech is within grasp, or so it would seem. Basically, a laser weapon works as the transfer of heat to a target. It's a silent killer, supposedly, or so the scuttlebutt goes, which is capable of burning the eyes out of a soldier on the battlefield, and from as much as a hundred miles or more out. Meltdown, evaporation of anything the beam is focused on, no shots fired in anger. Only now the next quantum leap would be to use it on aircraft and missiles. Or even satellites. That's where the microchips come in to help get the bugs out of high-energy X-ray lasers. Now, the ones DYSAT have produced—or so our informants told the FBI—can locate, identify, track and intercept satellite transmissions, anywhere, anytime."

"And disrupt," Brognola said. "There is nothing

wrong with your television sets, NORAD. We are in complete control."

"In a worst-case scenario," Kurtzman went on. "What our three AWOL contacts told us is called Ramrod Intercept is currently on the drawing board and is designed to shut down early warning of ballistic missile launches or air attacks. Akira and Hunt get all worked up when they start talking about excimers, carbon dioxide molecular transfers and gas exits, but it's essentially pulse radiation from what I can understand."

"I get something of the picture," Brognola said. "We're talking about the next step in silent, invisible warfare. Warfare directed from space."

"Or even from the ground," Kurtzman said, "if you have the microchips, a computer, the component parts of what the missing informants called a roving command center."

"We still have three more civilian brain suits who hacked into the Pandora's box, right? These college playboys running scared?"

"Carl," Price informed Brognola, referring to Carl "Ironman" Lyons, the leader of Able Team, "states he has them under constant surveillance. Alive and well, I might add."

Kurtzman grunted. "Carl's on a short leash, I have to tell you, Hal. Well, you know the guy's bulldog style. He says if he has to go into one more gentlemen's club and order soda water and watch everyone else having a grand old time while he's playing a poor man's Magnum with his thumb up his—"

"I get the drift," Brognola said. "He's about to go apeshit. And this is where, once again, I get the long hard pauses from the Man to the point where I nearly have to ask him if he's still there. He tells me, item— DYSAT is a legitimate Air Force–run classified project, funded, of course, by Congress. Bottom line he wants absolute, one hundred percent concrete proof there's a conspiracy before I send Lyons and Able Team crashing down the front door, kicking ass and taking no names."

"They're working on it," Price said. "And we have enough suspicion, handed to you by way of the FBI, that there is a conspiracy to get these weapons and the Ramrod Intercept technology to both the Sudan and the Iranians."

"Which brings me to Striker's status. Well?"

Brognola read into the anvil of silence. Mack Bolan, also known as the Executioner, was Stony Man's lone wolf operative. There would be no Phoenix Force or Able Team this time out watching his back. They all knew that, days ago and going in.

"Limbo, to quote you, and holding," Kurtzman said, "at a U.S. air base in Saudi."

"I haven't quite gotten the particulars yet on what he's supposed to do or how he's prepared to get into Sudan, a country hostile, to understate it, folks, to the West."

"Once we receive the green light," Price volunteered,

"Striker will be air-inserted inside the Sudanese border, a HALO jump from a Starlifter C-141."

"I'm waiting for the good news."

"I've arranged for a CIA contract agent to meet him, roughly twenty kilometers northwest of Port Sudan. One call on a secured satlink from the Company, and the contract agent will be there to pick Striker up, on-site and waiting. Striker will have a passport stating he's an Iranian businessman who deals in Persian rugs and jewelry, if he finds himself facing down Sudanese soldiers while in-country."

"That's thin, Barbara. Especially if he's confronted by the Sudanese authorities at a roadblock and they decide to lock him up until they can check him out. They tend to skin Western spies over there alive and feed them their own flesh."

"It was the best we could do, Hal," Kurtzman offered. "Since we have an ongoing situation in Port Sudan, and since we strongly suspect DYSAT is funneling the high-tech goodies through the country—"

"And with the Company contract agent as an escort," Price quickly put in. "It's dicey, I know, but Striker insisted he go. Shake some trees and see what falls. He said…he'd figure it out."

Brognola had to smile at Bolan's balls-to-the-wall philosophy. "Tell me why I'm not surprised he said that."

He and the others dropped into silence as each of them hashed over the enormity of not one, but three separate missions. Just the same, three or five doors to bulldoze through, Brognola could see the dots beginning to connect all over the map.

The only thing left was to take decisive action, start putting the old boot through some doors and find out what waited on the other side.

The clean-and-simple approach.

"Is he dropping in with a full bag of necessities, Barbara?"

"One commando knife, his Beretta, just in case."

"God knows…"

"Once he's inside Port Sudan, the contract agent will land him the requisite hardware."

Brognola rubbed his face. "Okay, so I guess we just work it out as we go along."

"The usual," Kurtzman said.

"Right. What's new?"

Brognola found Kurtzman studying the world map on a monitor, suddenly as grim as hell. "What is it?"

Kurtzman cleared his throat. "Well, we have a window for about, well, another two hours, tops."

"Meaning?"

"Meaning if we don't get the call, we'll have to wait another full twenty-four hours—or rather Phoenix will have to wait. If we're going for a dawn strike it has to get under way ASAP, according to the timetable we've laid out. And there's another piece of bad news, Hal."

Maybe it was nerves or just plain weariness, but Brognola sounded off a grim chuckle. "Oh, this is getting better by the minute. Do tell."

"At roughly six o'clock, Madagascar time, the ONI-1 satellite is going to have to get moving on. Akira tells me there's a Russian satellite moving in the same orbital path."

"A collision course with a Russian satellite? How in the…? Never mind. I never understood how the Russian mind works anyway. You're telling me no one on either side can move either satellite's orbital path from down here?"

"Not can, but will they?" Price posed. "I've been stonewalled at Langley, and no one at the DOD has an answer."

"So," Brognola said, "Phoenix is on their own, and we're blind to what they're up against because the Russians…unbelievable. It's outer space, folks. You mean to tell me…they can't…or won't…"

"We'll still have the satlink," Kurtzman said, but his grim expression told Brognola that was little comfort.

The silence was hanging for long moments, thick enough to reach out and grab it, when the red phone trilled. The big Fed nearly bit his cigar in two as he felt their eyes boring into him. A deep breath, expecting more bad news, and he lifted the receiver.

Brognola recognized the voice as the Man said, "A few items we need to go over first, and I want to make certain we are crystal…"

He wasn't sure if high anxiety hit the air or relief was lighting up their faces, but he knew they were reading the gleam in his eyes, stone-cold frozen and watching.

Brognola didn't even hear the next few words, but he knew enough, reading into the Man's tone. He gave them the thumbs-up.

CHAPTER TWO

"Every day's just one big party for these guys. Cars, broads, blow, not a care in the world. One big tits-and-ass joyride. I tell you what—"

"Oh, shit."

Rosario Blancanales knew that god-of-thunder voice for what it signaled. Trouble was on the way, mayhem imminent and aplenty and just around the corner, but so far Carl Lyons was keeping his temper reined in.

Barely.

Blancanales was edged out some himself, all the waiting and watching eating at nerves demanding action. Still he regretted the slip, not wishing to incite Lyons to blow before the time was right for a real showdown.

"What was that, Pol?" Lyons growled from the shotgun seat.

A wry smile worked its way over Blancanales's lips.

"Nothing, Carl. I was just having a heart palpitation. Might just be heartburn from lunch."

Lyons was the leader of Able Team, which was comprised of the former L.A. detectives, Blancanales and Hermann "Gadgets" Schwarz. They were all friends, tried and tested commandos who would make the ultimate sacrifice if need be, and for one another if it came down to that. It wasn't that a wrathful Lyons made Blancanales especially nervous or even intimidated—no, berserker outbursts were simply wasted energy as far as he was concerned. Try telling that, he thought, to Ironman. Best just to let him vent some steam, clean the pipes out, then get himself refocused. Men, he knew, who fought and killed the enemy side by side, who knew what it was to face down death and walk out the other side of combat had a way of coming to read and gauge each other's mind-sets and moods better than most couples married for a lifetime.

"I'm getting sick and tired of all this sneaking and peeking around," Lyons growled, his gaze fixed on the strip joint across Sunset Boulevard. "Watching a bunch of goddamn playboys acting out their own Hollywood Babylon. They take two hour cocktail lunches in Brentwood, sashay out the office lobby before four, then go piss the night away gaping at ass and getting hummers in back rooms 'reserved' for their candy."

Blancanales groaned against his will. "Oh, man…"

Lyons fixed him with an eye that was glinting between mocking and irritation. "Another heart palpitation? Maybe you should go a little easier on all that hot sauce I watch you drown your tacos in. We're not getting any younger, my friend. We can't assault our systems the way we used to, you know."

"I'll take that under advisement."

Lyons went back to glowering at the front doors where two of their DYSAT exec targets had just entered to begin a long night of trolling for fun and games. "These thousand-dollar-suited pricks are starting to annoy the hell out of me. These guys, every time I see them get a lap dance they throw at least a twenty-spot away, go skipping up to the stage, same deal. A bunch of twinkle toes with shit-eating grins. Their cash is trash. Big shots."

Blancanales looked into the rearview glass, caught Schwarz grinning from his control console in the back of the van. He put a glare into his eyes, softly shook his head, but, damn it if Schwarz didn't barge ahead with it anyway.

"If I didn't know better, Carl, I'd say you were sounding a smidge jealous."

"You're right—you don't know any better. And jealous of what? I just got a full head of steam, three days and nights out here, doing grunt dick work while we wait on Hal to tell us the Man finally made the hard call. We know these guys at DYSAT are dirty. I mean, two pigeons vanished off the face of the earth just as Hal's Justice suits were marching to scoop them up. Two and two still add up to four where I come from, guys."

"We still have three to watch," Pol said.

"Baby-sit, you mean," Lyons said. "And, you know, I somehow don't get the whole scam. If this DYSAT is run by spooks and former air commandos, why hire a bunch of kids damn near fresh out of business school? Still wet behind the ears, but given the keys to the kingdom."

"I think I have a pretty good hunch why," Schwarz volunteered.

"That right? Well, Pol and I are all ears."

"They were handpicked, chosen."

"You're telling us," Blancanales said, "they're sacrificial lambs."

"Something like that. I'm thinking they were sought out on purpose, with the specific intent of becoming scapegoats if the arms and high-tech wheeling and dealing was found out by the Feds. Your basic fall guys. The former air commandos, with their service records, would simply shrug it off, lie their way out of it, go to ground until the smoke cleared and the college boys were safely on their way to the big house."

Blancanales saw Lyons bobbing his head, hashing it over.

"Makes sense, in some twisted way," Lyons said. "And the marginal lifestyles they lead, it wouldn't be a stretch for the top brass to point out these guys had serious vice problems."

"It's the only thing that fits," Schwarz said. "We know they are simply numbers crunchers for the most part, moving the parts of the goodies around, writing up the manifests, using the contacts of the real powers to create safe transport lanes for delivery. They figured the civilian workforce they hired would be too naive to figure it out."

"How wrong they were," Blancanales said. Then he saw two big men in dark suit jackets and buzz cuts going for the doors to the gentlemen's club, rolling out of the night shadows, flashing lights jumping about like winking halos around them from this lit-up neon stretch of clubs and bars. "Hey, heads up. Our playboys are about to get paid a visit by your friendly neighborhood DYSAT goons."

"Yeah," Lyons said. "They were at the last club, too, where Collins disappeared. Only I counted up three the last stop."

"I know their vehicles," Gadgets said, watching his monitor, the image being relayed from a minicam mounted on top of the van, the rolling command center handed off to Able Team courtesy of Hal Brognola's Justice contacts in L.A. "I photoed them and the plates yesterday when they came out of the garage of the office complex."

"So, go find them," Lyons said, "and stick another of your famous tracking boxes so we can stay glued on their tails. I see a parking lot down the street, the direction they came from. Let's rock and roll, Gadgets. I'm going in. Pol, keep the engine hot. The looks I just read on the goons' faces…let's just say I've got a bad feeling about this."

Blancanales cleared his throat as he watched Lyons secure the mini-Uzi in a special rigging beneath his loose-fitting windbreaker, the Ironman's .357 Magnum Colt Python snug in a shoulder holster on the opposite side with a clear bulge. *Subtle* wasn't found in Lyons's vocabulary. "Easy, big guy. We still haven't been flashed the green light."

Lyons shot Blancanales a cold grin, checked the load on his Colt Python, then slid the big piece back into shoulder leather. "Relax. I've got a few extra bucks on me to throw around. Maybe I'm just rolling in there to have a couple laughs, check out the girls. Let 'em know big daddy's in town."

Lyons was out the door, into the night. Schwarz rolled back the side door, gone to play his role as bug planter.

Now Blancanales felt a real heart palpitation, and it wasn't the aftereffect of hot sauce and too many tacos. This wasn't good, he thought. Hell's bells, he could almost feel the angry energy, trailing Lyons as he crossed the street.

A human time bomb, looking for a place to blow.

No mistake, he could feel it all about to hit the fan, and maybe go straight to hell before the mission even got official status.

JACK ROSWELL DESPISED his current task, or, more to the point, the kind of flunkies he was hunting. The former air commando and black operative for the NSA had his orders from up top, and he would carry them out even if he couldn't fathom the logic in the whole scheme from the very beginning. This whole mess, he thought, could have been avoided long ago. Now he had been cut loose, a stone-cold killer, on the march to silence wagging tongues.

As he weaved his way through the gaggle of suits and howling throngs of half-drunken lechers, Morton on his left flank, he wondered where it was all headed. It was the colonel's show, just the same, from day one, and he had often considered broaching the subject. Such as why hire on a pack of twentysomething guys to do the dirty work of moving the prototype high-tech goodies around the globe? Such as why allow them access to classified files? Such as why let them run all around Los Angeles, having the Sodom and Gomorrah time of their lives, a couple of them coked up half the time, six figure salaries to a man? Flash, showing off, now flapping loose lips.

Worse still, the backbone, the real movers and shakers behind DYSAT, had the boot heel of the Justice Department stomping down on it, putting on the weight, ready to snap it in two. At last count, three of the pretty-boy executives were dead and accounted for, with three more that he knew of still running around, making little whispered noise about blowing the lid on the whole plan to one another. Well, the Feds had come running, and Roswell knew they were even right then in the neighborhood. No, it wasn't all that difficult to spot the black van bristling with antennae, parked across the street for what it was.

Official G-men were on the prowl.

He hoped they came running, trying to close the net. With some cunning and a little brazenness, he could lead them outside, a dark alley maybe, where he could send a message to the Feds. When they came and picked up what was left of the bodies, he didn't figure they'd just pack up their surveillance and leave town, tails tucked between their legs. No, they'd turn up the heat, but that was just fine with him. Things were reaching a critical mass anyway, and only a swift and decisive counterattack could save the DYSAT kingdom.

After dogging the marks around for days, where they wiled away their nights in gentlemen's clubs, paid cash for quickies and huffed up blow in back rooms, he was starting to feel mean, and dirty. Midforties, he was somewhat surprised to find a craving for younger girls boiling in his loins, an urge he hadn't known existed until now. But this was business, and he had no time to indulge any amount of seething lust.

He needed relief, though, and he was content enough to find it through the barrel of his sound-suppressed Beretta 92-F.

Maybe when this whole dirty business was cleaned up he could return to one of these clubs, peace of mind intact, and spend some of his hard-earned cash indulging the fire.

He spotted them beyond the next stage where three girls were gyrating the creamy goods to heavy metal thunder, in their faces. The swirling light show lit up their baby-smooth features, eyes glittering, and it angered Roswell to find the executives ready to laugh and lust the night away while prepared to stick it to DYSAT. They had secured a booth, nothing but Heineken and top-shelf booze for those guys.

Roswell gave Morton the nod. They knew the drill.

And they had their marks squeezed into the booth before they could wonder what the hell was happening.

Grogan had his bottle poised near his lips, eyes darting all around. "You guys…"

"Yeah, us guys," Roswell said. "There's good news and there's bad news, ladies. Bad news—Collins, Hurley and Samuels found new employment…in hell. Good news—you guys have a chance to stay breathing, but only if you talk to us and give us everything you even think you think you know."

Caldwell was the first to want to spill it. "Not a problem, guys, just let us explain…"

"Not here," Roswell said. "Nice and quiet, we'll all get up, one big happy family, out the back door."

"We've got a problem. Twelve o'clock."

Roswell followed Morton's stare out to the party sea of lights and noise and AWOL husbands. In Roswell's experienced estimation of human nature, separating what was what from who was who in the interest of self-preservation, the big guy was falling way short of trying to blend into the crowd as another rooster on the loose away from the wife and kids. For one thing, there were the twin bulges under the windbreaker, the first tip-off a hunter had walked in, trying to close the gap, quick and quiet. He didn't quite have the look of a Fed, Roswell decided. There was something too cold and menacing to conclude he and Morton would simply hear the guy reading off their Miranda rights.

The big guy with icy eyes stuck to the Mr. Cool routine, just the same, ordering a beer at the bar, grinning around at the female amusement park. Once the bottle was settled in front of him, he picked up his march, shouldering his way through the suits.

Moving with purpose.

Roswell grabbed Caldwell by the arm. "Let's go."

LYONS WAS twelve to fifteen steps away from the hardmen when he was spotted. They were hauling the playboys out of the booth, the two buzz-cut thugs seeing him without seeing him. Tweedledee and Tweedledum had the eyes, too.

Which meant they would just as soon kill him as look at him.

He could have radioed Pol for backup, as he saw the foursome weaving through the crowd, angling for a gigantic bouncer guarding what Lyons supposed was the doorway to whore paradise. The Able Team leader decided to go solo, do it his way.

The hard way.

He deposited the beer on the edge of the bar, brushed past a scantily clad waitress who scowled and bleated an oath at his backside. They made the door, and Lyons saw Tweedledee slip a crisp bill into Godzilla's hand, mouthing something in his direction.

Rolling on, as the foursome was swallowed up by the gloom beyond the door, Lyons already knew where this was headed. Godzilla was all evil eyes, watching as

Lyons marched up to him. Getting tensed up to go on the muscle, Godzilla sizing the opposition.

"It's a private party. Take a hike, Pops."

Lyons gave Godzilla a quick measure. Late-twenty-something, all muscles, the kind of arrogance in his eyes that told Lyons he had never done much more most likely than toss a few drunks out the front door.

"You're telling me this is members only, son?"

Godzilla was about to lose it, his eyes turning mean. "What part of 'take a hike' didn't you understand, Pops?"

"How about none of it?"

It came from the heart to begin with, the tried-and-true warrior backed by experience, all the pain and disappointment a man could know, choke down and file away along the course of his life coming together in a critical instant to do the deed. It boiled down, essentially, to a man versus a punk. Physically it came from the legs, a coiled spring that cut loose up his lower back, up the spine, an explosion down the arm until his forearm shot up with all the force of an erupting land mine. Lyons saw the light nearly winking out as Godzilla was lifted an inch or so off his patent leathers, head snapping back on wilting rubber from the forearm pile driver to the jaw. Figure he'd spent a few more hours in the gym lately, pumping more iron than Lyons had his entire life, and he saw the need to follow up with a sweeping left hook. It damn near scared Lyons to hit the guy that hard, his fist driving through jawbone, head snapping sideways, out and back. For a second, Lyons wondered if he had decapitated Godzilla. When the man went thundering off the floor, down for the count, Lyons checked his pulse, found a weak beat. A scan of the party crowd and he found his luck was holding up for a change. They were too busy playing grab ass to notice the incident.

"Pops" Ironman Lyons freed his Colt Python, then hit the door.

CHAPTER THREE

Schwarz found the black Lexus parked in the shadows of some white-facaded structure gone to seed with weeds and vines. There was no gate around the lot, permitting quick and easy access, no valet he could find with a search of the naked eye. And the surging party mass along Sunset was too busy trooping in and out of all the rock, comedy and gentlemen's clubs to pay one straggling shadow any mind.

Or so he hoped.

He was deep in the lot, but felt an unseen watcher hawkeyeing his back, radar from some invisible force homed in on his march, lining him up. He started to feel an itch between his shoulder blades as he gave the line of vehicles a long probing eye.

Nothing stirred.

Okay, he was in, but something felt off-kilter, and he found himself planning his exit already. Still he had a job to do, but as he was forging toward the black Lexus, he couldn't help but feel Lyons was on a headhunting tour inside the club, a sense of urgency to get back to the van burning him up. Three days of lurking all over town, watching their targets live it up like piggish royalty. For some reason he couldn't quite pin down, he felt it was set to blow up in their faces.

Lyons wasn't the patient sort.

Schwarz picked up the pace, feeling that heart palpitation Pol mentioned, wondering where the black SUV that carried at least two of the other thugs was parked. He'd settle for one out of two, at worst, even though Ironman wouldn't appreciate a half-assed outing. It wasn't that Schwarz intended to come up short on his task. Rather, he felt a strange anxiety, some omen hanging out there in the buzz and babble of nightlife. Speed and a quick retreat made more sense than wandering about, checking out vehicles, casting about the paranoid eye like some potential car thief in the neighborhood.

He made the Lexus, fixed the small magnetic tracking box under the starboard front fender. He was suddenly thinking of his choice side arm, the Beretta 93-R, when he sensed a presence behind him. It was pure combat instinct that sent Schwarz springing to his feet, propelling himself into a flying leap over the hood as the pistol sounded a cracking retort from behind, a bolt of hot lightning burning over his scalp. The round chipped off a fleck of stone above his head, the screaming ricochet flying off into the night. Smart money told him a cop would have at least identified himself.

That left the missing third goon.

Schwarz had the Beretta out, came up, glimpsed the thug in question and capped off a round to let the guy know he was no easy tag. He missed badly, a hasty shot with no time to line it up, winging it for effect, the thug dropping beneath the roof. The windshield of a Jaguar downrange absorbed his wild round, a neat hole punched through to give the missing driver some mystery to ponder over later.

Schwarz hit the pavement on his belly, somehow kept the wind from getting punched out of his lungs, adrenaline doing all the work as he knew there was less than a second to clean it up before he was the only mess left behind. It was nothing more than a flash, feet scampering up the opposite side, but Schwarz tapped off a 9 mm round that scored flesh and bone, chopped the guy off at the ankle. Even in the heat of battle, he gave the opposition some credit for not screaming out, the hardman hammering the ground, but holding on to dish it back and fight it out.

The microsecond of begrudging admiration ended in the next eye blink as the thug turned wildman, opened up to throw his own play back in his face. Rounds were whining off the asphalt, lead hornets buzzing and banging off the chassis. Schwarz hit the front end, the tire punched out in a thud followed by a long hiss of exhaling air, then he went for broke.

Schwarz made a snap decision to steal a page from the Ironman manual on combat tactics. It was akin to charging the hill, all balls and brazen defiance, but Schwarz knew there was no choice but to go for it.

The opposition was still blasting away on the blindside when Schwarz threw himself onto the hood, rolling up the windshield as more wild rounds then came erupting through glass, the shooter trying to line him up, professional cool under pain and fire, the faceless hardman trailing all the racket of his weight slamming metal with screaming lead. He was up and sliding down the roof, skidding on his butt off the back end when the shadow shooter figured out the play too late. It could have been white-hot agony clogging up the works, keeping the fallen shooter from twisting to line him up. It could have been he'd burned out the clip by the time Schwarz was dropping off the trunk and going for it.

It didn't matter either way in the end. Schwarz hit his feet, pumped a 9 mm sendoff between the shooter's eyes just as the hardman was swinging the pistol his way.

The curtain might have dropped on one out of three, but Schwarz knew the real trouble had only just started. So much for high-tech intentions.

War had just been declared on Able Team.

Schwarz was scanning the vicinity, retracing his steps back through the lot. They were still laughing it up out there on Sunset, unaware death walked among them. Schwarz kept the Beretta out and leading the way. He was thinking of Lyons, some uncanny instinct tugging him toward the club. He pulled out his handheld radio, raised Blancanales and told him, "We've got problems."

ROSWELL DECIDED the alley would mark the big guy's final resting place. A deathtrap was in order, something quick and neat, since he'd just seen their pursuer slip through the doorway, a large revolver in his hand. Something had gone wrong, the fifty spot he'd laid on the bouncer wasted money. Just before hitting the far back door, Roswell thought he'd caught the sound of a falling body where the bouncer had stood guard.

Whoever the big guy was, he had a look about him that warned Roswell they were being tracked by a mad dog who wouldn't rest until the choice beef was in its mouth. And now he wasn't only moving with more purpose, but he was also kicking ass and taking names.

A quick scan of the wide alley, and Roswell nodded toward the garbage Dumpster behind, told Morton, "I'll get his attention."

Roswell needed this nailed down, five seconds ago, then get on his way back to the colonel's office. A long night of grilling two more of DYSAT's loudmouths was going to prove a task grim enough. Much wailing and gnashing of teeth was on the menu, on hold for the moment, but the last thing Roswell needed was some armed bulldog chasing them all over Los Angeles, growling and biting at their heels.

Enough. Time to make a stand.

Roswell grabbed Caldwell by the scruff of his neck,

then jammed the muzzle of his sound-suppressed Beretta against the base of Grogan's skull. "Both of you. Slow. Turn around. Any squawking, any sudden cute moves, I just as soon shoot you both and leave you for the garbagemen in the morning."

THE STINK of sweat and stale sex in his nose, Lyons advanced down the long hallway, tuning out all the moaning and mewing from behind closed doors on the way. Moments ago, he'd spotted his quarry going out the back door. Colt Python leading the march, Lyons made the door, listened to the silence beyond. If they were gone, he could only hope Pol had a visual, Gadgets delivering the tracking presents. If they were waiting…

Lyons shouldered his way out the door. Two steps beyond and into the alley, he heard, "Hey, over here!"

It was too easy, and the old saying about something looking too good to be true saved his life. He was lurching back just as the first two or three rounds were barking his way. Lyons had the setup mentally gauged, as slugs tattooed the doorway in a flash of sparking steel. Tweedledee was using the DYSAT playboys as human armor, with Tweedledum down the alley, looking to wrap this up, no fuss.

Screw it, Lyons thought, crouching, swinging around the big hand cannon. He was lining up Tweedledee's leg when the howling of men in anguish raked the air. The Beretta was blown out of Tweedledee's hand in a burst of crimson, then Lyons made out his back-door cavalry.

Schwarz.

Maybe it was the sight of watching his comrade in kidnapping going down as his head was cracked open by one well-placed round from Schwarz's Beretta. But Tweedledum's head popped over the edge of the garbage Dumpster, eyes bugged, and Lyons pulled the trigger, erasing the picture of confusion forever.

The playboys were grabbing air, hopping around, snapping out the questions. Lyons was already on his radio, rounding up Blancanales. "Pol, get your ass in the alley."

Schwarz was sporting a wry grin, stepping up to the DYSAT executives. "Good thing I was thinking about you."

Lyons matched the look as Blancanales roared the van into the alley. "Something just told you your old pal would need a helping hand, huh?"

"You know, Carl, you ever think about cutting back on the red meat?"

"WHERE TO?" Blancanales asked as he headed the van west on Sunset.

"Find Santa Monica Boulevard," Lyons answered. "That will get us in the general vicinity of Century City. I think it's time we paid their boss a visit. Assuming he keeps longer work hours than the hired help."

Lyons was scrunched up beside Gadgets, and their two songbirds were in back. The plastic cuffs had already been snapped on their wrists, and Lyons read the fear on their expressions as they sat on the floor.

"Right, you two are in a world of hurt."

"Are you cops?"

"Not exactly. Right now we're the only thing that stands between a bunch of guys like the ones we left back there in the alley, and your permanent retirement from DYSAT."

"You want us to talk about what we know?"

"You sound like a smart young man."

"What's in it for us?"

Lyons chuckled. "Now you're sounding not so smart. All I'm telling you on a deal, is that it depends on what we hear. Bottom line, that's not my call to make."

He was about to unleash the flurry of questions when the phone with its secured line beeped from its hookup on the console. Schwarz fielded the call. Lyons waited, heard Gadgets grunting.

"Yeah…uh-huh…right…just a second…"

"It's Hal," Schwarz said, his hand over the mouthpiece. "He said we have a green light—sort of."

"What the hell's sort of?"

"There's conditions. What do you want me to tell him about our situation?"

"The truth."

THE TRUTH SENT Brognola digging out the packet of antacid tablets. He washed three of them down with coffee, then moved deeper across the Computer Room. Akira Tokaido and Hunt Wethers stopped their cyber sleuthing on pertinent background data on the key

DYSAT players long enough to catch the grim update on Able Team.

"Carl says it was self-defense," Brognola said. "Schwarz says his guy came in, likewise blasting."

"The bad guys know they're targeted," Kurtzman said from his workstation. "Maybe that's good. Now that the opening guns have sounded, the top dogs will get nervous, maybe try and pack up their toys, whatever the latest shipment, and bull ahead."

"Or pull up the drawbridge," Price stated.

"I don't think it's exactly what the President had in mind," Tokaido put in, "when he alluded to turning up the heat a notch. But we all know Carl can get a little antsy."

"Well, antsy or whatever, the heat is on, people," Brognola said. "The only question is who burns first."

"And the DYSAT lab facility in Idaho?" Wethers asked. "Is it still hands off?"

"For now. Okay, where are we?"

Brognola checked the large monitor that displayed a tract of the Indian Ocean where the minisub was taking Phoenix Force to the Madagascan shore. Tokaido commented on the visual capacity of the state-of-the-art high-energy X-ray laser tracking beam that was monitoring the minisub and anything else moving in the water from space. Just like an X-ray it outlined the sub, twenty feet below the surface in a hazy gray frame.

"Two more minutes and they're out the hatch," Price announced. "They're right on schedule."

"The problem is that damn Russian satellite," Brognola groused. "We're going to be blind soon, and we won't have another satellite pass over until they're wheels up in the Spectre."

"Five hours before it has to move on," Kurtzman said. "And we still can't get any answers from our side or any contacts we have in Moscow why a Russian satellite is up ONI-1's rear. We'll have to do this the old-fashioned way. Over the phone."

"Hal, I know I'm getting a little ahead of the program," Wethers said, "but I've been poring over the sat imagery of the situation in the Strait of Hormuz. At some point I think we need to address it again. I mean, I have a clear and growing military buildup, far exceeding anything the Iranians have done to date. The key islands in the strait, Larak, Henqin, Sirri, Qeshm and the Greater Tunb Islands…well, they've moved in an additional sixteen pieces of antiaircraft hardware, including surface-to-air missiles. Now, one-third of the world's oil supply is tankered through the Strait of Hormuz. I'm not pushing any panic buttons, but we're looking at some connection between DYSAT, Sudan, the Iranians in Madagascar and the latest renewed military buildup on the islands. Say the Iranians pull the trigger? A 130 mm gun is more than plenty to sink any one of twenty tankers that pass through the strait every day. A wall of fire, a massive oil spill would shut the strait down. I don't even want to begin to imagine the damage to the economic infrastructures of Europe, Japan, and, of course, the United States."

And thus phase two.

"The President's aware, Hunt, of the potential enormity of the problem. Depending on what happens with Phoenix in Madagascar, and if Striker's able to link a few of the missing pieces together...let's get Phoenix through Phase One. The Strait of Hormuz situation remains on the back burner."

Brognola was watching the X-ray beam tracking the minisub when he saw it. It came at the minisub, from the south, moving through the water, on a collision course.

Kurtzman muttered a curse as he recognized it for what it was. "How close are they to shore?"

"Three hundred yards still," Tokaido said. "Oh, my God."

Brognola nearly lost his grip on the coffee cup, fingers clenching so hard around the cigar he nearly snapped it in two. "Please, people, someone tell me that's not what I think I think it is."

CHAPTER FOUR

It was the dreaded demon, the alpha and the omega, he thought, of any SEAL's worst nightmare.

It was a white shark, and it was a big one.

Calvin James nearly leaped off the bench, as soon as the thud struck the hull from above, the black ex-SEAL scrambling toward the control console when—

He froze, heart lurching into his throat as he caught sight of the massive tail slowly stroking, fanning the murk, back and forth, out to the port side. Yellow light from the minisub outlined the creature, framed its white underbelly from which it got its name.

The sub's driver, a blacksuit brought from the Farm, watched until the distant darkness swallowed up the great fish, his eyeballs nearly popping out of his skull.

Gone but hardly forgotten.

"Sir, that was at least a sixteen—"

"No," James said, "more like an eighteen footer, four,

maybe five tons. A submarine with teeth." The former SEAL turned and read the grim fear on the faces of his comrades in Phoenix Force.

T. J. Hawkins was watching the dark gloom, intent as hell, as if the behemoth might come back for another look at the minisub, or worse—ram its head straight through the reinforced glass bubble. "Cal, I'm thinking they probably never told you what to do about something like that in BUDs."

"Pray."

Rafael Encizo, donning his frogman suit like the other commandos, said, "Beyond the Our Fathers and the Hail Marys, what's the plan?"

David McCarter, the leader of Phoenix Force, stepped up to the control console, reading the depth gauges. "How close can you get us to shore?"

"Another fifty, sixty yards tops, then I'm cutting it close to hitting the bottom."

And, of course, they were warriors, with a mission on the table. No one, even if the thought fleeted through his mind, was about to say out loud, "Hell, no, I won't go."

"So, that leaves us how far a swim?" Gary Manning wanted to know.

"A little less than a hundred yards."

"Fire the torpedo," McCarter told the blacksuit. "All right, mates, everybody has a knife. We swim in a staggered formation. Slow and easy. Give yourselves six feet apart, I'm thinking, breaststroke it in, blade in one hand."

Space enough between them, which meant they

wouldn't accidentally cut each other with their knives while stroking.

"Gary and I will watch the flanks and the rear. It shows up and wants a late-night snack, go for the eyes."

"I suggest we swim to the bottom, hug the deck all the way in," James said. "When they strike, they usually come up from below."

"Understood. Keep the headlights on us to light the way in," McCarter told the submariner. "All right, mates, let's saddle up and hit the hatch. No fish is going to keep us from going to the dance."

BROGNOLA RAISED McCarter just as Phoenix Force was fully suited up, lined up and set to go out the hatch. He gritted his teeth until the blood pressure throbbed in his eardrums, the mere thought of what waited for them outside the minisub cutting a primal terror through the Justice man, the ungodly likes of which he hadn't known in some time. A part of him wanting like hell to tell McCarter to scrub the mission for the time being, they'd find another way.

"I don't like it, David," Brognola said, checking the sat imagery from the X-ray eyes in the sky. "It's either left the area or gone too deep to pick up on our end. We'll be out of touch until you reach shore. You don't even have a weapon—except a commando dagger."

"We're here and the troops are tired of sitting around, cooped up on a sub, Chief, thumbs up the old sphincter. We're gone. I'll phone home as soon as we hit the beach."

"Good luck, and godspeed," Brognola muttered, but he was talking to dead air.

"Torpedo just went ashore," Akira Tokaido announced, but no one in the Computer Room looked hardly relieved by that minuscule piece of good news.

Brognola watched the monitor as, one by one, the five white ghostly shapes of Phoenix Force left the hatch and started swimming for the bottom. A hundred yards, he thought, the length of a football field. It might as well be a hundred miles.

THE END OF THE LINE, of course, for each and every man or woman was death. The journey along the way shaped, forged and revealed a man's character before the Grim One rolled the dice and the man crapped out, ticket yanked.

No problem, as long as a man was somewhat in control of the journey, and could die on his feet, in battle, with honor intact, he thought. Thomas Jackson Hawkins, as a warrior, never had a problem with the concept of his own death. He never dwelled, much less brooded, on the idea of a world without him tomorrow. He was in the business of death, after all, preferably dispensing it, but he knew someday, somewhere he would go down and not rise up. As a warrior, dying in combat was accepted going in, part of the high-stakes game of being a balls-to-the-wall commando. Combat to him was as natural as breathing.

The problem he had, as he breaststroked ahead, knife in hand, was being chomped in two by a creature three times his length and fifteen to twenty times his weight.

Something as old as the earth itself, which knew no fear, and had no known enemies.

Something that had put the fear of God into him, and any human being, he imagined, who had ever laid eyes on it. It always galled him, he thought, when some skipper and *National Geographic* types hit the waters off Australia or South Africa, in search of man's greatest fear, camera ready, Budweisers in hand. Spouting off— in nervous laughing voices from the safety of their deck—how white sharks were misunderstood, weren't really the ferocious man-eaters the uneducated believed them to be. All of it just myth, you see, fabricated by folks with too much time and imagination on their hands. So, why, then, he wondered, did they always go down into the water in titanium-reinforced cages?

Call it twenty, twenty-five yards tops of visibility on the flanks, with James and Encizo beside him, Manning and McCarter on the far outsides, the big Canadian and the former SAS commando lagging a little behind, doing a slow circle to watch their rear.

Ten inches of steel against a submarine with teeth. Man alive, he thought, they had to be crazy.

It was a straight plunge of roughly thirty feet to the ocean's bottom, the halo of yellow light from the minisub losing its glowing shield the more distance he put from the craft…and closer to shore. Could the monster home in on the hammering of his heart? Could it smell the undeniable and understandable fear, leaking out in great streams of sweat beneath his wet suit?

Don't think about it. He knew he wasn't alone.

Small comfort, to be damn sure.

The sandy bottom began to run off on a gradual downward slant, and he was thinking another fifty yards or so.

An eternity still.

He decided to look back, found McCarter falling behind, eyeing their rear through his mask, as if he sensed its presence.

And the massive shadow of the great beast appeared, materialized out of the darkness beyond the minisub. For some reason the monster was taking another look at the minisub, holding, some black demonic apparition, then slowly worked its massive body around the craft. Hawkins felt a tap on his shoulder. He looked at Encizo, the Cuban shaking his head, indicating with his knife they keep moving.

Not a problem. But why was McCarter trailing them? he wondered. What the hell was he doing?

A moment later Hawkins saw the ex-SAS commando fall back in, resume stroking with a renewed burst of energy.

IF THE MONSTER CAME for them, McCarter decided he would sacrifice himself if that meant the others could reach shore in one piece. He knew they wouldn't allow that, not if they wanted to get up the next day and look themselves in the mirror. But if the creature started ripping him limb from limb, he could only hope primal fear and good sense would take hold of the others and send them shooting like human bullets for the beach.

It was a false hope they would leave him to die one of the most horrible deaths he could imagine, but the mission was more important than the life of any single man on the team.

Still the behemoth appeared more curious about the minisub, circling the craft, nudging it with its great torpedo head. He gave the blacksuit submariner a mental salute. The guy was staying put, lighting the way to shore.

Nothing but steel balls. There was never any doubt.

McCarter turned toward shore, figuring another thirty yards or so, arms sweeping, legs scissoring. The team had pulled ahead, with James and Hawkins looking back, peering at him, aware, most likely, of what he was thinking if it went to hell. A few more strokes and McCarter was in line, but craned his head around every few yards. It wasn't much longer and he felt his knees scrape bottom, his head poking out of the surface. Twenty yards and they surfaced to a man. As luck would have it, they caught a decent wave, and began stroking now like Olympic swimmers as they rode it into shore.

Rebreathers were out and tanks were stripped off. The heavy breathing of Phoenix Force slashed the calm quiet of the beach as flippers were removed and they made solid land.

McCarter gave the smooth glass surface out to sea a search. No giant fin knifing out of the water, just a soft glow of light beneath the surface where the minisub was parked. He checked the troops, and his chuckle carried a heavy note of grim relief. "Anybody have to change his shorts first?"

Stony Man Farm, Virginia

BROGNOLA COULD BREATHE again, but it would take a few minutes, he knew, before the trembling left his hands. McCarter was on the satlink. "All present and accounted for. We're changed, locked and loaded. Titan on the way back to the mother ship."

"Grimaldi will be wheels up in two minutes, David," Price said. "We'll monitor your march and alert you to any locals or army units on the prowl."

"Well, in that case, we'd better shake and bake. A ten-klick hike will be cutting it close to sunrise."

"Understood," Price said.

"Shouldn't be a problem moving double-time. I can still smell the adrenaline after our close encounter with Jaws. We'll be in touch. Out."

Brognola lifted the stogie in a shaky hand. "Air drops. For a while, at least, only air insertions. That, folks, was way too close for this old guy's heart."

They were smiling, nodding, but their relief, Brognola knew, sweet as it was, would prove short-lived.

The worst was yet to come. Getting in might have proved the easy task.

Century City, California

"YOU BOYS AREN'T really telling us much more than we already know."

Lyons was laying the evil eye on Grogan and Caldwell as Blancanales punched in the access code that lifted the door to the underground parking garage.

The van was rolling, going down into the subterranean labyrinth where the office of DYSAT was housed in Century City. Schwarz was monitoring the police bands with his scanner, had informed Lyons units were already on the scene of the carnage back in the alley. No firm ID on suspects. No description of their vehicle.

The way Lyons figured it, from there on it was time to crank up the heat, put some serious fire to the tails of the so-called board of directors. Grogan had put in the call to the boss. The man in question, James Lake, ex-colonel in the Air Force air commandos, was hunkered in his office, calling the shots.

Literally.

"What more do you need to know?" Caldwell sputtered. "We accessed the classified files, it was something of a fluke, an accident. We found out they're using a cutout in Thailand to ship the merchandise from there to Port Sudan. The microchips are prototypes, samples."

"And this Benny Goodman..."

"Godwin," Grogan corrected.

"Whatever. This clown somehow lifted the samples and is sitting on them at his girlfriend's place in Malibu."

"Along with the information we downloaded about the operation," Caldwell added.

"What's our next move, Carl?" Blancanales asked.

"Find a space in DYSAT's turf and park it. Me and you are going to have a little chat with the board of directors."

"How come the sound of that puts me a little on edge?" Blancanales said.

"Because these assholes are traitors. Because I can't stand traitors. From now on, we do it our way, and if the President squawks he squawks. Hey, what's the problem anyway? These guys tried to draw first blood. We have 'official' status as special agents of the Justice Department. I can walk up to the guy's office now and start slapping the crap out of him, if I want, threaten him with about twenty-five to life and back it up."

Lyons watched through the windshield as Blancanales motored deeper into the garage, found DYSAT painted on a stretch of concrete, slid into a space that was isolated from other vehicles.

"You're going to need my magnetic swipe card to get through the door," Grogan said.

"Where is it?"

"In my wallet."

Lyons was his usual gentle self, clawing a talon into Grogan's shoulder, shoving him around and bending him over a little to yank the wallet out of his back pants pocket. He found the card, slipped it in the pocket of his windbreaker, dumped the wallet in the guy's lap.

"Then what?"

"Well, you have to go up the steps to the lobby. You can't take the elevator from down here."

"Meaning a rent-a-cop encounter."

Grogan grunted. "He'll want to see your ID."

"No problem."

"He'll call up to Lake."

"Again no sweat."

Lyons reached into the weapons bin and handed an Ingram MAC-10 to Blancanales. "Gadgets, you're on baby-sitting detail. If we get a bunch of attitude from these clowns when we go up, you'll be the first to know."

"Meaning it's hit the fan," Schwarz said, sporting a grim smile.

"Let's rock, Pol."

CHAPTER FIVE

James Lake knew the end of DYSAT would come, had to, in fact, and from the very beginning when he'd helped conceive it, put the pieces together and get it launched as part of the Pentagon's Special Access Programs. It was designed to go down in flames on purpose, make certain an avalanche of badges and subpoenas came crashing down on DYSAT, all the sound and fury of the Justice Department, trumpeting out the intimidation, offering guys immunity in the Witness Protection Program and the like. But also in mind from the start would be the final conflagration, stoked and brewed to critical mass, while he skipped out the door, all the way to the bank.

The genius of it all was it had been worked out by his own cunning and the toil of spilled blood on his hand.

Everything in life ended. Everyone died. Survival was not necessarily for the fittest.

Survival was simply survival. They said that after the big one dropped, only the cockroach would inherit the earth. Mindful of that disgraceful tidbit, just how special could man be?

Not very, he thought.

If there was no hope for humankind, there was also no redemption, and certainly no salvation. Armageddon was inevitable; it just needed a decent shove in the right direction to ignite the fuse.

He sat in his large, deep-cushioned swivel chair, scanning the massive office suite, an amused smile tugging at his mouth. Beyond his teakwood desk, the size of three grand pianos, Grandahl and Preuter were busy on their secured cellulars, trying like hell but failing to dial up their hitters. He wanted to believe no news was good news, but the whole deal was unraveling fast. He could feel it, a noose dangling over his head, ready to drop and put the squeeze on.

It was time to clean up the garbage and bail.

Yes, he had wanted this whole venture to fail from the start. Failure, he once heard said, was often the measure of a man's success, but he never bought into that loser's philosophy. Granted, he had failed in three marriages, with seven children he never saw spread all over the country, but what could he say? Women were women, and a man needed far more in life than the comfort and stability of some suburban purgatory.

A man needed conquest, honor and respect. It was either the bliss of heaven or the agony of hell; nothing in between was acceptable. And, no mistake, never again would he fail at anything. DYSAT was his baby, and if he had given it life, he could most certainly take it away. He had always believed the real power in the world came from the left hand of darkness anyway, the true father of light. Even the devil, he believed, had real feelings and needs. It was simply a question of having those wishes honored by the legions of faithful subjects. Meaning they had to be prepared to not only sacrifice their lives for him, but also sell him their very souls.

Still, he often thought life would have been much simpler, easier if he had been, say, a biker. Riding in the wind. A big middle finger jammed in the eye of society at large. Wheeling and dealing guns and dope… Well, he could at least claim he was something of an arms dealer, an outlaw, to be sure.

And outlaws only had to care about and look out for number one, which was why his stint as an Air Force air commando had been brief to the point of ridiculous. Search-and-rescue missions didn't mean much more than a gob of flying phlegm when a man didn't care if human beings lived or died. On then to a number of years working as a special black operative, guarding classified Air Force installations where they were building the future of super high-tech. Grooming contacts and, of course, quietly removing any thorns in his side on his climb to the top.

Well, Jim Lake had finally arrived. His big deal was on the table, in the wings, ready to fly. The college kids had been nothing more than pawns, mere toilet paper, he thought. Bring them on board, unleash a few secrets, here and there, fat salaries so they could indulge their every whim and petty earthly desire. He always knew a couple of them would have cracked under the strain of uncovering knowledge of high-tech espionage, state-of-the-art goodies being delivered to so-called enemies of the United States. Truth was, he had counted on them to go running, pants wet, to the Feds. By the time the real law figured it out, he would be long gone, a whopping numbered account overseas, engineering grand schemes to bring on some doomsday from a remote tropical paradise. It would be a sort of in-their-face gesture, proving to every American man, woman and child, from the hallowed classified halls of the Pentagon all the way to Silicon Valley, that Jim Lake was just a little smarter, tougher and, yes, better looking than they were.

That Jim Lake wasn't only his own man, but a god among mere mortals to be worshiped.

He was scanning the bank of security cameras hung from the ceiling over his desk when he spotted the two men in the lobby. The bigger one was haggling with the security guard, flashing a wallet packet, looking as if he were poised to fly over the desk and start slapping the man. A Fed, on the muscle, only if that guy was a Fed he was Gandhi.

"Gentlemen, I believe we're about to have company."

"I don't like the looks of those two," Grandahl said, craning his neck some to stare up at the camera bank.

He was fingering his goatee, running a nervous hand over his shiny dome. "I can't raise Morton or Roswell. We should have heard from them by now. We know the Justice Department was set to bag—"

Lake sounded a long deep chuckle, a hollow knell that seemed to swell up the suite with the sound. "Relax. We'll deal with them. It's time we wrapped this up anyway. We have one more pigeon out there on the run to take care of. We have a backup security force in town, which you just put out the call to, on standby." He leaned up, smoothed out the arms of his silk jacket, punched a button on his phone. "Giddell, I've got company on the way. They look rather unpleasant."

"Yes, sir, I saw them, too."

"Stand by but make yourself available next door. There's going to be some noise, then we're bailing."

"Understood, sir."

Lake wheeled back a few inches, reached under his desk and slid the Uzi submachine gun from out of its special mounting. He checked the load, cocked the bolt, then took a peek at the Beretta 92-F in shoulder rigging. If it wasn't enough, there was an arms cache in a hidden wall panel, twelve paces to his right.

"When we're finished here," Lake told his hitters, "we go pay this little snip Godwin a visit. I'm hearing he got his filthy paws on the Ramrod Intercept microchips and data manual. Without those, gentlemen, my deal may fall through. If I can't retrieve them, our whole timetable will be altered."

"Meaning?" Grandahl asked.

"Meaning we'll have to go the lab in Idaho and pick up another batch. I had planned to do that anyway. One last shipment has already been arranged through a CMF."

"A classified military flight," Grandahl said, nodding. "Sweet."

"Standard procedure. Look alive, they just hit the elevator."

Of course, he took the obligatory alerting phone call from the security guard.

"They had badges, Mr. Lake, looked official, meaning they looked real enough to me. Special Agents from the Justice Department, they're telling me. Carl Lemmon and Rosario Bocales. I—"

"Not a problem, there was nothing you could do. I'll handle it. Thank you."

Jim Lake leaned back and sounded off another death knell chuckle. Life, he thought, was just about to get real interesting.

And what was real gain, true triumph on the way to glory without risk?

WHEN LYONS AND BLANCANALES stepped off the elevator to the DYSAT floor, they found yet more cameras monitoring their every step.

Lyons led the march toward the mammoth teak doors with the gold-plated Jim Lake, President hung as large as a Vegas neon sign. He could feel Pol's nerves mounting as they closed on the doors, the mirrored walls reflecting their grim looks, the cameras catching them on the roll. Lyons felt his own personal time bomb ticking away in his gut.

It was time to start spreading the misery around, kick a few of the top dogs in the teeth.

"How come I feel like raising a middle finger salute to one of those?" Lyons growled.

"How do you want to play this?"

"Straight and to the point. Just follow my lead."

"I was afraid you were going to say that."

They reached the DYSAT gates to the inner sanctum. Lyons was about to bang on the door when a chuckle that sounded as if it came from the bowels of hell filtered out the small intercom beside the doors.

"It's open, 'Agents' Lemmon and Bocales. Please, enter. Please, fear not."

Lyons considered going through the door with his Colt Python out so they could get quickly beyond any friendly preamble. He opted to leave the big piece where it was for the moment, until he got a firm read on what was what. He led Blancanales through the door and found himself moving into a sprawling suite fit for a king. Big leather couches. Wet bar, giant-screen TV. Two inches of white carpet, wall to wall. Long black marble conference table. Soft white light fell from the ceiling, framing a handsome face he recognized from the Farm's intel pac on Jim Lake. As he moved deeper into the suite, he was somewhat curious why a former Air Force colonel would wear his jet-black hair down to his shoulders, like some wanna-be hippie or biker. Go figure how the mind of a traitor, or an insane demon worked, he thought.

He took a measure of the two other men standing off to the side of the desk. One was a Van Gogh–type gunslinger, goatee, but no hair on his head, the face gaunt and weathered, the eyes sunken black pieces of coal. The other guy was a buzz-cut issue like the men he'd gunned down in the alley. The eyes of both men warned Lyons they had itchy trigger fingers.

Lyons took up turf in front of the desk, hauled out his Justice credentials. And Lake gave him that deep chuckle, in his face.

"Please, don't insult me."

"How's that?" Lyons growled.

"Okay, we'll play it your way for the moment. What can I do for you, Agent Lemmon and Agent Bocales?"

JIM LAKE KNEW a bulldog when he saw one. In fact, wildmen were the only kind he wanted to hire on as security. Guys, yes, who could go through a door loud or quiet, in search of blood and wearing somebody's guts for a necklace, either way they charged in. No fear, just do it. To even consider losing made a man a loser before the proverbial feces even hit the fan.

The one called Lemmon wasn't the kind to tap dance or dream of losing. "Here it is, Colonel," the big guy said, with a contemptuous note dropped on "Colonel." "Three of your buzz-cut Dirty Harrys were eighty-sixed.

They tend to want to shoot people on sight to make their day. They tend to seem to not care if they're civilian or like us, with the Justice Department, which already dumps you in a world of feces. This is what we know, and this is what we're going to do. We know you're running a scam to unload high-tech weapons and technology overseas somewhere. We know you were using your executives and think tankers to draw out the wolves, my guess is so they could be scapegoats when you left Dodge. You've gone for broke, and you lost. Now we have two of your employees who want to turn songbird under our care and protection."

Lake knew what had to be done. He steepled his fingers, rubbed his eyes and blew out a long breath.

"What? Am I boring you assholes?"

"Uh, Agent Lemmon, let me speak frankly, so we can get past all this macho posturing and palavering."

Lyons sensed the whole mood change around him. It was as if a dark veil had dropped over Mr. Chuckles, some rage clamped down on before then, churning over now, building heat, the pot of his black soul simmering. Van Gogh and Buzz-cut Issue had to have been clued in to the sudden shift in Lake's demeanor, and Lyons read the squaring of the shoulders for what it meant.

It was set to blow, loud and hot. It was going to get messy, and the mere fact Lake was prepared to go for it told Lyons the guy had backup somewhere, ready to bolt town to pick up the pace on whatever his dark agenda.

"Well, Agent Lemmon, I guess there's not much left to say, except I can't recall the last time I saw a G-man walking around in rubber-soled combat boots. I didn't know government issues, the official kind, trooped around with compact submachine guns in special swivel rigging beneath oversize windbreakers. To answer your suspicions, yes, I have a deal, a major deal in the works that could change the entire destiny of the world. Yes, my employees were nothing more than human chess pieces to be moved around at my wish, to take the fall, as you put it, while I fly off into the sunset. You know what my problem is—"

"I'm not your shrink, Colonel. I didn't come here to listen to how you were an abused child and all you need is a little love."

The big chuckle again. "My problem is I don't like wrinkles in my plans, large or small. My problem is, when I don't get my way or what I want, I become extremely agitated."

And Lyons was already searching out some immediate cover, aware he and Pol were caught in the coming cross fire. It was something in Lake's look and voice, a new darkness sinking to still lower depths, that warned Lyons to make a scramble to save his skin.

The Able Team leader was in the air, flying over a couch as the Uzi appeared, like some sorcerer's trick, in Lake's hands.

CHAPTER SIX

The Uzi subgun was out and flaming 9 mm parabellum rounds before either Blancanales or Lyons could free his own hardware. Lake beat them to the punch. Instead of standing his ground in some grandstand suicide play, pulling iron and blasting back at the face of death where he stood his ground, he opted to take a running dive over the conference table. The sprint and flight stole him a few precious moments. Only pistols were barking now, chiming in the deafening symphony of weapons fire, hot lead scorching the air, seeking out his scalp like angry hornets.

"You're fucking with the wrong air commandos, ladies!"

Lake, bellowing like some fire-and-brimstone preacher hungover on Sunday morning, the long-haired crazy man pounding out the lead, marking his turf behind the desk, defying to be shot. Blancanales skidded off the table, hot slipstreams of lead tearing past his

scalp, tugging at his shoulders. On the way down he un-
leathered both the Beretta 92-F and the stubby Ingram
machine pistol, and got busy dishing it back before all
was lost. A shaved head with goatee came shooting
around the corner of the table when Blancanales cut
loose with a double burst. The Van Gogh shooter was
capping off rounds from his own Beretta when Blancanales was rewarded by a scream of pain. Van Gogh
lurched back, out of sight, grabbing at the red smear on
his upper thigh, cursing up a storm.

"If you're Feds, I'm the prince of darkness!"

The way the madman was pumping out the lead,
screaming in berserker fury, Blancanales didn't find the
statement a stretch.

Lake was stone-cold insane.

A swivel chair was absorbing a flurry of 9 mm rounds
when he popped up, and let it once more rip with twin lead
barrages. It was luck, more than skill, winging the rounds
out when he tagged the buzz-cut gunner, sent him crashing down on Lake's desk, bleeding and flopping all over
polished teakwood surface like some giant gutted salmon.

"Nice shot, son!"

And Lake seemed to slap home a fresh clip in a
nanosecond, not missing a beat.

"You want the best, you've got the best! The hottest
Colonel in the land. Jim Lake!"

THE GUY WAS hung out there but good, off in some land
of insanity that even caused Lyons to balk for a full sec-

ond or two. He was shooting up his own office, which told Lyons he didn't plan on coming back here. Whatever Lake's personal vision of greener pastures, Lyons didn't intend to let it become reality.

Not on his watch.

Not this night.

The mini-Uzi and Colt Python out, Lyons skirted on a hunch away from the tracking line of autofire that was eating up the couch, a storm of insatiable lead locusts buzzing in his ears. He came up, just in time to find Blancanales nailing the buzz-cut gunner and cut free with hand cannon and subgun to give his friend a much needed helping hand. The mini-Uzi hosed the desk, but Lake was already ducking, the curtained window behind him, drawn to block out some bird's eye view of the city skyline, taking a few hits. It fluttered a little as holes were punched through the window to let some traffic noise filter in from far below.

On his two o'clock Lyons found Van Gogh was shooting on the move for the wet bar when he assisted Blancanales in waxing the guy off his feet. Four converging points of fire turned Van Gogh into a bursting sieve, painting him crimson from the neck down to his crotch. He was airborne next, snarling out the pain and rage, before he sailed over the wet bar and brought down the top-shelf booze.

Lake jumped back into the game, back on the trigger, screaming out something about abortion pills marking the end of civilization, how civilians were all too willing to serve bastards and whores.

What the hell? Lyons thought.

The Able Team leader was going down behind the couch when the ex-colonel fired another long burst his way, then shifted his aim and drove Blancanales down behind the conference table.

Then a shadow with a massive autoshotgun whirled around the corner where some slat appeared in the wall near Lake's desk.

The cavalry, riding onto the scene, out of nowhere.

The curse was choked off in Lyons's throat as he flung himself away from the couch on the peal of thunder. Lake's subgun spray came back and helped chase Lyons to cover behind a wooden cabinet, the expensive teak scarred as tracking rounds began eating up the facing. A roaring boom and half of the cabinet vanished in Ironman's face in razoring wood splinters.

"See you around, ladies!"

The dark hole swallowed up Lake and Mr. Autoshotgun as Lyons broke cover. The slat was closing and Lyons, jacked up on adrenaline, hit the area with a .357 round and a half-dozen 9 mm projectiles from his mini-Uzi.

Wasted effort and ammo.

Lake was gone.

Lyons was feeling the wall for some button or latch that

would open the slat. Nothing. There was no space either where he could dig his fingers in to force the slat open.

"Time to boogie, Ironman. Something tells me the cavalry's going to be waiting when we hit the hall."

Lyons grabbed up his handheld radio and patched through to Schwarz.

"WHAT MORE CAN we tell you? We've given you directions to where Godwin is holed up. I put the call through, like you asked. You know he's there, and he has the package you want."

They were sweating out the unknown, worried about little more than saving whatever might be left of their dicey futures, wanting nothing else but for their party to go on. Schwarz didn't have the time or the inclination to put their fears to rest, nor did he much care about their desire to keep the good times rolling. The more they found out about DYSAT and the goons who ran it, the more he felt the killing heat was only just getting turned up.

And DYSAT needed to go down the toilet.

"Hey, come on, mister. Cut us some slack here. We're cooperating. We didn't know what we're getting involved in. Hey, we came to you people. That should count for something."

Schwarz was watching the lot through the windshield and the monitor. He heard Lyons coming on his handheld radio, as gruff as usual, but now there was a definite edge of urgency in his voice.

"Gadgets!"

"Yeah."

"Round two's just started. Lake tried to turn me and Pol into human sushi with an Uzi he had stashed under his desktop. Two more of his shooters are down for the count. Lake and another goon with a SPAS-12 are probably headed your way. Maybe he'll pick up reinforcements on the way down. We're on the way. Look alive."

"I copy."

And Lyons was gone off the air, in pursuit.

Schwarz scrambled for the weapons bin, hauled out a Colt Commando assault rifle. One clip of 5.56 mm rounds up the snout and he took three more, jammed them in his waistband.

"Which one is Lake's car?"

"It's a black Towncar."

Schwarz searched the monitor, worked the stick to move the mounted minicam around. At that hour there weren't many vehicles left in the garage, but he was irritated it took him ten seconds before he spotted the vehicle belonging to the president of DYSAT. It was parked at the deep north end, sandwiched between a white van and Cadillac. Okay, he decided, move in on foot, take up position behind a concrete pillar down that way.

Lay in wait and ambush the bastards. Sounded like a plan.

"Stay put, no matter what," Schwarz growled at Grogan and Caldwell. "Try and run on me…"

"We understand."

Schwarz malingered, not certain they did. Something

was turning over in their eyes, but he didn't have a second to spare.

A couple of mad-dog shooters, or more, were on the way.

Schwarz was out the door, the assault rifle up and ready. He was almost clearing the van when a leggy blonde came through the doorway leading to the stairwell. Mouthing an oath, he was forced to wait until she vacated the combat zone he was sure was only moments away from erupting.

LAKE WAS LIVID as he stormed into the security room. He was raising Burrows, part of his security detachment from the next floor down, when Giddell hit the button on his private elevator. Lake scanned the bank of cameras, watched as the two human freight trains rolled for the doors.

"Burrows, you and Jackson hit the main hall. Our friends are right now coming out. Do not worry about noise or making a mess. Just get it done."

"Aye, aye."

Just get it done, he thought. Seething, as the door to the car opened, he couldn't understand where it had gone wrong in the office. He was certain he'd gotten the draw on them, but they moved in an eye blink, as if they'd anticipated his killing play or could read his mind, which was impossible.

No, it was something else that had saved their skin. Experience, he decided. Those guys were pros of some kind. But what? And from what agency?

There would be a few moments to kill before the elevator reached the garage. In that span he needed to raise the reinforcements, get his thoughts together about their next stop. Malibu. Godwin and girl. He owned a private hangar in an airfield south of L.A. proper that was used exclusively for ferrying military brass, and DYSAT people. Once he had the data manual and the Ramrod Intercept microchips...

First he needed to clear the premises. He couldn't be sure, but he didn't think Burrows and Jackson had what it took to take out the freight trains. If nothing else, they might slow them, long enough for him to make his Towncar and ride on.

He checked the Uzi's load, half-empty, then gave himself a mental pat on the back for having the foresight to take two spare clips from his desk. It occurred to him next the freight trains might have backup, even a small army waiting for them when they hit the garage. No problem, he decided. He was shooting first anyway, so why change the program now?

THE LADY DAWDLED in her Mercedes, lighting a cigarette, sitting there, dreaming. She looked pensive, for damn sure, as if the smoke was helping to get her nerves under control after a long day at the office.

"Come on, come on."

He knew he couldn't very well just roll out into the great wide open, assault rifle in full view, the lady probably armed with a cell phone. Panic would take root, and she'd be on the blower, dialing up 911.

L.A.'s finest was the last thing Able Team needed to see, he knew.

Finally, she was backing out, dropping the expensive sports car into gear. Schwarz hugged the far side of the van, dropped back a couple of paces as she motored by, rounded the corner of the ramp.

Another search of the garage, and he found he was clear.

Schwarz was breaking into a run when the door to the stairwell burst open. Whether it was combat instinct or plain old paranoia jacking them up, Schwarz couldn't say. But they homed in on his dash, two steps out the door, and opened up with weapons fire.

TWO MORE PROBLEMS cropped up just as Lyons and Blancanales were marching past the receptionist's bay, but the Able Team commandos were geared up for any surprises once they hit the hall.

The human trains kept on rolling.

A black guy in flattop and a muscled hulk the size of the *Titanic* were already capping off with their Berettas. Lyons and Blancanales returned fire, twin-fisted style, heads lowering, but surging ahead. The mirrored wall cracked, then came apart in raining shards behind the Able Team commandos. Call it luck of the freight trains, but Lyons and Blancanales scored out of the gate. Lyons gave them credit for holding their ground, just the same, as they brazened it out.

Straight to the grave.

Two pistols against four weapons didn't stand much of a chance, not when the commandos of Able Team were stoked on full heads of steam and hearts pumping with righteous anger and adrenaline. Flattop got the mother of all haircuts, his skull vanishing in a scarlet halo before he plunged to the carpet. The *Titanic* went down harder, listing to the side, triggering off wild rounds as his chest and face bore the brunt of four punishing impacts.

"The stairwell," Lyons said, leading Blancanales down the hall.

They ran on, whirling, covering their own six.

"I don't know, Carl, but something's telling me Gadgets isn't real happy to be on his own right about now."

SCHWARZ HAD TO WONDER when the hell his comrades would show up and lend a helping hand. He nearly didn't make the concrete pillar, as they let rip in unison. The SPAS-12 was all flame and thunder, driving a crashing roar through Schwarz's eardrums like hot needles. The Uzi subgun sounded merely a bleat, as the one he recognized from the Farm's intel as Lake tried to tag him on the run. The concrete pillar was assaulted by screaming ricochets, lead and 12-gauge rounds creating a blanket of potential man-eaters around Schwarz, forcing him to cover. He went low, came around the corner and held back on the trigger of the assault rifle. Lake was already behind the wheel of the Towncar, turning over the engine on an angry rumble. The SPAS-12 hardman had to have been ordered, Schwarz decided, to lag behind, cover the boss man's retreat.

Good enough. Schwarz intended to see him land on permanent vacation, but if Lake fled the premises...

A quick burst from his Colt Commando and Schwarz blew out the luxury vehicle's back windshield. Lake was gone to his sight, hunched low behind the wheel, fueled, no doubt, by a crazed desire to get the hell out of there.

The thunder of the autoshotgun kept swelling the garage, forcing Schwarz to think about his next move. The pillar was taking hits, chunks vanishing in his face, as the shooter kept Schwarz pinned, the Able Team commando unable to get off even a spray and pray if he wanted to keep his face intact.

Schwarz brought up his assault rifle, trying to get a fix on Lake as he tore by on a shriek of rubber. He was just about set to go for the wheels, if nothing else, when the Towncar was shielded by a line of three vehicles. He rode out two anxious seconds, figuring he would get one more shot when...

Schwarz nearly bellowed his outrage. Grogan and Caldwell were down there, hopping away from the van, shouting Lake's name when the Towncar plowed through them, sent them flying down the garage, broken scarecrow figures in thousand-dollar suits. The Towncar raced on, then Lake hit the brakes, piled out the door. Distance and the fact Lake was blocked from sight next by a minivan kept Schwarz from stopping what he knew was coming next.

"Goddamn it!"

His curse and the stutter of the Uzi was washed away by more SPAS-12 rolling thunder.

LYONS TOOK A READ on the situation, on the run, through the door. The autoshotgun had Gadgets at bay behind a pillar, the shooter running out of rounds, no time to reload. The hardman was digging around inside the Cadillac, coming out with an HK MP-5 subgun when Lyons and Blancanales let him have it.

He also took a few rounds from Schwarz, whose Colt Commando showed around the pillar and flamed out a long fusillade, a stitching burst that drove the hardman down the side of the Cadillac, dousing the wheels with a fresh red paint job. Once again, Lyons bore witness to the sheer toughness and tenacity of the opposition. Even though he was taking hits, up and down his torso, ventilated to red ruins, he shouted in rage, trying but failing to take somebody with him. The SMG was jumping around in his hands, blood spattering his face, as he hopped around, as if wired to high voltage. It took the remaining two rounds in Lyons's Colt Python, burning up the rest of the clip of his mini-Uzi, but the hardman finally sagged on boneless legs, crumpling to the ground.

Able Team linked up, rolled on for the van. Lyons cursed when he saw the two dead DYSAT executives. He went and checked their pulse, but found they were well on their way to the other side.

"Sorry, Carl. I should have closed the side door."

"Forget it. I take it Lake's flown?"

Schwarz was clearly angry that he'd come up short. "Just before you showed up."

"Let's roll, guys," Lyons said. "There's one left. Looks like we're going to the beach."

CHAPTER SEVEN

The arrogance of Iranians never failed to amaze General Fateh Arakkhan. It wasn't so much what they said; rather it was how they said it, and, closer to the point, how they looked when they spoke. Usually—almost without fail—they talked about their own demands and wants, beliefs and intentions.

In short, themselves.

When speaking, they grew fire in the eyes, the voice rising with each passing word, the whole mounting diatribe clearly meant to warn against any denial or defiance of their wishes, any aversion, scathing or otherwise, to the Islamic point of view. In many, perhaps all ways of speaking and acting out, they were like little children to him. They wanted what they wanted when they wanted it. He could understand that kind of thinking, to be frank with himself, but sometimes like personalities could clash, and people of like kind could wake up one morning and discover the block wasn't big enough to accommodate them both. Or in this case the abandoned but sprawling French villa—now established as his command post—perched just beyond the western wall of the garrison. The longer the Iranian's sullen silence, the more the study seemed to shrink, swell with rising angry heat by the minute.

The general decided to lean back in the heavy-cushioned leather recliner, sip his French brandy, puff with some degree of apparent contentment on his Cuban cigar. He was relaxed, or trying to give the impression all was sweetness and light, while Bahruz Fhalid chugged down two snifters, gnawed on his own cigar like a man losing all faith and confidence in the situation, the future, himself.

The study, for the most part, was barren, like the rest of the villa, and the general often found himself wishing for more lavish surroundings. The recliner, brandy and black-market Havanas were a personal indulgence, shipped in from his home in Khartoum after he'd fled when the West dropped a bounty on his scalp. He had planned to ease the pain of his fugitive status in advance, before flying on from Khartoum, aware of the primitive conditions he'd find himself plunged into when he landed on Madagascar.

Impoverished hand-to-mouth existence was meant only for those masses to be ruled and serve their master, he believed. Madagascar, he had seen, really wasn't all that different than any other African country, despite the fact nature had separated the fourth-largest island in the world from the African continent some two hundred million years ago. The few wealthy still ruled the poor wretched masses, fisted the reins of power through violence and intimidation, backed by armed, uneducated thugs who had pretty much, he thought, just fallen out of the trees.

Alleged warlord with a track record of mass murder and genocide or not, he wasn't about to shuffle around in squalor, deprived of the few things in life he still enjoyed. When the French packed it up in 1973, he knew they took anything of value that wasn't nailed down from there all the way to the capital city. The Tana government stepped in next, naturally, decided to convert the villa into a radar and tracking station when Communist insurgents and rebels became a little unruly in the countryside and visions of landlocked African countries flying out Russian MiGs pushed fantasy to the shadowy borderland of paranoid delusion. The great African invasion never happened. On the plus side, since things had settled down after communism the equipment had been updated since the French bailed out. Meaning Arakkhan could feel safe and snug from lurking enemies, shadow gunmen skulking in from parts unknown to claim his scalp for the Western bastards.

The general was grateful, if nothing else, that Fhalid hadn't reminded him how important Iran was to any future ambitions he was dreaming about. The Sudanese general knew all about the Iranian incursion in his homeland anyway. They were everywhere, like mice, scurrying about, scores of soldiers stationed from Port Sudan all the way to the scrub wasteland of the south, where the Iranian agents had set up numerous training camps for "freedom fighters." It was something of a pact with the devil, he thought, but what could he do, short of telling them to pack up their toys and go home? Iran had roughly seventeen years' worth of leases left on its bases in the country. They came with smiling faces, full of all manner of flattery and promises for a greater Sudan.

Guile aside, they came bearing gifts of weapons, supplies and hefty sums of cash from oil money siphoned out of Tehran nonetheless. Sudan got weapons and money, while the Iranians staked out chunks of real estate to plan the coming great revolution of their jihad. The Iranians even dumped hefty cash contributions into a radio station in Port Sudan, where, daily, the holy trumpet sounded, that call to arms to the Islamic masses to rise up, strike down the Great Satan wherever he was found. The propaganda was even fed, beamed via satellite, all the way to Sudan's northern neighbor, Egypt. Since Sudan was just over seventy percent Muslim, the Khartoum government didn't squawk when the faceless talking heads incited the masses from behind the safety of a microphone. Truth was, the Khartoum powers encouraged the venomous railing against the West. It was, after all, "us" and "them."

Islam versus the West, death to all infidels.

"I would like a time frame," Fhalid said, the hint of

a fire building in his eyes, as he poured himself another glass of brandy. "My men and I grow weary of this island, just to name one inconvenience, the sitting around, killing time, waiting for something to happen, to get done. I have my people to answer to, and they grow anxious for news. They wish to know when they will see this 'big' shipment of your high-tech gold mine."

"I understand your impatience, but with every crisis there comes an opportunity."

"Do not patronize me, General."

Here we go, he thought. Already getting confrontational. Arakkhan smiled around his cigar. "Never. You have men inside my country who have proved invaluable to me. They have been my eyes and my ears. I am grateful to your fellow freedom fighters. Without them," he said, jerking his cigar toward the garrison, "there is no telling how much damage those three might have caused. Speaking of which, I've been meaning to ask…"

"Does it disturb me that they are dead? No. They were less than jackal dung."

"And the manner in which they died?"

"The punishment must fit the crime. I expected no less from you."

The general chuckled, hoped the anger he felt toward the implied sleight was missing from his voice. "Meaning my reputation preceded me."

"Back to the future. Your intentions?"

"I had believed they were clear between us."

"Refresh my memory."

"Very well. I have powerful allies, a coalition of soldiers and officers in Sudan who are paving the road for my return. I have, sad to report, also accepted a degree of help from our common enemies. Sometimes the road to victory is paved even if a man must hold hands with the devil."

"The CIA?"

The general shrugged, puffed, took a deep swallow of brandy. "Who knows who these men really are? I hear NSA, FBI, CIA, British MI-6. What I know is that they have their own agenda, most likely involving the accumulation of wealth. My money has seen its way into their hands to get some of the weapons, component parts, thus far."

"And my money, or the money of my sponsors, is tied up with your money."

"Yes, that much is true."

"I get the impression you are leaving something out."

"My own time frame has been carefully arranged. I have my own people inside Sudan who, as we speak, are prepared to hand over a final payment to acquire the technology we agreed on as part of our deal."

"And you wish to use Iranian agents to help you with your revolution in Khartoum?"

"Yes. A storming of the palace. It gets no more simple than lopping off the heads of my enemies, men who stabbed me in the back. Men," he said, and realized he was now the one with the fire in the eyes and voice, "who used me as a scapegoat to conceal their own crimes, this so-called genocide against the black Christians in the south, the SPLA thugs who would destroy my country. I understand, I respect your fire, your holy mission to slay the enemy. It, too, burns in my heart. But I am asking for a little more time."

"How much?"

"Two, three days at most."

The general could tell the Iranian was about to blow, patience an alien concept to the man, and decided it was time to show some good faith on his part. "I have a shipment of the laser weapons here on the compound."

The fire was gone now, replaced by a strange glowing light.

"No, I was not holding back. Come," he said, and stood, snifter in hand. "I will show you just a small portion of all that we have sweated and labored to obtain. I will prove to you I am all that I claim to be."

"Which is what?"

"A conqueror, a twenty-first-century Napoleon, shamed by traitors, who will return in glory and slay his enemies. No more, no less."

MCCARTER COULD SENSE the memory of the great beast still clinging to their thoughts, and the Briton could well appreciate even the specter of total grim recall. It kept them moving swift and hard, just the same, weapons and high-tech instruments in hand, the hardware fanning the heavy darkness of the hill country while the small gizmos monitored their surroundings for unwelcome visitors. Their combat harnesses in place, ammo pouches stuffed with spare clips and grenades, with Beretta 93-Rs as side arms, a curious mix of relief, tension and precombat jitters hovered in the muggy air as Phoenix Force marched on, deeper into the high plateau country, steering clear of dense forest, farmland and a smattering of Madagascan villages. Here and there, a few heads of cattle turned up in the green illumination of their NVD goggles, but no sign of any two-legged creatures. Yet.

The pace inland was swift, five armed shadows in the dead of night, hauling it double-time, a sense of urgency mounting with each klick knocked off and bringing them closer to their end game on the island. Encizo, an M-16/M-203 combo in one hand, with the Multi-round Projectile Launcher hung and slapping between his shoulder blades, was the pointman. The Cuban moved them ahead, up the rugged hills that spined Madagascar, using the Magellan GPS module to guide the way. Hooked into NAVSTAR, the satellite then beamed its transmission back to Stony Man Farm, where the team there could mark and monitor their progress, alert them via their com satlink to any unforeseen meandering problems. Thanks to Price and Katz, McCarter knew the way was already paved, as they took the easiest route possible, navigating, with NVD goggles in place illuminating the brisk march ahead, through the least populated areas. He gave the Farm crew a mental thumbs-up for making life a tab easier on the way in.

A smooth but adrenalized jaunt.

They had already passed the bullet-shaped huts of Merina tribesmen, the largest and most feared of the Madagascan tribes. Skirted a French Catholic church. Up and down three rice fields terraced into dark volcanic hillsides. No sign of life.

No armed interference.

Manning was next in line behind Encizo, the big Canadian's com link removed for the time being as he listened to the night, courtesy of a sound-amplifying Game Ear. Basically an earplug, it magnified the slightest noise up to two hundred yards. Manning wasn't the sort to jump at leaves rustled by a nervous lemur, but he could damn well discern long in advance any approach of human traffic on foot or by vehicle. Calvin James was number three, the ex-SEAL likewise toting the M-16/M-203 combination, checking the infrared heat sensor in one hand, which would show two-legged life up to three hundred yards. While Manning was volunteered by McCarter to pull sniper duty, his HK-33 assault rifle was a reliable piece of hardware in his capable hands. Hawkins claimed the fourth spot in the rolling march, had the task of wielding the big M-60 machine gun. The man-eater was already belted, Hawkins's chest crossed with bandoliers of 7.62 mm ammo for the squad killer. Hawkins and Encizo also had rope, with fixed grappling iron, curled around their shoulders to get them over the courtyard wall.

Conventional covert wisdom when operating in foreign countries, McCarter knew, either for deep-cover operatives or headhunting commandos, called for the use of weapons that would never indicate a fallen warrior's origin of state. Dead was still dead the last time he checked his own field manual. And since the President's hope was they bag a few trophies to take back to the States to stand trial before God and the world, McCarter knew it was pointless to cover up any hint of Western identity. They skipped the black warpaint, too, since there would be nothing stealthy about their attack.

Spectre would lay waste to designated targets. While the sky dropped on the compound, Phoenix would move in and start tagging or bagging.

Nothing cute, nothing tricky.

Basic slaughter circus. And if they wanted to be taken into custody, willingly, that was fine with McCarter. The ex-SAS commando, however, was anticipating the bad guys holding their ground, going out with a roar, to a shooter.

Sounded like a good deal to him. Hell, it was the only game he cared to play, in their face, take them down and out.

Encizo raised a hand, signaled they pull up and gather round. The Cuban was pointing up the rise of the next hill, toward two baobab trees. The so-called upside-down trees had already been marked by sat imagery as the gate to the compound on the other side of the hill. Over the top, from there a descent, then a walk into the valley of death.

McCarter keyed one of three buttons on his com link, patched through to Grimaldi. "Phoenix One to Sky-Hammer, come in, SkyHammer."

"SkyHammer here. Go."

"ETA?"

"Thirteen minutes. I can see shoreline now."

McCarter knew it was time to ratchet up the pace another notch. They needed to be in position when Spectre started the fireworks.

"We're in their backyard, SkyHammer, and rolling on. You know what to do."

"Roger, Phoenix One. We aim to please."

"See you on the other side, SkyHammer, over and out."

McCarter lifted and dropped his arm, and the five heavily armed shadows hit the slope. Thirteen minutes and counting, the Briton thought.

Then it was only rock and roll, but he could damn well be sure the blokes on the receiving end weren't about to like it.

FHALID HADN'T BEEN fully truthful with the Sudanese general. But truth, like beauty, he thought, was in the eye, or on the tongue, of the beholder.

Yes, it disturbed him deeply that men who had served the revolution faithfully up to then had turned traitor. Yes, it angered him greatly the obscene manner in which they had been executed. Well, the general had mentioned something about a man forced to sometimes join hands with the devil to fulfill his own goals, see his enemies eventually trampled in the dust or left standing only to serve the victors. History, he thought, was always meant to be rewritten in the blood of the vanquished. In that light, Fhalid was beginning to think of Arakkhan as the devil. The man was as ambitious, as self-centered and self-serving as any he had ever seen, bloated on ego, indulging himself with his toys flown here from Khartoum while the Iranians ate little more than rice and bread and slept in filth. No, he didn't trust Arakkhan any farther than he could spit, certainly not now, after witnessing three of his own people getting impaled, as if the general was showing off his blood lust, hoping, he suspected, to make the rest of them cringe, or bow and scrape to his every whim.

On the plus side, Fhalid was in daily contact with his sponsor on the island in the Strait of Hormuz. The satlink came into his hands, thanks to Chinese bene-factors, who, of course, monitored every transmission beamed from the island to Qeshm. Yet another bargain struck up with devils.

A day of victory, of judgment against the infidels was coming, and he would do whatever was necessary to see his people gouge at least one eye out of the Great Satan. If nothing else, Fhalid understood the dire importance of acquiring the Western technology that involved dis-rupting satellite transmissions, the use of high-tech laser beams that could melt the engines of ships, tanks, even fighter jets and render them useless junk. If they even existed. Simple, though, was always cleanest when killing the enemy, as far as he was concerned. He would have preferred a mass shipment of chemical or biolog-ical weapons. Or a twenty-kiloton-nuclear package, hauled along in a suitcase, set off in some American city. But his sponsor, his imam, was clear, emphatic to the point of desperation. A deal had been carved out, behind his back, and he would carry his orders through, even if it meant martyrdom.

He was following the general toward a large stone structure—the armory—when he thought he heard some distant rumble.

Like rolling thunder.

"They are component parts for chemical laser weapons," the general said, beaming around his cigar. "The problem is I need the data manual on assembly."

"Sudan, again."

"I have contacts there who assure me it is being delivered as we speak."

Fhalid glanced at the three Madagascan soldiers trailing them to the armory, their AK-47s leftovers, no doubt, from the days of communism. He wasn't sure why, but he kept searching the skies around the compound, ears straining as he thought the thunder was now pealing louder, bearing down. Aware he was weaponless, he felt an inexplicable urge to head back for the barracks and rouse his men from sleep, or those who somehow managed to drop into slumber after viewing the hideous spectacle still suspended in the courtyard.

The general was rambling on about something called the Ramrod Intercept, how once whoever was in possession of the state-of-the-art high-energy X-ray laser could ID, track and break into satellite transmissions.

"Let us just say they are 'bankrupters,'" the general said, chuckling. "Without their eyes in the sky watching you, troops can be amassed, anytime, anywhere. You will seize the advantage, say, if your country chose to attack its hated neighbor, Iraq."

It wasn't all that simple, Fhalid thought. Nothing was that simple.

"What is it?"

Fhalid noticed he had stopped in his tracks, the general looking concerned as the thunder sounded in long rolling peals from the north, a great wave of noise washing toward them. He was about to shake his head and fall back in step, thinking it had to be some aberration of nature, when a Madagascan soldier came running from the communications building.

"General! A large aircraft is flying for the compound. They do not respond to our calls."

Fhalid felt his heart lurch. He was about to curse the general for incompetence or negligence when he spotted the craft in question.

And it was a behemoth, filling his eyes like some vision from hell, coming in low from the north.

For the compound!

He couldn't say one hundred percent, but Bahruz Fhalid knew some undetermined enemy had come to destroy them. A moment later, his suspicion was confirmed as the cannon on the port side of the winged leviathan began pounding out its doomsday payload.

MANNING SECURED a roost in a narrow swath cut in the hillside. Waist deep in the hole, he settled the HK-33 on the edge, taking in the compound below. Their chronometers in sync with Spectre, all that was left to do was wait for Grimaldi and company to hit the scene and get the big show started.

Soften things up down there, he knew, while the other commandos moved in, mopped up, and maybe bagged a few big shots.

Enemy compounds, he once again noted, were always much larger and more sprawling in real time than they looked on sat imagery. The French garrison was no different. The gruesome handiwork of the Sudanese general—one of the more notable cannibals they had come there to snap up—was in full view, planted smack in the middle of the courtyard. Klieg lights, spaced around the parapets, seemed to home beams directly on the impaled figures, as if they were trophies to be admired. A bad way to go, he thought, long and painful.

Soon enough, Manning knew the misery would get spread around.

Panning on, Manning spotted the shadows of Encizo, McCarter, Hawkins and James moving in on the wall. They were already splitting up, Hawkins and James veering off to hit the wall from the north, McCarter and Encizo ready to put the clamp down from the south. Each team lugged along one grappling hook. Once Spectre announced doomsday, they would go over the wall and let it rip.

It was something of a pleasant surprise to Manning they had gotten so far in such a short time, sticking to the timetable laid out by the Farm. No roving patrols, not even a sentry on the walls, but satellite monitoring had already shown them the enemy force was slack when it came to the finer details of military life.

Their problem.

Manning raised the assault rifle, adjusted the scope on the group taking up real estate beyond the west wall, call it two hundred yards and change. He framed the face of the Sudanese general, then moved on, catching an eyeful of one Bahruz Fhalid. The infamous Iranian terrorist was looking at the sky, ears prickling, Manning could well guess, at the rolling thunder coming from the north.

Counting down.

Manning didn't have to wait much longer. The winged behemoth showed up, boiling out of the black sky, right on schedule, and got the party started.

CHAPTER EIGHT

Malibu, California

Considering the circumstances, that the end of life in his world as he knew it could come to a screeching end, Miles Godwin should have known better, but he couldn't help himself. He needed relief, bliss, in fact, and he needed it now. The problem with smoking cocaine was that, yes, it provided bliss on tap, he knew, but relief was about as attainable as catching a fistful of the wind. There was the usual paranoia, of course, the merciless, agitated craving to keep doing more and more. Only this night he felt jacked up to new extreme heights he'd never before known, soaring out there, somewhere in the ozone, flying along on electrified senses that felt pricked by hot needles. Settle down, he told himself, lifting his glass of whiskey off the coffee table, taking a deep slug, smoothing out the razor edges so he could enjoy the next fat monster bomber. Thank God, he thought, he was in Malibu, among the idle rich, safe from the madness of the city. Removed, no less, from the black widow's web of DYSAT and those crew-cut thugs who would give the Terminator nightmares.

The mini-propane torch in hand, Sally hit the rock, melting it down until the bowl swelled up like a white balloon. He was always amazed how much smoke the woman—all five foot four and one hundred pounds of her—could take in. When she held it, then blew out a never ending stream, Godwin figured there was a cloud thick enough to walk on, clear across the living room, unfurling all the way to the balcony overlooking the Pacific.

She had some pair of lungs on her, he had to admit, inside and out. She should, he decided, she was a former porn star, after all, with looks that would make a saint gawk and consider all manner of pleasures of the flesh. He glanced up at the giant-screen TV, where Sally had popped in one of her "classics," killing time until she saw fit to hand over the pipe. The sound was off, but Godwin was enjoying an eyeful of her work, just the same. It was a lesbian scene, and Sally looked to him to sure enjoy her work. No actress, she also liked to prance around in the raw when smoking up, and he felt a brief tug in his loins, wanting to reach over and lay her down on the couch. Well, the other problem with smoking rock, he knew, was that it would take four, maybe five days before he glimpsed even the hint of a half erection.

Well, life could be tough like that, he decided. It was all pressure, the need to unwind, let it go, then fall back into the routine, he believed. This was Hollywood anyway, where stress and performance demanded a vice or two, just to stay sane, in the game.

Rocking up was a weekly ritual for Miles Godwin. He needed to unwind, at least once, sometimes twice a week depending on how the mood swung him. The rigors of working for DYSAT, finagling arms deals off the books, was enough to test even the moral resolve of say, he thought, Job. This was his sanctuary, his slice of heaven. The split-level, three-million-dollar pad overlooked the ocean, perched on a rocky precipice, away from the so-called Colony, that monied-up enclave of the rich and famous who partied up a storm behind secured wrought-iron gates, her posh abode likewise far away from the wanna-be stars who were crammed into those choked rows of beach houses down Pacific Highway.

Sally had inherited the home after her former boyfriend, a major player in the Hollywood coke scene, was burned by the Feds and went upstate, he believed, the name of the penitentiary escaping him. The house had been put in her name, and she was now locked in an ongoing court battle with the Feds for possession of the home. Swell guy that he was, Miles Godwin knew she was lonely these days, her man locked away for the next fifteen to twenty-five in a cage where reputation in the outside world didn't mean squat to some gorilla who wanted his cellmate to put on a dress and wig. That in mind, he supposed life could always be worse.

At the moment, it was bad enough, but he was doing his damnedest to try to forget.

She finally parted with the pipe, and Godwin figured it was time to load up a white nugget the size of his thumb. He went to town, the whiskey kicking in, the expected instant jolt taking him straight to heaven on Earth as the smoke flooded his brain.

"Take it easy, we have all night, Miles."

How could he fully relax, he thought, with what he had inside the leather-bound briefcase at his feet? Stolen from a courier, no less, his pals in the company vanishing all over the place, every shadow or motorist on the freeway a potential armed killer or a Fed.

On the upshot of life in the fast lane, he knew she wasn't concerned about running low on the good stuff, eighty percent Peruvian flake. The flying narc squad had been more than happy with the ten kilos they found in the bedroom, missing the two-key stash squirreled away beneath a floorboard under the kitchen sink.

Godwin felt funny, rose from the couch, wobbly, nauseous. He was shaking, his coiffed-up two-hundred dollar haircut feeling as if it were wilting from the heat radiating inside his brain. Trembling, he set down the bowl, pluming still with smoke.

"I need some air."

"Miles, you've been acting weird since you got here. I mean, you keep looking at your briefcase…like…I don't know, there's a bomb or something in it."

Oh, that was rich, he thought. Like the muted scene on the television he had the urge to tell her she was a much nicer person when she kept her mouth shut, that she should be seen and not heard.

"Miles? Miles, are you all right?"

He couldn't find his tongue, a frozen lead weight in his mouth. He was shimmying toward the balcony, felt the sharp pains, a giant slicing dagger in his chest, his heart doing some weird fluttering dance, when a shadow swept through the curtain. He was sucking in deep breaths, gasping for air, as he felt the bones melting out of his legs. Maybe it was terror at the sight of the last man on earth he wanted to see, but the world started to rush around him on a carousel.

"Mr....Mr. Lake."

"That's Colonel Lake to you, son."

And the lights blinked out for Miles Godwin.

THE ADDRESS off Pacific Coast Highway, handed off to Able Team by the late DYSAT playboys, was right on the money, but the setup felt all wrong to Carl Lyons. He could feel the enemy beyond, something evil in the air, a heat hovering around them with a life of its own.

The van was ditched in a canyon cutting close to the foothills of the Santa Monica Mountains. A brisk jog in for the beach compound, the commandos loaded down with Colt Commando assault rifles, and Lyons broached the march into the drive. Problems right off, and Lyons knew what waited. The gates were wide, the control panel jimmied open, wires crossed.

They were late for the party.

The commandos stuck to the lush vegetation, single file, legging it swiftly twenty yards up the driveway, until the split-level home loomed into sight.

Silently, spying the Towncar, two vans and Mercedes that were jammed into the circular driveway, Able Team melted into the dense undergrowth.

Hunched, Blancanales and Schwarz hemming him in, Lyons told the commandos, "Full bore. Gadgets, hit the front door. Pol and me will go up the balcony. If it's armed, drop it. If they grab up our boy here, don't hesitate and get locked into a dance with these guys. Shoot to kill. I want home runs out of the gate."

And Able Team surged ahead for round three. A crazy colonel and his mad-dog shooters were on the grounds. Lyons wasn't about to stand around and hope he could talk some sense into these guys.

It was time to yank Lake's ticket.

HE WAS STILL ALIVE, no stroke finishing him off, and he was grateful to be clawing his way back to the land of the living. At first, Godwin thought they'd dumped him in the ocean, cooling him off, reviving him with a brisk dunking in the Pacific. Then he felt the warm stream splashing him in the face, smelled the bitter taint digging deeper into his nose.

"He's coming around."

A voice he didn't recognize. Then Lake, "Get up, son. Get your sorry ass up."

He was almost afraid to, the real world nothing but

a place of darkness and nightmare, but somehow Godwin managed to open his eyes. And found the colonel standing over him, zipping up his pants.

Lake was grinning, holding some sort of submachine gun. "Didn't Mommy ever tell you drugs are bad for you? Whatever happened to Just Say No? Now I understand why personnel was always howling about all the sick leave you were taking every other week. Oh, well, welcome to Hollywood, huh? All the beautiful people. Everyone doing their own thing, passing off garbage as art, brainwashing the little people. You ever stop and think all the money the idle rich throw away on this garbage they could feed the starving masses in some North African hellhole?"

His head feeling stuffed with cotton, his shirtfront slick with bile, Godwin let himself get pushed toward the couch, where he stumbled and landed next to Sally, Lake sounding off with a rolling chuckle. She was getting more than a few approving stares, and he couldn't decide if she was terrified, indignant or craving a quick fix.

Lake claimed a seat across the coffee table, eyeing the bag of flake, the paraphernalia used to base it up. Godwin was trying to get a read on how many gunmen were roaming about, saw two on the balcony, counted two more staking out positions near the bar. As if, he thought, he could actually do something heroic. No action hero of film lore, he knew he was stuck, trapped. He needed to find some angle, some way to smooth talk Lake into thinking he could play ball, keep his mouth shut, life could carry on. But what? One read into those eyes, and he feared Lake wouldn't accept the Holy Grail from him.

"Johnny Carson your neighbor?" Lake said, chuckling, examining Sally like some exotic animal in a cage. "I always wanted to meet Johnny. That new guy? He's a little too PC for my taste. Anyway, relax, both of you. Go on, help yourselves. I understand. Everyone has something to hide, everyone has a monkey on their backs."

Godwin felt the chill walk down his back. He had always only seen this man in board meetings, in control, level but firm, the president in charge of the company, interested in the bottom line of business, progress. This was another side, Godwin thought, a dark side, raging out of the closet. Lake's eyes didn't even look human, just two orbs of flames, peering into…no, he corrected, "through" him.

Godwin almost couldn't believe it, but didn't expect much less as Sally loaded up a bomber and went to work, handing off the pipe after a deep pull.

"Go on, son," Lake encouraged when Godwin hesitated.

This time around he took a smaller hit, drawing just enough smoke to wash out the sludge from his blackout.

"Feel better already. Good. Now, I'll take back what is mine," Lake said, and grunted at one of the henchmen who stepped up, claiming the briefcase.

Godwin felt those awful eyes again, the chuckle filling the living room. "I hate thieves, Miles. I hate liars, cheats and I especially," he said, boring the look into Sally, "hate little suck-bitch coke whores."

"Hey…"

Sally, courage obviously fueled by her high, edged up on the couch, ready to pound out her anger, then seemed to think better of it, as Lake lifted the subgun an inch off his lap.

"Here's the deal, boys and girls. You see, I have a vice myself, an urge, an impulse I can't control. I've actually been created by the society we live in, but I don't expect you to understand. My problem, my addiction, it's called killing people, specifically those liars, cheats and whores."

Godwin thought he was going to be sick, or faint. "Mr. Lake, Colonel, please, I can—"

"You can what? Explain? The company's finished. Your future, eveyone's future at DYSAT no longer exists. I was always going to bail, leave you pretty boys, or so I hoped, holding your puds in your hands for the Feds. This way, it's much cleaner. You know, just think of yourselves as the unborn, never born, gone to limbo by way of this new abortion pill. Popped out into the toilet, flushed away. You know, I really have seen the end of civilization. Sometimes, I think I can even hear the devil laughing, hard at work from his fiery little cubicle, telling all you people what you want to hear, giving you all you want, indulging your sick desires, as you sell your souls like the whores you are. Right now, I'm seeing the end of your world. Fear not, however. At least you'll die at the hands of a real man, a warrior."

"Oh, God, no," Sally cried, "you can't...you can't just kill us. I don't even really know him...or what's going on. I have no idea."

Lake let the chuckle fly. "And thus the whore reveals herself. Take a look at what you pandered to, son, and for what? Say good night, Gracie."

Godwin was on his feet, heard himself begging for the man not to do it, there was some mistake, he'd make it right. The eyes were nailing him as soon as he started flapping his lips, judging him as he squawked for mercy, then he saw the submachine gun coming up, its nose flaming. He felt the impact of bullets tearing into him, a fiery pain carving him up, driving him down. He heard the cry of his own horror and pain, ripping out—the injustice and insanity of it all—then fading out to some dark, soundless point far away, calling him down. Then the black curtain dropped over his eyes, telling Miles Godwin he was already gone.

CHAPTER NINE

Blancanales had been volunteered by Lyons for the dubious honor of moving in on their quarry from the east. While Schwarz went through the front door, Lyons scaling the long flight of steps toward the balcony from the west, Blancanales crept in at damn near a snail's pace, Colt Commando up and searching for enemy meat. The problem, the way he saw it, was the rocky precipice, the house nearly jutting out over the cliffside, right on top of Pol. One errant step, and Blancanales would find himself doing a header off the cliffside, a straight swan dive some hundred feet or more for the bed of boulders getting a harsh pounding by the sea far below him.

Already he heard the shooting from beyond the balcony, at some point inside what he figured was the living room. A man and a woman, screaming for their lives to be spared, then the unmistakable stammer of the crazy ex-colonel's Uzi.

Lake, no doubt, had gone berserk once more.

The second problem, going in, was Able Team had no fix on the number of shooters on the premises. Judging the seating capacity of the combined vehicles out front, assuming one of them belonged to the late lady of the house, and he surmised a ballpark figure of eight, ten shooters tops.

Any more armed buzz cuts in the wings, and they were pushing lady luck to throw them a beanball to the head.

He didn't think they built homes on the cliffside, raised on stilts in California anymore, due in no small part to the wrath of Mother Nature. An earthquake, or a mudslide, and the whole structure would go plunging for the Pacific, crushed to matchsticks on the rocks below. It didn't really matter in his final analysis what the architecture, but he needed to take a few more treacherous steps farther out on the precipice if he was to line up his own shooting gallery.

Lyons wanted a straight bulldozer approach, nothing but heavy metal thunder, gloves off. Well, let there be rock and roll, Blancanales thought, easing away from the balcony, the sound of pounding footsteps washing over him from above.

And he lined up two heads out of the gate.

The shorter version of the M-16 raised, Blancanales took up slack on the trigger and went to work. The first two lines of 5.56 mm slugs stitched one, then number-two hardman up the crotch, zipping crimson holes on the way up to savage windpipes to ragged meat. Now that he had their attention, as a shadow gunmen leaned over the railing and started winging out the subgun fire, he scampered beneath the balcony. The muzzle velocity of his Colt Commando rounds was in the neighborhood of 880 meters per second. Plenty of punch to get them tap dancing as he sprayed the flooring of the balcony beneath their feet. He got lucky, drawing third blood, making somebody sing soprano, as a piercing howl was swept out to sea, then heavyweight hammered off the deck. He had to have nailed a foot, maybe cleaved off a pair of family jewels, since the thrasher above was cursing vicious enough to make this week's rapper flash-in-the-pan blush.

A moment later, he became aware of the stammering autofire from the stairs to the west.

Lyons was hard at work himself, squeezing down the lead clamp.

Blancanales wished the big guy luck, but knew Ironman had a way of creating his own unique brand of charm.

LYONS WAS HALFWAY up the steps, mentally kicking around the architect genius who decided a raised balcony, this stairway to heaven—giving an eagle's-nest view of the Pacific for as far as the eye could see—might up the market value of this patch of real estate. He didn't even bother counting the number of steps, just swiftly hauled his bulk up higher, closing down, the heads of two goons coming into sight when the screaming and the shooting inside the house started, then ended abruptly.

Blancanales got the killing match for the home side under way, chopping up two sea-gapers closest to the railing. They came running through the balcony door next, Lyons meeting Lake's wild-eyed stare for a brief moment.

"You guys again! I'm getting real tired of you assholes! You're like that one fly in the room you can never get rid of!"

And Lyons let his Colt Commando do the talking for him. Another buzz-cut issue was toppling, Lyons figuring Pol was rearranging the deck from below, the hardman's foot all but disappearing in a dark crimson mist. Lake was holding his ground, the defiant one again, triggering his Uzi, and Lyons was forced to duck as lead sailed over his scalp. The deck getting a lead termite savaging made them change their evacuation strategy as Lake surged back through the balcony doorway. Lyons bolted up two more steps, glimpsed a hardman lugging a briefcase and hit him in the chest with ten to twelve rounds. The guy was dancing back, hosing the sky with his HK MP-5, twitching and gaping out his shock and horror. Momentum and the impact of Lyons's crashing lead wall sent him bulling on his way through the railing, briefcase sailing out to the dark night.

"No! You bastards!"

Lake. Catching the sight of whatever goodies were

in the briefcase going down the cliff, Lyons gathered, to be swallowed up by the sea.

No time to cry that even the good guys were striking out all over the map, losing songbirds and high-tech merchandise over half of L.A.

Any butt-chewing was on the backburner for later, when Brognola got the scorecard, and found Able Team had struck out when the bases were loaded.

Zero stoolies.

Shit happened.

Lyons topped the steps, and pinned the fallen hardman with a 3-round burst to the chest. He was moving for the open entrance when Lake, all bellows and curses, hosed the jamb, smashing out the glass with tracking autofire. With any luck, Lyons figured Schwarz was right now rolling in on the enemy's six, going for the blind-side slice and dice.

SCHWARZ HIT THE FOYER running. He was surging around a corner, spotting them folding in a human wave back into the living room, when he gave them another rude jolt, mowing down three hardmen with a long burst of dicing autofire. Lake was either blessed with pure dumb luck, or some unholy dark angel was holding the guy's hand, Schwarz thought. Somehow, he was hemmed in by a phalanx of his shooters, by chance or design, Schwarz couldn't say. By the time Schwarz tagged the trio, dropped them, crimson human dominoes, Lake was a bolt of lightning, dashing around the corner of some adjacent room.

Three shooters left, and they proved hell-bent on covering the insane ex-colonel's flight out of there. He figured Lake was searching for another avenue out of the house, a garage perhaps.

Then the ex-colonel rejoined his hard force, directed a sudden burst that nearly scalped Schwarz. A trickle of blood hit Schwarz in the eye, as he flung himself for immediate refuge behind the couch that marked the final resting place of their last and very late songbird, and playmate.

"I don't know who you assholes are, but you can't beat the colonel!"

Schwarz hugged the carpet as lead hit the couch with a drumming thud.

"You girls don't understand one simple fact of life! Even God has sympathy for the devil! God just can't stand the guy's pride! Or maybe the devil's a woman! Imagine that! Makes sense to me!"

"Oh, man," Schwarz muttered to himself. "This joker's out there. Fruitcake."

The leadstorm abated in lessening degrees, as a cry of pain lashed the air and they started pulling their aim. Schwarz crabbed a few yards farther down the couch, then popped up in time to see Lyons had swung his assault rifle low around the balcony entrance to score a castrating crotch shot on a buzz-cut issue. The guy was hopping back, the HK MP-5 falling from hands more concerned with caressing the source of his misery, the end of his bloodline. Lyons eased his pain forever in the next moment with a rising burst to his chest, flinging him into a stereo cabinet.

Two shooters were dropping back, alternating their subgun sprays toward the balcony, then the couch. Schwarz caught a face full of blood as wild rounds tore into a corpse on the other side.

Standoff, while Lake fled, he knew.

A fresh clip cracked home, and Schwarz poured it on, chasing the shooters to cover in the adjoining room. When Blancanales's Colt Commando poked through the entrance, opposite Lyons's blazing weapon, three streams of autofire merged, eating up the wall, then scoring flesh. A belched grunt of pain, and the follow-up crash of a body told Schwarz they were nailing it down.

That left one shooter.

"Carl!" Schwarz shouted above the racket of autofire. "I'm going after Lake!"

Lyons was his typical understanding and compassionate self, Schwarz thought, and felt the grim smile hit his lips as his teammate roared, "So, get your ass moving! We'll finish this one scumbag!"

"WHO ARE YOU calling scumbag? You're talking to a goddamn air commando hero!"

Lyons hadn't intended to get the guy riled up any more than he already was, or push some emotional button to stoke his rage into a fatal careless move. But it happened that way, and Lyons had the self-proclaimed hero dead to rights.

He came cursing out of the dining room, all snarls and flaming subgun. Unfortunately for the raging braggart, he borrowed one too many pages from Lake's manual on anger management and reckless rebellion in the face of long odds, and flunked the whole course.

"I got more commendations and medals than you got hair on your nuts!"

"Nuts this!" Lyons roared back, and slung the barrel of his assault rifle low around the edge of the jamb. Holding back on the trigger as a round slashed the assault rifle and nearly ripped it from his hand, Lyons fired blind, marking the voice, mentally gauging the suicide march. The shooter's rounds were suddenly going high and wide, the sound of rage and agony reaching rock-concert decibels. A quick look and Lyons found he'd scored a knee. It was over in the next flung curse, as Blancanales assisted Lyons in a twelve-to-fifteen-round overkill, scything the hardman to scarlet ribbons, a dancing puppet that didn't want to go down. Before the boneless sack was even plunging for the final fall, Lyons and Blancanales were charging across the living room, homed in on the double stutters of autofire out front.

SCHWARZ WAS FORCED to beeline for the cover of some dense shrubbery. He was off the steps, veering for dicey cover, at best, as Lake leaned out the window of his Towncar, sweeping a long burst, reversing it out of there.

Lights out, Lake held back on the trigger of his Uzi. Schwarz felt the slipstream of hot lead hornets buzzing past his ears, the foliage eaten up, in his face.

"Try me on for size in Idaho, honey!"

Everything but an I-dare-you, Schwarz thought, plowing through the undergrowth as he heard tread shriek and claw at concrete, the roar of the engine seeming to grow louder by the second.

Schwarz came out of the brush, moved on down the driveway in a loping roll, triggering his Colt Commando. One second he was sure he had Lake's face lined up, then there was nothing but a shadowy veil as the guy's long mane flowed up when he dropped to a hunch beneath the steering wheel. Schwarz drilled three, maybe four spiderwebbed holes across the windshield, then the Towncar was whipping past the gate, an angry crush of brakes sliding it deeper into the darkness of the road beyond. A roar of the powerful engine, and the vehicle vanished.

Schwarz heard his teammates running up. He turned, looked at Ironman and Pol, both of them steaming in silence, mirror images of the frustration and anger he choked on.

"This guy's starting to really bug me," Lyons growled.

Lake was already long gone, and Schwarz knew by the time they retraced their steps to the van he would be well on his way.

"Idaho," Schwarz said.

"What?" Lyons growled.

"This guy's got a pair the size of Godzilla. Get this," he added, and relayed Lake's parting quote.

"Is that right?" Lyons said. "Well, I've always liked a challenge. Especially when the opposition's got a bull-dog way that makes me look neutered."

"But will Hal get it past the Man?" Blancanales said.

"Speaking of Hal," Schwarz stated, "who's going to be the messenger of all the bad news?"

FOLLOWING LYONS'S update and signing off to await further orders, Brognola hung his head. Sitting in a chair at Kurtzman's workstation, the big Fed sounded off a chuckle that rolled and hung like a death knell in the Computer Room, ripping out from a belly full of grim anxiety that would need a full packet of antacid tablets to smooth out. Two missions launched, well under way, but problems were rearing ugly doomsday mugs so fast the Justice man figured he might need a calculator to keep score on all the snafus.

"Why am I not surprised it went to hell in Holly-wood?" Brognola posed to no one in particular.

"It sounds like Able had no choice," Kurtzman offered.

They were monitoring the situation, via satellite, in Madagascar. It was already bombs away on the garri-son, and Brognola needed to focus on Phoenix Force. For the next few hours, Able Team was on hold.

"Lyons said Lake came right out and damn near chal-lenged them to try and hit the Idaho facility," Kurtzman said. "I say we get them cut loose, Hal. It's clear DYSAT is dirty. Time to send in the cleaning crew."

"As soon as Phoenix is wheels up, I'll get in touch with the Man," Brognola said. "We've made some preliminary arrangements on an incursion into the Idaho facility, right, Barbara?"

"All that needs to be done is to fly in the special package Gadgets requested," Price answered. "Beef up their ammo at the same time. It can be done in a few hours from our end."

"If," Tokaido said, "the President allows us to move on what he still thinks is a legitimate classified military facility."

"Able's up against a bunch of black-op, mad-dog killers," Brognola said, chomping down on his cigar. "I'll convince the President to give us the green light, don't you worry."

But Brognola wasn't so sure he could sell the plan of having Able Team storm the gates of the DYSAT complex, which was funded, in large part, by the Pentagon's Special Access Programs. Brognola had some grim experience in the past with black projects, Striker having dismantled in his own way classified military high-tech sanctuaries that believed they were above the laws of man and God. It would be a hard sell.

"Okay, people, let's focus on Phoenix for now."

And, Brognola thought, keep their fingers crossed the five commandos pulled off the seeming impossible. Sudan was up and on the board next, but the big Fed didn't even want to begin dwelling on Striker kicking ass and taking names, while traipsing around countryside that was as hostile to the West as the worst in Iran or Afghanistan. Striker, all but hung out there, alone, on his own.

One man, on deck, against God only knew how many thugs, cutthroats and killers, saboteurs and double agents. Brognola quietly chuckled to himself as he recalled what Bolan had told Barbara.

He'd figure it out.

So, Brognola thought, what was new?

CHAPTER TEN

Madagascar

Gary Manning made his decision for Big Brother, God, country, the free world and—last but hardly least—Phoenix Force to take the opening shots, bring down two heavies off the bat. It was only the grim beginning, the first of several snatch-ups of bad guys for Phoenix, he hoped, to tow back across the Atlantic for hard justice, Uncle Sam style. The justice end of any bagging of known killers here, of course, would ultimately fill only the eye of the judicial beholder, would come down in due course from the gavel of, hopefully, a hardballing judge.

Already he could see the media feeding frenzy when the smoke cleared and the stench of death and destruction here wafted all the way back to the States. He could already hear all the talking heads squawking every night on end over the moral prerogative of American military muscle squeezing the clamps on "alleged" international terrorists, all that who was really who and what was really right.

Not his problem.

The talking heads and Monday-morning quarter-backs weren't here on the firing line, probably never had much more to worry about in their day aside from what four-star restaurant they'd sashay into, and they could kindly kiss his Canadian ass. Like the other commandos of Phoenix Force, being a deniable expendable for covert operations out of Stony Man Farm damn near ranked him as a ghost with a license to kill, nothing more or less.

Five killing shadows, indeed. No headlines, no glory, nothing but pure guts on this end, and the knowledge of a job well done, that the world might be a little safer, brighter place when the mission was wrapped.

Manning's sniping task was about to end all discussion before it started. When he did it, they would need a doctor first, and soon, plus a heavy dose of painkiller for what he had them lined up for. In the plus column for the big Canadian, there would be no tense scene in the office of some wet-behind-the-ears D.A. two months out of Yale and who believed the glove didn't fit, had to acquit. No judge spouting off how he violated their constitutional rights, bleating out the nonsense, such as where did he get off torturing suspects, denying them medical attention, all that crazy shit that made the legal community go hunting for the scalps of men who put their lives on the line to dump the scum on their doorstep for what was, sadly, all too often a gentle slap on the wrist.

The choices were everywhere, no question, bursting out of the barracks, scurrying pell-mell from the disintegrating rubble of radar and tracking structures, and Manning made the first call of many in the name of justice.

So many savages. So few bullets.

The face of the Sudanese general was a picture of utter panic, so close in the mounted telescopic sight, it looked as if Manning could reach out and touch him.

He did. Considering the many crimes and atrocities committed by his first two marks, he could have opted for doling out some serious agony. Such as blowing off an elbow, or maybe putting a 5.56 mm castrator through the man's package. Instead, he chopped Arakkhan off at the ankles, and in a very real literal bloody sense. Unlike Hollywood tripe, a bullet tearing through sinew and muscle and nerves hurt. And when a round shattered bone, through and through, the appendage generally required amputation. The general was down, thrashing, his shrieking lost to the sound and fury of the Spectre eating up the world around the enemy. There was little question in Manning's mind that the Sudanese general would lose that foot, at best. The Iranian butcher from his memorized photo lineup was next, frozen at the sight of his fallen dark angel, framed in the crosshairs when Manning lowered the sights, took up slack on the trigger and let another 5.56 mm round fly. Muzzling along at nearly one thousand meters per second, the round all but blew off Bahruz Fhalid's foot, a dark mist swelling up the sights in Manning's scope.

The Iranian cutthroats were now charging out of the barracks, hurling out the panic in shouts and bellows, armed with assault rifles. They started winging off some rounds at the winged behemoth, but they might as well, Manning knew, blow spitballs at the aircraft. Grimaldi and company returned the favor, softening it up some more as planned, the Bofors cannon, manned by two blacksuits, pounding out a wake-up call that leveled half the troop quarters in a line of rolling fireballs.

The sky was, indeed, falling.

And Manning stole a second to admire the Spectre's handiwork. The big Canadian had seen the mammoth warbird in action before, the mother of all flying destroyers, as far as he was concerned. The racket of the combined fury of the 105 mm howitzer, twin 20 mm Vulcan Gatling cannons able to pump out 3000 rounds per minute and the Bofors was the ultimate message of doomsday from the sky.

Of course, Manning's preference would have been going into the gory mix with his buddies, side by side, running and gunning. But McCarter had laid out his role, which was no less critical than the four commandos mopping it up on the floor show, wrapping the plastic cuffs on those with more good sense than murderous defiance. A few well-placed shots, and Manning could bag some notorious names in the terrorist scene for interrogation and trial. Or so the scheme went.

So far it was working out, all dark light and bitter sweetness for the first two down there, rolling around and howling out their misery. Not only that, but Manning could cover their flanks, their rear if some cutthroat popped up on their blind side.

He lifted the assault rifle and went back to searching for more savage game.

THE PAIN NEARLY MADE him weep. The noise of the assaulting warbird, uprooting his command post, the radar and tracking station, was so loud, endless peals like thunder from hell shattering his eardrums, Arakkhan couldn't tell if he was, in fact, crying or screaming. Looking down through the burning mist in his eyes, he saw his left ankle was hanging by a few strands of tendons, pieces of bone looking stark white in the flashing halo of the warbird's firestorm. He looked around, thinking he was about to throw up from the pain and the horror, wondering what the hell had happened, who was attacking them with such ferocity, such audacity.

He needed to get to the airfield somehow, even if that meant crawling like some snake on his belly all the way there.

He hadn't seen the shot that had brought him down, the bullet that had claimed a foot he was certain he would lose to a surgeon's knife. That meant some commando force had moved in, he suspected, from the hills, marching even then into the garrison. Thirty Iranians, and nearly as many Madagascan soldiers...

They had to be enough to repel the invasion. How many enemy soldiers could possibly storm the garrison anyway? The warbird was a monster, no question, and he was thinking perhaps they had landed by parachute. The size of the winged beast, and he put the number of enemy soldiers in the fifty to seventy range.

"Help me up!" he hollered at the Madagascan soldiers, then watched as all three of them fled, leaving him to lie there and choke on his agony, concerned only with saving their own hides. He was cursing them for cowardice, when he heard another oath flung from somewhere in all the sound and fury.

"You incompetent bastard!"

Fhalid, he saw, was down and raging, part of his foot missing, a dark pool spreading in the red dirt of the courtyard.

"We have to get to the airplane!"

"How!" Fhalid somehow shimmied to stand, then started hopping toward him on his good foot. "They'll destroy our aircraft, you fool. They are Americans!"

"How do you know?"

"That's an American aircraft! It's over!"

"We must leave."

The general noted the fire in Fhalid's eyes, and it went much deeper than pure agony. He was insane, casting blame, looking to punish the man he believed responsible for this disaster. There was no point in attempting to reason with the Iranian, explaining the need to bail, fly on, regroup, try to get the deal launched another time and place. Fhalid's hands turned to claws as he hobbled closer, his face twisted in hate.

"I'll strangle the life out of you."

The thought of dying cleared some of the pain away, as Arakkhan fumbled to free the Makarov pistol. He was swinging it up, finger curled around the trigger when—

At first it felt like a beesting, then, before the pall of

shock could fully settle over him, he saw the pistol was gone—along with his trigger and middle fingers. He was about to cut loose with a bellow of pain and rage when he spotted Fhalid hopping around, twitching like some crazed dancer. Blood was spurting from his legs, Fhalid howling as his thigh absorbed a round or two, then his knee was lost to another silent bullet.

The general felt the bile shooting up his chest, a pitiful-sounding chuckle in his throat at the sight of Fhalid going down. If nothing else, he decided his misery enjoyed the Iranian's company. Whoever was sniping them could have killed them outright. Whoever it was, he was sending a message.

Stay down.

At the moment, any amount of pain was preferable to death, and lying utterly still seemed like the wisest option.

Arakkhan covered his head next as the flying rubble from the massive explosions rained down around the courtyard.

THE CANNIBALS WERE intent on devouring each other. It happened like that, Manning knew, when the world of the savage was threatened to get snatched away, all twisted dreams and ambitions getting shoved down their throats. It was simply the nature of the dark force to cast blame, search out scapegoats, lash out.

Working on that instinct, he checked back, found his first two big tags ready to eat each other up as their world came crashing down, and doomsday was in their face.

They might bleed out, of course, lapse into shock before the four commandos could rustle them up, but he'd made the call to keep them down and breathing for now.

Roundup was later.

Right now, he saw his four friends were set to go over the wall. The problem was a bunch of cutthroats were waiting close by, on the other side from both teams.

It looked like it was time, after all, he decided, to start the turkey shoot.

"TAKE OUT the transport and the executive jet, Jack," Brognola heard Barbara Price order Grimaldi. "We're showing some runners heading toward the airfield. How do you look on fuel?"

"Even with the payload we brought to the show," Grimaldi reported back over the satlink, "not too shabby. Time allowing, I might fuel up, though, in case I have to take the long way back to Tanzania."

Which meant, Brognola thought, flying out to the Indian Ocean, beyond any radar net from Tana.

"Spare the fuel bin, but take out those birds," Price said.

"Affirmative."

"Stay in the sky and give Phoenix air support on their way out of the garrison."

"I copy. Time to get back to work. SkyHammer, over and out."

So far, so good, Brognola thought. The sat imagery showed the main radar and tracking housing, the command post were demolished ruins. Now the tough part, he knew. The butcher's work was up and coming as Phoenix Force scaled the wall to move in on foot. Outside Striker, they were best at what they did.

Killing the enemy, and in droves.

He could only sit by and hope that this time out the best was enough.

MCCARTER WAS over the wall, going into the twelve-foot drop, braced for impact when he saw the first group of Iranians take notice of his encroachment. He hit the soft red earth, stumbled some, then tapped the trigger of his M-203. Encizo landed next, as the thunderclap rocked the group of terrorists. The fireball blew a few of them this way and that, mangled stick figures sailing away to crunch up in smoking heaps, but the problems were only just beginning to crop up. The Briton was already hosing down two nearby Iranians who flinched at the blast with a blanket of 5.56 mm sendoffs, kicking them back in a jerky dance of spasming limbs.

They were spinning, falling fast and hard when Encizo linked up and they surged ahead together. The multiround projectile launcher in hand, Encizo blew away a pack of hardmen with two 40 mm fireballs. The way ahead, as they angled in on the barracks, was clear, but McCarter knew that was about to change any second.

The compound was rocking, flaming debris dropping from the sky, the Spectre having left nothing but smoking craters where the main structures to the west once stood.

Voices sounding the alarm in Farsi were raised in the distance, beyond the south edge of the barracks. Things were just getting heated up, McCarter knew, as he made the corner with Encizo by his side, and started counting up the armed opposition.

Some alert hardman, whipped up into a frenzy by both terror and adrenaline, was wheeling toward the two invaders, pointing and shouting.

Striking up the band, McCarter thought, as maybe ten Iranian cutthroats lifted AK-47s, going for broke.

Holding back on the trigger of his M-16, Encizo chugged out the 40 mm payloads of mass death, as the rest of Phoenix Force opened up.

As many as Phoenix Force mowed, McCarter saw just as many boiling up, edged out there and braced to go for it.

The slaughter show, the Briton knew, was only in the first act. From there on he knew damn well it would only get uglier.

CHAPTER ELEVEN

Calvin James knew it would never make him any less courageous, certainly no less of a warrior. But he could still feel his nerves on fire, the fear some lingering aftertaste following their close encounter with the great fish. Fear was a good thing, he knew, a tool, in fact, if a man let the feeling move him toward action, using it much like a carpenter would a hammer and saw.

Or in this case an assault rifle and raw determination, moving on, into the fire, nerves of steel, balls of iron.

The ex-SEAL had the dubious honor of going over the wall first—or, rather, legs draped over the edge, catching the big M-60 chucked up by Hawkins, who then scaled the rope in two seconds flat. The kind of brutal training a special class of soldier underwent before knowing the honor of becoming a SEAL, or, in Hawkins's case, an Airborne Ranger, never quite left a man's memory. In fact, it remained in the heart, forever more, something that lived on, an anchor of the soul, an anvil of the warrior character that never faded away, no matter what life—or the threat of death—threw his way. A warrior, he knew, used fear, even pain to motivate him, dig deeper, push himself even harder when he thought he had nothing left to give.

Such was the heart pounding, the spirit moving in Hawkins, who was on the wall in two shakes, M-60 plucked from his buddy, and they were going over and down, free-falling together.

They landed, and not an eye blink too soon.

There were armed targets aplenty, scampering dead ahead, and James and Hawkins got busy racking up a few quick scores. Three Iranians had whirled their way, for whatever reason, and there was no time to wonder if it was plain animal instinct or some fluke of battle-field psychic intuition. Veering away from each other, presenting no packed twin easy pickings, James opened up with his M-16 while Hawkins got the flesh-shredding M-60 cranked up. Three toppled right off, screaming scarecrows chopped to ribbons. Two more fanatics came flying around the north end of the barracks, nearly had the two Phoenix Force commandos dead to rights when slick fingers of crimson were jetting out their shattered skulls in a lightning one-two punch.

Thank you, Gary, James thought, you'll have a Bud on me, and rolled on.

A wave of terrorists was now beating a jagged flight across the courtyard, James noted, the more sensible opting for the bailout. James hit the corner while Hawkins cut loose with the M-60, sweeping a heavy metal burst of thunder across the courtyard, cutting down a quick six or seven runners, all rubber limbs and sharp grunts and free-flying AKs leaving lifeless hands. Two of the Iranian tags were bulled ahead by the ex-Ranger's wall of 7.62 mm NATO man-eaters, and bowled down the impaled, landing in tattered heaps on top of their already dead brothers in jihad.

They had the plastic cuffs brought to the party, but the way it was shaping up, James was having serious reservations whether they'd make the President proud with a big catch or two.

They were locked in but good and ugly with the enemy, and these guys didn't strike James as wishing to find themselves sitting in some American courtroom, facing twenty life sentences or so.

Work to do.

James flung his M-16 around the corner, spotted something of a standoff at the far south end. A few of the more terrified and less battle-hardened types thought they could become human rats digging a burrow into the smoking wreckage of the barracks where the Spectre had sounded the reveille of Armageddon.

Okay, James figured he'd do it the hard way, a frag bomb or two leading the way before he went into the dark ruins and dug them out.

First, McCarter and Encizo looked as if they could use a helping hand.

"T.J.! Cover me! I'm southbound! Our buddies down there need a little help from their friends!"

"Gotcha!"

DEMOLITIONS, namely the gutsy art of defusing, was primarily Manning's claim to military expertise. Of course, setting off the fireworks had been left to Grimaldi and company, so he stuck to the game plan, out of both discipline, loyalty and to make sure his comrades walked out of there in one piece.

On his worst day he would never indulge such an emotion, feeling cheated of showing off his talents, since Manning knew any bruised egos under fire didn't make it out to see the other side, for one thing. The Sudanese general and Fhalid were two cases in point how stung pride always came back to slap a man in the face.

Tough lessons, all around, and class had only just begun.

At the moment a suicide wave had mounted on the far southern edge, a pack of the Iranians whipping about, obviously alerted by now to the threat on their six. Two of them had RPGs up and aimed at the spot where McCarter and Encizo had taken up a firepoint. Enemy gunners were dropping all over the place out there, as James and Hawkins made the stage, but for some reason—call it the chaos and confusion of battle— the RPG boys were going unmolested.

Until Manning took them out with head shots, one of

the warheads launched but sailing over the wall, a thunderclap echoing from some distant point to the south.

That was too close for his comfort.

He took a read on the situation on the airfield, stealing a few seconds, as the Phoenix Force commandos locked horns with the Iranians. The demolished ruins to the west were now getting consumed by secondary fires, sparked by tongues of brilliant flames leaping away from the pulped matchstick shell of the armory. The jumping umbrella of meshing fires outlined the Madagascar soldiers hitting the airfield to the distant west, going for the big transport plane and the smaller executive jet.

Manning didn't have to wait long, as the dark bulk of the Spectre, after cutting a half circle to the south, came back and hit those grounded aircraft with a symphony of pounding cannon fire, splitting the night once again with fire and thunder from hell.

That got the attention of the Madagascar runners, no mistake, as Manning saw them hit the deck when whatever they might haved used to fly on was vaporized before their eyes.

Back to work.

Manning chose his targets with minimal discrimination, searching for any more rocket men, but finding only the bad guys going for broke with their AKs. Five scores later, and he sensed he'd helped break the back of the suicide charge.

It was far from over, he knew.

The Iranians looked hell-bent on going down to the last man.

That was fine with him. He had four clips to spare, two of the bigger human sharks already in the net.

Manning lined up another fanatic in his sights, and erased that look of rage and hate in a crimson splash, sent the guy on his way, a martyr for his twisted version of a holy war.

McCARTER HIT THEM with short precision bursts from his assault rifle, keeping the selector switch locked on full-auto. Call it a dozen martyr wanna-bes, fifteen tops, and McCarter and Encizo were more than able and willing to indulge the enemy's wish to go out with a roar.

And they weren't cooperating, willing to go out quick and easy.

No problem. McCarter was there to help.

The Briton popped away from the edge of the barracks, fresh clip cracked and racked, as Encizo chugged out the last of his twelve 40 mm hellbombs, then took up his own M-16. They shaved the charge down to four takers, streams of Farsi oaths and bellows hurtled into the face of death. From somewhere midway down the barracks, the distinctive stammer of Hawkins's M-60 was going to town, while James locked in on the martyrs from the north, driving them deeper into the jaws of death.

They didn't want to go down, McCarter saw, even as he raked them, port to starboard, breaking the line, one here, two there flopping to the ground, Manning's sniping kicking four, maybe five off their feet as dark mists hit the air in gory halos above shattered skulls. He had to give them a brief mental salute for their tenacity, just the same, then it was back to the butcher's work. The few standing Iranians bulled ahead into the converging leadstorms, finally toppled as the scissor of bullets snapped them in two.

A few runners of Iranian origin had made the west gate, were now darting out of the courtyard. Going for God only knew what, McCarter thought, as a Mount Everest of fire climbed into the sky from the direction of the airfield.

Autofire snagged McCarter's attention as he broke into a jog, crouching beneath curtained windows. As previously outlined in the battle strategy, James shouted key phrases in memorized Farsi, booming it out, so his voice carried deep into the rubble. He ordered them to surrender, hands up, and they wouldn't be killed.

As another burst of weapons fire chased James to seek cover beside a mound of rubble, McCarter knew they'd have to this the old-fashioned way.

The hard way, all blood and guts.

McCarter took up position opposite James and Hawkins, plucked a frag grenade off his webbing, then gave the nod all around for everyone to palm a steel egg.

"On three."

They pulled the pins.

"One."

Spoons falling, hands filled with live ones.

"Two."

Braced for the quadruple pitch.

"Three."

And let them fly, the commandos homed in on the source of all the Farsi tirade and autofire over a hill of debris. It was short in coming, a second and a half tops, then the darkness blew and swelled the night with noise and the screaming of men shredded by countless bits of steel.

ENCIZO JOINED Hawkins, moving in behind James and McCarter, up the rise of rubble and shards, a dangerous trip over flimsy wood and stone, forced to watch his step and keep his senses tuned in to any sudden sound below. They dropped off the debris, Encizo finding they were inside a scaled-down wasteland, with rubble and shattered boards blocking the way, or hiding, he knew, a potential wounded and very much rabid fanatic. They split up, McCarter and James angling off to the left, hunched and sliding through the gloom. Encizo and Hawkins took their march to the right, going in and up, weaving through the maze of jagged garbage, toward the back when a bloody thing staggered from the smoke. Nothing but the whites of the eyes showed, burning with pain from behind a slick mask of crimson. He was also holding an AK-47 over his head.

"Surrender! I give up!" the Iranian shouted.

"Drop the weapon!" Encizo barked.

"Surrender! I surrender!"

Something changed in the eyes, as the AK came

down. Encizo anticipated the suicide stand and hit the Iranian at near point-blank range in the chest with a burst of autofire, kicking him back into the jagged teeth of some shattered boards.

More shooting sounded from McCarter and James's way.

Hawkins was on the move, and Encizo was in lockstep two seconds later. A group of three Iranians had to have tried the same dumb tactic of extending an olive branch with their assault rifles. They were getting waxed by McCarter and James, but Encizo and Hawkins joined the slaughter for good measure, nailing it a few moments later as the screams were whipped away by relentless autofire.

It took a few minutes, but they covered the ruins, alert to any sound or movement, rooting around while Hawkins and James covered the digging.

"We're clear," McCarter announced, then raised Manning, and told him to come down.

Time to walk out of there, and, he thought, get the hell off what was really now a great red island, awash in the blood of savages.

McCARTER WAS TREATED to the usual barrage of questions and acrimony when the commandos reached the Sudanese general and Fhalid. Encizo snapped the plastic cuffs on their prisoners, manhandled them to their feet.

"We'll chitchat later," the leader of Phoenix Force told their captives when they launched into another round of abusive language. Calvin James was the team medic, so assumed the chore of tending to their wounds, making sure they didn't bleed out. One look at their crippling wounds, and James wasn't bashful about giving them the good news and the bad news. The good news was they were alive, and would stay that way if they cooperated. The bad news was that both of them were going to lose a foot. The immediate problem was lugging along their human cargo, since they were unable to walk on their own. McCarter shot Manning a grim smile.

Manning nodded, returned the look. "Right. I made the mess...."

After James performed immediate first aid, the big Canadian slung his assault rifle, then took a handful of each prisoner's shirt between the shoulder blades. They grunted, cursed Manning as he hauled them onward, no gentle touch for these butchers.

McCarter raised Grimaldi and told him to bring it down, they were moving out for the airfield.

Time to go.

Only the Briton suspected evacuation could prove touch-and-go, especially if the Madagascan soldiers decided to stand and fight. The Spectre was armed with state-of-the-art radar tracking and jamming goodies. And the Farm's sat recon of the island had turned up all of six fighter jets, he knew, somewhere to the north near the capital city. If the alarm was sounded, McCarter knew he'd hear something from either Grimaldi or the Farm.

So far, he figured no news on that front was good news.

ARMED RESISTANCE greeted Phoenix Force at the air-field. It was the same ploy McCarter had seen in the ruins of the barracks, and he began to wonder just how stupid the Iranians thought they were. Kick a guy's butt, he thought, and then they walk up, all apologies and ex-tending their hand, no harm done.

Shake this.

Five Iranians kept their AKs over their heads, shuf-fling ahead, calling that they gave up.

"Drop the weapons!" McCarter shouted, the faces of the five Iranians framed in the dancing light of the firestorm devouring the edge of the runway. "Gentle-men…"

"We're on it," James said.

Maybe the Iranians thought the odds were even, five on five, but the fanatics were bringing down the assault rifles, even as they professed they would surrender.

They gave it up, all right, as Phoenix Force mowed them down where they stood.

Done.

McCarter searched the airfield, saw the control tower that would have housed any radar or radio setup crushed to fiery ruins by some more of the Spectre dusting.

And the great warbird of prey rumbled in, hitting the runway to start its long roll.

McCarter couldn't find any sign of enemy gunners, but figured they had vanished into the hills, unwilling to risk their lives for their Sudanese and Iranian guests. That was fine with him, likewise hoping those fighter jets stayed grounded up north. The word from Farm intel was Madagascar was real slim on any flyboys skilled enough to take to the air for much more than a peek at the AC-130. Sometimes intelligence, when it came from a source other than the Farm, got it wrong. Sometimes it didn't.

Well, they would out soon enough, one way or another.

Their terrorist load was grunting up storm of pain and anger, stumbling along.

"Rafe," McCarter told Encizo, "give Gary a hand with those two."

When Phoenix Force was treated to another round of cursing, McCarter thought the first thing he'd do when they boarded the Spectre was to find a bar of soap, and wash out their filthy mouths. After the show the five of them had put on here, he figured they were owed just a smidge of respect.

Stony Man Farm, Virginia

BROGNOLA DIDN'T LET loose with a sigh of relief when McCarter touched base. Phase one was a wrap, but this was just the beginning, he knew, of some killing game that could well lead to a major conflict in the Middle East.

On the plus side, Phoenix Force was wheels up, nothing on the radar nets of their monitors showing a hostile jet taking to the air in pursuit. And two of the bigger catches were in the bag, good guys all present and accounted for. The big Fed would have liked a few more heads to hand on the silver platter to the Man, but figured two was better than none. And who knew? he thought. With any luck under some intense Q and A from McCarter, and they could be staring at a gold mine of intel.

He looked around the Computer Room, then Price sought him out, disconnecting the satlink to Striker.

"Well?" Brognola prodded the mission controller.

"One minute to the DZ, and Striker jumps."

Brognola felt his heart lurch, reached for his packet of antacid tablets, but knew nothing would calm his stomach or his nerves for some time to come.

Nothing, that was, except success in the field. And his people alive and in one piece, coming home.

He read the big question in the eyes of Kurtzman, Tokaido and Wethers, searching him out. What next?

"We wait and see what Striker turns up," he told them. "And depending on what Phoenix learns from this Sudanese butcher and the Iranian."

"It's going to be a tough sell, Hal, either way," Kurtzman said.

"Tell me about it," Brognola groused. "We're talking maybe a full-scale surgical strike on the Iranian military bases on those islands in the strait. You want to talk about giving the Islamic fundamentalist world not only a major kick in the teeth, but setting the table for God only knows what in the future. Maybe renewed terrorist attacks in retaliation for what we're proposing…"

"If," Price pointed out, "DYSAT is linked to a Sudan connection, which is then funneling the laser weapons and this Ramrod Intercept technology to Iranians on those islands, I don't see where we have a choice."

"That kind of technology in their hands," Kurtzman said, "could definitely tip the scales in their favor. You wouldn't need to launch a missile. Just point a laser beam at, say, a passing tanker and you can disable the engine."

"I've got some idea of just how dark the future would look if that happens," Brognola said. He leaned back in his chair, as Price informed him they would have to wait a number of hours before Striker checked back. Something about the contract agent having a satlink modem, courtesy of the CIA, but stashed away in a safehouse in Port Sudan. A number of hours, he thought, and gnawed on his cigar.

He didn't want to even think it, but the thought crept in, eating into his rising anxiety. He couldn't help but wonder if he'd ever hear from his old friend again.

There was nothing left to do, but wait, ride it out, he knew, hope for the best.

Bolan would figure it out.

CHAPTER TWELVE

Sudan

Mohammed Nhoubaff pondered the new course his life was about to take. It was dangerous enough, being a contract agent for either the CIA or the DIA, juggling alliances between the various splinter groups of the National Islamic Front, the Iqwhan or the day's top military brass thuggery, stroking the egos of human sharks on all fronts, wheedling information about weapons shipments, Iranian troop movements or terrorist camps set up in the desert, and the like. Then, since he was never certain which American intelligence agency buttered his bread, informing the shadow men of who was who and what was what in Sudan. The danger of talking out of both sides of his mouth was that he never knew when one of the more fanatical leaders of the NIF would discover Mohammed Nhoubaff was the eyes and ears of Western foreign agents, whereby he could start counting down his life, numbered in hours.

Now he was being asked to aid and assist another foreigner, an American, who was coming to Sudan.

To do what? He couldn't say offhand, the agent simply stating he was to pick up the American, bring enough weapons and gear to get this stranger started on whatever he was coming to Sudan to do. The stranger also needed information about recent shipments of weapons, the stories abounding in Nhoubaff's shadow world how they were high-tech weapons of the future, with microchips for some sort of prototype satellite-disabling system.

Sudan was a mess, he thought, to understate the sorry state of affairs in his country, and no amount of high-tech, even foreign aid was about to save the country. The violence knew no end, and he doubted there would ever be peace in the largest country in Africa. One man, he wondered, as he searched the predawn cloak of darkness veiling the wild frontier country of northeastern Sudan. What could one man possibly do? What were his plans? And how, Nhoubaff wondered, did he fit into whatever the scheme of things, other than being a chauffeur, a weapons courier, informant?

He had counted off the kilometers from an arranged point of departure from Port Sudan, driving due north for the Red Sea Hills. A check of his watch, and if the information provided him by the shadow agent was on the money, the stranger would have already landed. He wouldn't see the plane from which the stranger had jumped, of course, since he had to assume it had already flown on, heading back for Egypt, maybe thirty thousand feet or so in the sky.

Ahead, the baobab tree was framed in the headlights,

then a tall shadow disengaged itself from behind the tree. Nhoubaff checked the desolation he'd left behind. According to his sources there was a large Iranian camp, roughly six klicks west of his current position. He wondered if this rendezvous site was a simple coincidence, or if the stranger had arranged it that way. The problem right then was the Sudanese army Hummer he'd picked up on his rear, ten minutes back. For whatever reason it had fallen back, stopping at a distant point near a wadi.

If this was some kind of setup, Nhoubaff would free one of the two AK-47s hidden in the paneling of the van, make sure the RPG-7 was handy, just in case there were more soldiers prowling the area. It had been some time since he'd killed a man, but for a double agent to be taken in by the authorities...

Well, he knew there were fates worse than death.

He stopped the van near the tall shadow, and stepped out.

THE HALO JUMP from the Starlifter went off without a hitch, but Mack Bolan knew the easy part was behind him. Silent incursions into hostile enemy territory were routine for the man also known as the Executioner.

It was the getting-out part that always held a few grim surprises.

He'd landed forty-three minutes ago on the black lunar desolation, which could have been the face of the dark side of the moon. The chute was wadded up, covered up with scrub, hidden enough to escape a passing scrutiny by any patrol of soldiers. Beneath his loose-fitting tunic he carried only his Beretta 93-R, spare clips in his waistband, a commando dagger sheathed around his lower leg.

Nothing more at the moment, but the good stuff was supposedly on the way. He had the contact's name, nothing else. The soldier didn't know what to expect, but he made out the Hummer in the distance, waiting there as if the occupants were trying to decide on a course of action.

The VW van had come to a stop near the baobab, a slender figure in tunic falling out, approaching, uncertain.

"They said that God wept when he created Sudan."

The Executioner watched his contact, then delivered his own line to assure them both they were the right match. "They said God also laughed on the same day. So I've heard it said."

Bolan nodded toward the Hummer. "Looks like we have company. How much of a problem do you think that is?"

"Out here, in the frontier, with Iranian camps all over the place, I would say very much a problem. They will want to know who we are and what is our business. They will search the van. Whether they find the weapons…" Nhoubaff shrugged.

"Well, there's a saying where I come from about curiosity."

"I believe I've heard the one. Something about curiosity killing the cat."

"That's the one."

Madagascar

THE MORPHINE IV solution had eased their pain, but McCarter broke out the bottle of Scotch whiskey to help loosen their tongues some more.

Fhalid and Arakkhan had seen their wounds tended to by James. Under the circumstances, aware they were eventually going to go under the knife for amputation, they struck McCarter as amazingly calm. They were laid out on metal cots, and McCarter waited as they passed the bottle between them, the other four commandos of Phoenix Force grouped down the bench in a staggered seating line. The rumble of the Spectre's turboprops swelled the aft hold as Grimaldi headed them out over the Indian Ocean for the long way back to Tanzania.

"Here's how it is, gents," McCarter said. "You're eventually going to America to stand trial for an assortment of crimes against humanity. Depending on your cooperation and what useful intelligence you have, things may go easier on you. What I need is everything you know about any shipments of laser weapons, names, contacts in Sudan, shipping routes, the whole enchilada."

"And what do we get in return?" the Sudanese general asked.

"For starters, a little longer lease on your lives."

"You would just kill us outright?" Fhalid spit.

"No mercy. Wouldn't even blink."

Arakkhan mulled something over, hit the bottle and said, "I know the weapons are coming from America.

A middleman makes the arrangements. I have heard the arms dealer is called DYSTATE."

"DYSAT," McCarter corrected.

"Yes, that's the one. Now, how it was working…"

Sudan

THERE WAS SOMETHING ice-cold about the stranger that made Mohammed Nhoubaff uneasy. He was some sort of professional soldier, the manner in which he checked over the AK-47s—that much he could tell. But it was something in the eyes that wanted to tell Nhoubaff a thousand terrible stories of death and violence.

He couldn't be positive, not yet, but he sensed another bloody tale was about to go down in the stranger's personal history.

"They'll want to see your passport. I understand it says you are Iranian."

"That's what it says, only I don't intend to get bogged down in any lengthy discussion."

The man had told him his name was Cooper, but he could be sure that was an alias. He had ordered they move at an angle across the desert, veering away from the Hummer. It was as if he was either anticipating trouble, or looking forward to it.

The Hummer, as he had always believed it would, came barreling toward them on an intercept point, headlights hitting them in the eyes.

"Stop it here," Bolan ordered.

And he was gone, armed and out the door as soon as the three Arab soldiers disgorged from the Hummer. It happened so fast, Nhoubaff couldn't believe he was a witness to such lightning slaughter.

The soldiers were out, bringing their French-made FAMAS assault rifles to bear on Cooper when the dark stranger hit them at near point-blank range with a raking burst from the AK-47. He nailed them, left to right, mowing them down like torn and hapless stick figures, not flinching. It was incredible, he thought, the stranger just one fluid motion of dispensing death in about the time it took to blink. Next he claimed their weapons as the spoils of the massacre then was back in the shotgun seat, depositing the French assault rifles on the floorboard in the back.

"Get us some distance, then stop so I can inventory what you brought. Drive in the direction of the Iranian camp west of here."

So that was it, Nhoubaff thought, dropping the van into gear and lurching ahead. This man had come to Sudan to declare war on terrorists and their sponsors.

A disturbing thought settled like a cold chill over Nhoubaff as he glanced at the three sprawled corpses. The Angel of Death, he thought, had just landed in Sudan.

WHEN THEY FOUND a wadi suitable enough to keep any watching eyes out on the desert from wondering about them, Bolan checked his weapons. Two AK-47s, a dozen clips. There was also an RPG-7, four spare warheads. He was inspecting what he guessed was in the neighborhood of fifteen pounds of plastic explosive, checking the timers, when Nhoubaff said, "The C-4, that came from who I believe was the CIA."

Bolan stowed clips for the assault rifle in a small satchel along with the C-4. He climbed back into van, took a close measuring of the Company contract agent, decided it was time to spell it out.

"Here's the deal," the soldier began. "American weapons are finding their way into Port Sudan. I have a shopping list of potential suspects. I'm not here on any mission of mercy."

"I would have gathered as much."

"Just so you understand where I'm coming from. You bail on me at a critical moment, leave me twisting someplace, I have my own sources in the country. I will find you. If you stab me in the back, you had better hope I go down and stay down for good."

"I have seen you are not a man to be taken lightly."

"You're right, because I am heavy and I'm not your brother."

"I think we understand each other."

"Now, when I hit this camp, keep the engine running and wait for me to get back."

"You're talking about twenty-five, maybe thirty Iranian fanatics."

"I've faced tougher odds than those."

"Somehow I can believe that."

"I'm in the business of making believers of the bad guys."

"You are asking for my undivided loyalty?"

"A simple yes or no."

Nhoubaff paused, and Bolan could see the wheels spinning. The man was putting it all on the line for a foreign stranger, an American, no less, a representative of the Great Satan. At some point, the soldier would be leaving Sudan, but if word got around that Nhoubaff had paved the road to hell for his own countrymen...

"If I help you, you understand if I am discovered as your ally and thought of as a traitor, then there will be no hole big enough for me to crawl into and hide."

"Life's full of risk that way."

"Indeed. Very well. I will help you, whatever it is you require. No strings, as you Americans might say."

And Bolan settled back in his seat as the Sudanese Arab drove on, taking him for an engagement with Iranian fundamentalists. The sun wasn't even up yet, and already the soldier knew it was going to be a long and ugly day.

AS FAR AS A CAMP for the training of Iranian terrorists it wasn't much, in terms of the number of tents or the size of the motor pool. It was basic, primitive at best.

From his perch on a ridge on the hills to the north, the soldier counted three large tents, spotted two sentries nodding off where a satellite dish marked what he assumed was the command post. Three military-style

jeeps, a Hummer, parked near a fuel bin. And somewhere between twenty and thirty sleeping hardmen.

The motor pool and the fuel bin would mark his starting place to get the fireworks launched with some
planted plastique. AK-47 in hand, the RPG-7 slung
across a shoulder, Bolan took a look in the direction
where Nhoubaff waited in a wadi with the van. This was
the first of many tests, he knew, where Nhoubaff would
or wouldn't show his true colors. If he pulled a rabbit
act when the shooting started…

Well, it was a long walk to Port Sudan.

Under the circumstances, Bolan had no choice but to
go with his gut. Nhoubaff was in the game.

The sun would be up soon, Bolan already seeing the
first smudge of dirty light hitting the sky in the direction of the Red Sea.

The soldier had a name, gleaned off his shopping list
from the CIA source in Sudan. With any luck, he could
bag an Iranian colonel, formerly of SAVAK, put the
Q-and-A torch to his pants.

No time like the present to jump-start the mission, he
decided, and moved in to start the big bang.

CHAPTER THIRTEEN

Colonel Ehad Qassar despised his current assignment in Sudan, viewed it as a giant albatross around his neck. The jihad was spreading rapidly, a flourishing wildfire consuming infidels in Israel, Yemen, just to name a few countries currently under a renewed siege, with new targets being arranged to taste Islamic jihad vengeance by the day. His brothers in the holy war were on the front line, and it galled him to no end that he was handed off the task of training fighters for the future in what he considered the hellhole of north Africa.

But what could he do? he thought. His orders came directly from the island bastions in the Strait of Hormuz, which in turn came from Iran. And the word out of Tehran was the Saudi, bin Laden, had been fattening a few chosen bank accounts for several years, buying and selling arms, grooming contacts and gleaning intelligence, recruiting the troops for the jihad. Part of him couldn't understand why his fellow countrymen seemed to choose Sudan as their home base away from home, but reckoned it was the strategic port city of Port Sudan along the Red Sea that inspired the temptation to stake out real estate in Sudan. And yes, Sudan was seventy percent Muslim, no problem there.

But it was a country of extremes, as heaven was to hell, with fifty different tribal groups, something like one hundred different languages, a part of the human factors that created a vast sea of turmoil, chaos and bloodshed from the border of Egypt to Uganda. Then there was nature, and an economy that was at the bottom of the barrel. A poor country that held no real interest for Western trade, with the usual obscenely wealthy few keeping the masses under their boot heel. Cotton was the main cash crop, he knew, next to the selling of arms. But rainfall had been so rare the past few years the whole country seemed to have become one vast furnace, barren and unforgiving, as if God himself was angry with the Sudanese.

And the killing of the black rebels in the south went on. Business as usual, of course, but it was intensifying as the CIA and other Western intelligence agencies smuggled in weapons and supplies to the SPLA.

Now it seemed as if part of an agreement, mapped out without his prior knowledge, much less his approval, was for the Iranians in-country to begin training their own people to aid in the slaughter of the rebels. Then there were the fantastic stories of futuristic high-tech weapons landing in Port Sudan, every other week or so. The floating rumor was the weapons were coming from Americans, the Great Satan, of all the unholy alliances. He had yet to see one of these marvels of Western technology, since he was a great distance from Port Sudan, stuck in the middle of nowhere, in command of thirty recruits, none of whom was older than twenty.

The future of the jihad.

Another annoyance was the fact he couldn't sleep lately. He would lie in his bunk, toss and turn, mind churning with resentment over the fact he seemed to have been shuffled out to pasture by the higher brass, given a chore that any lower-ranking officer with far less experience could have performed.

Stuck, and steaming then, no options but to suck it up for the present, see it through, resentful or not. He decided to check on the two young sentries standing guard outside his tent. He rotated them every three hours, aware that guards on watch duty tended to become bored, even sleepy. And since these young soldiers for the jihad had no formal military experience, plucked out of villages on pretty much the whim of Tehran, he knew sometimes he had to watch the roost himself. Just last night he caught one of them sleeping like the dead, snoring loud enough to rouse half the camp. If that happened again...

He fired up a cigarette, trying to calm his nerves. He had grown up in a desert village outside of Tehran, long since adapted to the heat and the barren wilderness, but there was something almost sinister about the black nights of the Sudanese desert, as if some hostile threat was always close at hand.

That was absurd, of course, since the Iranians were pretty much greeted with open arms by the Khartoum government. And this was northern Sudan anyway, meaning any threat of black rebel incursion was far removed to the distant south.

He was thinking he'd give it another week or so, then ask for reassignment to one of the islands in the strait. He understood there was a plan in the wings to begin attacks on oil tankers, using TOW missiles, perhaps slam one of them with a gunboat full of suicide bombers, the whole works weighted down with six, seven hundred pounds of high explosives. A plan just like that was already on the board. The way he understood it, two of his contacts in Port Sudan were waiting on a final shipment of these great weapons. Once that was done, a jihad, he had heard, would erupt in the Persian Gulf.

He was drawing deeply on his smoke, striding toward the flap when the first explosion went off. He froze in midstride, thinking some careless smoker had tossed a cigarette near the weapons depot. Some dark instinct warned him that wasn't the case. Even if these were green recruits, no one could be that stupid.

He was picking up the pace when the explosions thundered on, sounding like a giant string of firecrackers. The way it sounded, so close the pounding was nearly on top of him, he knew the motor pool was going up.

Which meant he would really be stranded. It was a

long walk to the closest army outpost, but if some invading force was storming the camp, a grueling hike across the desert sounded far better than getting shot down or blown up.

Two more steps, tossing away the cigarette and he was grabbing up his AK-47 when the tent collapsed under raining debris.

THE EXECUTIONER DECIDED to leave the sentries standing for the time being. They were both nodding off anyway, and since they were too close for comfort to the front flap the collapse of deadweight might alert the commander of the camp inside before he had finished lining up his ducks in a row for the big blast.

It had been an oversight on his previous surveillance, missing the ammo depot behind the tent on the far west edge. He planted some C-4 there first, setting the timer, then moved on, fixing more plastique to each of the vehicles in the motor pool, finally the fuel bin. With any luck, as close as the whole setup was to the tents, the series of blasts would take out a large body of armed hostiles before they had a chance to venture outside.

It went down according to the soldier's plan.

The Executioner took up position behind a lone baobab, some fifty yards west of the coming firestorm.

He rode out the final few seconds, ticking off the doomsday numbers in his head, when the fireworks erupted. As hoped for, balls of fire and wreckage tore into the tents, some of the bigger slabs launched for the sky, then floating down to pound them from above. They were hollering inside the tent, roused from slumber into a sudden scramble, then the general stampede began as they boiled into sight, veering away from the raging flames.

Bolan kept moving, swift and certain, and began hosing down the first nine or ten with a long burst from his AK-47. The sentries were wide awake now, and the warrior, closing the gap, zipped them with a short precision burst, flinging them back into the collapsing tent of their taskmaster. Another burst of autofire and Bolan saw another four hardmen go down, all thrashing limbs and gurgled cries of pain.

The problem here was twofold. One, this sort of din of weapons fire and explosions would travel far and wide across the desert, rousing any roving army patrols to come have a look, armed to the teeth. Two, Nhoubaff could get cold feet over the sound of this slaughter, wondering if Mr. Cooper had bitten the dust, leaving him to hold the bag and explain himself to the authorities.

No time to ponder trouble that hadn't happened yet. Whatever showed up in the near future, he'd deal with it, figure it out on the running and the gunning.

Right now it was time to turn up the heat and punch a gaping hole through a part of the jihad's future schemes.

QASSAR THOUGHT they were under attack by a large force, wondering who in his right mind would come gunning for a campsite that was under the sanction and protection of the Khartoum government. A number of grim thoughts passed through his mind as he crawled out from under the thick canvas blanket, like some drowning rat, clawing for his AK-47. Had someone in Khartoum decided he had outlived his usefulness? But how could that be, since his training assignment had merely just begun? And why, if that was the case? Had his contacts discerned a note of resentment or hostility in his voice when he complained, maybe all of two times, about his woeful station in Sudan? Was this some lesson being taught him, that it was best to do as he was told, and like it? Was it possible even that a band of SPLA guerrillas had ventured this far north?

Whatever the case, it sounded like a full-scale slaughter was under way. Two more yards of digging himself out of the tent, and he came to witness his recruits getting mowed down as they emerged from the tent, which was now engulfed in flames. Two fiery scarecrow figures came shrieking outside and they were chopped down where they flailed about.

Qassar gave the grounds a search, wondering where the hell was the small army of shooters, when he spotted a tall shadow with an AK-47 on the move, going for cover behind the firewall. It was impossible, he thought, one man had wreaked this destruction, laid out this carnage at his doorstep? He looked all around, but couldn't find any other enemy gunners.

Secondary blasts were now belching off as fuel tanks ignited from the motor pool. He was moving off to the side, lining up the shadow with his assault rifle when a great weight slammed off his shoulders, knocking him off his feet to a curtain of sparking white stars.

AZIZ AHAD DIDN'T HAVE any interest in dying at the ripe old age of seventeen. He had been recruited, paid and, of course, promised a great future by the imam's man out of Tehran, but he hadn't signed on to get slaughtered in a foreign country he wasn't so sure he cared much about to begin with.

He was gripping his AK-47, running out the flap, ducking the tongues of fire, trying to will the shaking from his limbs, when he saw his fellow Iranians dropping all over the grounds. He wanted to fire back, on instinct to simply save his own skin, if nothing else, but there was no visible sign of any target.

Then he spotted the tall dark shadow, his assault rifle flaming on, drilling his comrades on the run. He couldn't accept the idea they were all being cut down by a single gunman. It was beyond incredible, he thought; it was obscene. Even if that was the case, the shooter had seized an edge by blowing up the motor pool, dropping raining debris on their tent as they slept.

He didn't think that was very fair.

He considered holding his ground and shooting it out, then good sense told him they had lost this fight to…

One shooter?

There had to be a way out of this disaster, he thought, but what?

The general chaos and exchange of automatic-weapons fire bought him precious few moments to flee the scene. He found a gap between the tents, slunk back, hoping he was far enough out of the firelight to become little more than a dark silhouette. He reasoned that when this was over, someone of authority in the Sudanese army would want a report, maybe a description of the shooter. But what could he tell them? A tall dark man with an AK-47, who seemed to move like a ghost, all fluid swift strides, not hesitating as he poured out death.

How many men like that were wandering around Sudan, anyway? He hoped the authorities would buy his version of events, that also would carry a tale of how he stood his ground under fire, but the stranger melted off into the night as he went hunting for him.

Seventeen, and so much yet to live for, he figured it was best to live to fight another day. The jihad was calling, and he was too young to die on the parched earth of Sudan.

The shooting went on behind him as he hastened his strides, urged along by the sudden deaths of his countrymen. The stranger, whoever he really was, may live out the night, but he determined the man would pay. Only an enemy of Islam, a devil in human skin, would carry out the kind of slaughter he had seen.

And there was no way a lone gunman could move at will and at large around Sudan. No way in hell, and hell, he thought, was exactly where the stranger deserved to go.

CHAPTER FOURTEEN

Youth held no distinct advantages on the killing field of this particular predawn hour, not in terms of speed, reflex action and certainly not combat experience.

The truth was, youth was a disadvantage.

The Executioner took full and merciless initiative, unleashing all the skill and experience at his disposal, no exceptions, no mercy granted whatsoever for the reckless foolishness of the Iranian young here who had sold their souls in the hopes of becoming tomorrow's mass murderer and international headliner for the Islamic jihad.

By now, maybe a half-dozen shooters were left standing out front of the burning tents. A few of the more brazen were now winging around the autofire, but the soldier was skirting behind the shield of flaming debris, their tracking lines of rounds flying high and wide. Any miss, especially a close shave under these conditions, didn't go unpunished.

Bolan rang up two more on the other side, when the survivors started scattering, beating hasty exit paths for the northern hills.

The soldier moved out from his fiery cover, on something of an intercept course, fresh clip in the AK-47, and hit them with precision bursts from the rear, stitching them up into crimson rag dolls.

Four more down.

He'd already glimpsed what he hoped was the camp's commander, going down under a raining slab of wreckage. If he was still breathing, that was fine with Bolan. If not, he'd simply vacate the premises, move on. His shopping list was long and extensive, his memory having filed away the photo lineups, the past crimes of the various thugs he was set to hunt down after the mop-up here. No mistake, there was plenty of work yet to do in Sudan.

He caught sight of yet more runners, shadows bolting from the rear of the tents, racing from the flames. The Executioner set off in pursuit for more human but very savage game.

The sun wasn't even up yet, but they wouldn't live to see it anyway.

NHOUBAFF CLAIMED a spot on top of the ridge and took in the massacre.

It was a one-sided slaughter, damn near taking his breath away, the tall American's ruthlessness, skill and audacity stunning to watch, a morbid sight to behold, in fact.

He made out the tall shape of Cooper, near the flaming ruins of the motor pool. He watched as the man mowed down Iranians on the rabbit run from behind. If he thought about it—which he really didn't want to, since this was a glimpse of things to come—the man was a killing machine, with guts and experience to back him up, all the way to the wall.

So, where did it go from here? How would he move about Port Sudan at large like this, shooting down his enemies, and staying free? He wasn't sure, but he decided after viewing the grim fruits of the man's death harvest, he would be there. That was if he wanted to live to see the next day.

Cooper didn't play games.

The tall American, however, didn't see the shadow playing possum rise off the ground. Nhoubaff decided it was time he joined the fray. He lifted the AK-47, gauged the distance, took up slack on the trigger and cut free with a long burst, stitching the possum up the side, the rising burst all but lopping off an arm just below the shoulder. If nothing else, he hoped that scored a couple of points in the trust column with the Angel of Death.

THE EXECUTIONER WAS whirling toward the source of the autofire, sprinting ahead, braced for the bullets to tear into him, when he saw the shadow topple after a jerky three-step dance to hell. A look up the hill, and he saw the silhouette lift and wave his AK-47.

So Nhoubaff was going the distance. The Executioner allowed a tight smile, then picked up the pace, edging around the rear of the tents. A few of the more hearty were swinging assault rifles in his direction when he poured on the message of doom, dropping them in their tracks. The firestorm in his ears, the soldier gave it a moment, waiting to see if any other takers emerged from the tents.

Looked like a wrap, just about.

It was then he spotted a distant runner, long gone, out of range of his AK-47. A lone survivor to tell the tale, but Bolan didn't think there was much he could relay to anyone who chose to listen. The Sudanese army would eventually head out here, comb the carnage, wonder what in the world had happened.

Of course, by then Bolan intended to be knocking, or, rather, kicking down some doors close to Port Sudan. He was a long way from any home stretch; in fact, it was just beginning to get ugly.

He moved back to the front, claiming five spare clips from the dead for his AK-47 on the way to see if Qassar was still among the living.

QASSAR COULDN'T BE SURE how bad he was injured, but the pain shooting down his back told him he was still alive. His mouth, though, was full of blood, and it took several long moments before he cleared the bitter fluid with a few vicious hacks.

He was pulling himself up on his knees, aware of some presence closing on him, when he reached for his AK-47.

"Uh-uh."

The eyes either mirrored the flames, or they were burning with raw determination. Whichever, the look froze him up.

"If you're going to kill me, may I stand up?"

"Slow and easy, hands in the air."

"You are alone? You are…American?"

"Yes to both. I'll ask the questions."

"You will kill me, then."

"Quick and easy, or long and hard. Your choice. It's a done deal for you, Colonel."

Qassar struggled to his feet, amazed for some reason how calm he felt, knowing he was going to die.

"What is it you wish to know before you execute me?"

BOLAN COULDN'T BE certain whether any roving army patrols were in the neighborhood, thus knew time was running out. He had several questions, and let Qassar know that the first time he even sensed he was lying it was over. Spelling it out next that a long painful death was the only offer on the table if the colonel even hedged around the truth.

"I understand some high-tech weapons of American origin have made it into Sudan."

Qassar nodded. "You understand correctly."

"Don't make me drag it out of you."

"I know of men in a suburb outside Port Sudan, others in the city proper." He rattled off several addresses, and Bolan put them to memory. "They are part of the National Islamic Front, and they work with agents of my

NO POSTAGE
NECESSARY
IF MAILED
IN THE
UNITED STATES

BUSINESS REPLY MAIL

FIRST-CLASS MAIL   PERMIT NO. 717-003   BUFFALO, NY

POSTAGE WILL BE PAID BY ADDRESSEE

GOLD EAGLE READER SERVICE
3010 WALDEN AVE
PO BOX 1867
BUFFALO NY 14240-9952

Get FREE BOOKS and a FREE GIFT when you play the...

LAS VEGAS
GAME

Just scratch off the gold box with a coin. Then check below to see the gifts you get! →

YES! I have scratched off the gold Box. Please send me my **2 FREE BOOKS** and **gift for which I qualify.** I understand that I am under no obligation to purchase any books as explained on the back of this card.

▼ DETACH AND MAIL CARD TODAY! ▼

366 ADL DVFD　　　　　　　　　　　　**166 ADL DVFC**
(MB-04)

FIRST NAME	LAST NAME

ADDRESS

APT.#	CITY

STATE/PROV.	ZIP/POSTAL CODE

7	**7**	**7**	Worth TWO FREE BOOKS plus a BONUS Mystery Gift!

Worth TWO FREE BOOKS!

TRY AGAIN!

Offer limited to one per household and not valid to current Gold Eagle® subscribers. All orders subject to approval.

country. They have rivals, the Muslim Brothers, or the Iqwhan, who are envious that the NIF has curried favor with the Sudanese intelligence agents. What I am saying is that these weapons could be spread among the two groups, a bribe here, a midnight theft of a certain crate or two on the waterfront, you understand."

"I'm familiar with the drill."

"A contact who established this camp, a Colonel Issad Bhoutami, leader of the NIF, is a feared man. He has the weapons, or most of them, I believe. He commands a small army of killers."

"Telling me I'm about to go swimming with the sharks."

"Man-eaters. Big ones."

"I've been there before."

Qassar's grin was ugly, the eyes telling Bolan that his life was numbered in hours. Or so he was hoping. "The colonel is an especially brutal and ruthless man. He has even been known to forcibly take young boys from local schools as cannon fodder to go kill or be killed against the black rebels to the south. Those young men, teenagers, who do not wish to go are shot and sent back in a trash bag to their parents."

The soldier knew the name, had the file on this particular savage stored to memory. "He's the AWOL General Arakkhan's boy, right?"

"Boy?"

"Stooge. Spy. Contact. Word I hear is he's set to pave the way for the return of Arakkhan. An overthrow of the government in Khartoum, a number of assassinations lined up to land him the throne."

"Yes. I have heard the same rumors. You will want to speak with a man named Gamil Abu Said. He, I understand, knows who has these weapons. I also hear a shipment is en route for Port Sudan from these American suppliers, perhaps even as we speak. High-tech goods. Microchips, a data and technical manual that help assemble some sort of prototype satellite-disabling system. My countrymen have already bought and paid Arakkhan and his 'boy' the money for delivery of this merchandise."

"And you're saying there will trouble in paradise if they don't get what they paid for."

"The streets from Port Sudan to Khartoum will run red in blood."

The game plan was shaping up in Bolan's head. In short order, he would start lighting some fires around the suburbs of Port Sudan and the city proper. He already had a list of locations for various butchers, arms dealers and the like, gathered for the Farm, courtesy of the CIA and the DIA. It never hurt his cause, though, to dump a few extra heads on the chopping block.

"Beyond what I have told you there is little else."

The Executioner believed it, after a deep probe into the man's eyes. He was drawing a bead with the AK-47 on Qassar's chest, the moment of truth, when the Iranian decided to go out with a roar. The Iranian was reaching for a holstered side arm when the soldier cut him down.

One terrorist training down for the count. There were others spread around Sudan, he knew. Time and circumstance allowing, the Executioner decided he might pay one or two more a courtesy call.

Of the killing kind.

NHOUBAFF WAITED until the final shots rang out, then ventured down into the camp. The overpowering stench of death was the first thing he noticed. It was a mixed shroud of odors, ranging from cooked flesh to emptied bowels and bladders, that wanted to knock him off his feet. He had seen death before, plenty of it in a country awash in violence, witnessed cold-blooded murder, in fact. But this was something else altogether.

This was a microscopic vision of Armageddon. No, he corrected himself, this was pure hell on Earth.

The bodies were strewed everywhere, eyes wide open, brimmed with shock and horror, searching for answers that were only now coming in the next life. Burning fuel and the acrid clouds of smoke added to the odor, the deeper he forged into the killing field. He had just seen Cooper gun down Colonel Qassar after a couple minutes of getting some answers, more fuel for the killing machine's tank, no doubt. He was beginning to think he would live to regret ever having been marched out by the agent from Port Sudan to aid this Cooper. But the thing was, he was also starting to believe he would probably be safest if he remained glued to the dark stranger's hip.

Where was Cooper? he wondered, having seen the

stranger vanish at some point between the walls of fire eating up the tents. What in the world was he doing? Searching for wounded, who might be able and willing under the threat of death to beef up his information log on who was doing what in Sudan? He couldn't believe the big American would get lucky again, finding a live one to grill before...

Executing him. But Nhoubaff had seen the colonel reach for a weapon. Would Cooper have shot him down even if he hadn't gone for his gun? He would never know, and he could be sure it didn't make much difference in the final analysis of this lopsided massacre. Qassar had been a dead man all along, just like the Iranian youth who had been shipped here to become future killers for the jihad.

That was something else about this Cooper that was unnerving Nhoubaff a little. The man seemed to be pulled along by some...what? Divine force? Steering him toward evil that needed to be eliminated? Along that train of thought, if that was true, then Qassar and these misguided youth had been destined to go to the afterlife long ago.

The tall American finally materialized, rolling just past the crackling tips of flames reaching out, acting as if not even the firestorm could touch him. Or as if he was simply part of a living fire.

"Let's go," Bolan said. "All done here. The thing is, I lost one. A rabbit made it out."

Nhoubaff grimaced. "That could be a problem."

"Understood."

"If he reaches the nearest army outpost, about eight kilometers to the south, and he has your description…"

"I don't have the time to waste on worry."

And that was that. Cooper would deal with that particular problem, if and when it reared up. He didn't want to admit it, but Nhoubaff was starting to admire the way this man handled himself. Cooper simply rolled on, a human juggernaut, ready to deal with both the known and the unknown.

Yes, Nhoubaff concluded, in Sudan, a country rife with nothing but fear and uncertainty, with death and sabotage and misery all around, he was much safer sticking it out with the American.

IT WAS SOMETHING of a fluke, catching the faintest sounds of the explosions to the northeast minutes ago in the wind lashing him through the open window. It was a sound that made him aware some sort of battle was well under way in the distance, and they were late for whatever was happening.

But Captain Nafi Hassan had set out with a squad from the Wad al-Orawa post when he'd first heard the report of a strange Volkswagen van lurking about in an area that most Sudanese knew to stay out of, unless they wanted to spend a few long hours under interrogation, and sometimes worse. When Sergeant Hafeh hadn't reported back, the alarm bells began chiming in his head.

And thus he was out there, moving in the APC toward

the Iranian camp. Without question, he knew something was wrong in this off-limits sector of the Wad al-Orawa.

There would be consequences and repercussions from Khartoum, Hassan knew, if foreign spies nailed down the location of the Iranian training camp. In fact, Hassan would suffer more than a simple demotion if it was learned the CIA had uncovered the whereabouts, learned the numbers of recruits and sang another tale of horror to the Western intelligence agencies how Sudan was harboring terrorists. The way the jihad was shaping up recently, Hassan knew the rumors were abounding how the Americans were shipping out whole teams of black-ops commandos to hunt down and kill terrorists wherever they were located these days. The Iranians, he knew, shelled out good money, lots of it, to use Sudan as a safe haven to conduct the training and deployment of freedom fighters. The Iranians wouldn't be pleased, might even trim back on their payments, if even one of their camps was attacked.

He was cradling his AK-74 when he spotted the sheen of headlights hitting a rise where the desert tableland broke for higher ground.

A moment later the VW van in question came to a lurching halt along the rise, sitting there, and Hassan could almost feel the occupants planning some strategy, some way to run from the approaching APC.

When the van backed up, vanishing down the other side of the rise, Hassan felt his pulse race. They had a definite problem here. Someone with nothing to hide didn't run. Hassan barked at his driver, "Step on it!"

Hassan clutched his assault rifle. He hadn't seen much action in the province, other than driving away a few cattle herders, and he was beginning to wonder whether or not his lack of performance was the reason why he hadn't yet been promoted. If the occupants of the van had attacked the Iranian camp, then he needed a big kill, a fat notch on his belt to take to the provincial commandant.

He needed a victory, and blood on his hands to show he was worthy of swift promotion, to seize the spotlight for his own day in the sun.

BOLAN WASN'T about to slow, get bogged down or sidetracked by any prowling army patrol, no matter what the numbers. The mere fact they were heading in the direction of the graveyard he'd left behind spelled trouble.

Time to dial up some more killing heat.

The Executioner had given the order for Nhoubaff to drop the van back over the rise, sit tight while he went to work to take care of another unforeseen problem.

He was out the door with the RPG-7, a spare warhead clutched in his hand, the AK-47 hung across a shoulder, when the lights struck the rise. Bolan was on the run, veering away from the point where the APC would show. Figure a full squad in the troop carrier, two men in the cab. Fourteen, sixteen guns tops.

The Executioner got lucky, found a shallow swath cut into the slope. He hunkered down to wait it out. It wasn't more than five seconds before the APC came barreling over the rise. The driver then put on the brakes when he spotted the van waiting on the other side.

Bolan didn't intend to dance around with this bunch. The APC was slowing, stopping, a billow of dust boiling up from the rear, when he let the 40 mm warhead fly. The fin-stabilized, shape-charged HEAT round was capable of cutting through 320 mm of armor. He didn't think the Sudanese version of the APC had that much protective shell on it, and a moment later he was certain one round could have done the job. The warhead plowed into the engine housing, cleaving up the hood, and demolished the engine works in a fiery thunderclap. The cab all but disintegrated, sheared off from the troop housing in a jagged cloud of metal and body parts, ripping away the canvas covering of the hold, flinging a few stick figures into the air. In two shakes, Bolan had another charge loaded up and streaking on. They were tumbling out the back end, hacking and flailing away when the second missile vaporized the troop hold.

Even then, a few survivors managed to clear ground zero.

The Executioner was up and surging, holding back on the trigger of the AK-47. Two shadows, staggering about, trying to get it together but losing reflex time to various injuries and a certain loss of hearing, were chopped down first under the impact of Bolan's stream of 7.62 mm rounds. A few yards closer to the fire and smoke, the Executioner finished it with a few short bursts, dropping two more just as they plunged out of the smoke. Closing in, swift and senses tuned to the slightest groan or hack, and the soldier made a full circle. One gunner was minus an arm, scrabbling through the hard-packed earth for his AK-74. A quick stitching, and the Executioner pinned him to the ground.

Bolan malingered a moment among the snarling wrath of the firestorm, then realized it was finished here.

CHAPTER FIFTEEN

Major Thalib Ghaziz was having some serious diffi-
culty swallowing the young Iranian's version of what
the youth was calling the great slaughter. No, actually
this Aziz Ahad was sitting there, squirming around in
the metal chair, calling it the mother of all slaughters,
as if he'd heard that so many times from Saddam it
was the phrase of the ultimate warrior who had survived the ultimate battle. But who among even the
wisest of older men, Ghaziz thought, could account for
either the wild imagination or the simple inexperience
of the young, who thought they both knew it all and
were invincible?

In truth, he knew they were neither. He had been
around for a long while, and he had learned the hard way
whatever truths there were in life. The young, like this
Iranian, like his own children, tended to think of only
their own role in whatever scheme of things were the

day's events, how they matched up, how they looked, how they came out of it.

Self-centered.

They also believed, he thought, they could lie to their elders, those placid old goats who had been around for decades, feeble and decaying before youth. But he saw himself as a stalwart agent of reality, bred out of hardship and deprivation, climbing the ladders of life's success before this Iranian was even a twinkle in the eyes of his father.

Such foolishness for this Iranian boy, not much more than eighteen, if he judged the smooth, unlined, near babylike features correct, to think he could dupe, scam a man, no, a soldier who had personally killed in battle with the black SPLA rebels more men than he had wet dreams.

Ghaziz made himself look interested, rapt and ready to buy it all. There were pieces of the puzzle missing, Ghaziz was certain, and it had more to do with the youth's sudden wish to look heroic than anything else, the Iranian all but tipping his hand on his cowardice.

One other thing Ghaziz understood about human nature. Most people created their own problems. In this case, the Iranian youth, by fleeing and leaving his comrades to do the dying, had created a nightmare for himself. He couldn't possibly know it yet, but this Iranian wouldn't live past breakfast.

Ghaziz leaned back in his swivel chair behind his desk. Behind the youth, two of his soldiers were working with a fury trying to raise the two patrols who had left the base hours ago. No luck. Ghaziz could be sure something had happened to them, but what, and how they met some violent end he couldn't say.

"So, it is as I said," the youth continued, in his panting voice, glancing with worry over his shoulder toward the soldiers.

"Interesting. Go on. One man, you say?"

"Yes."

"American? Arab?"

"I did not hear him speak. There was so much shooting, the explosions, it was all I could do to fight my way out of there and come to you with this report."

"Interesting. Perhaps you were too afraid to notice if there were other gunmen running about."

"I saw only the one gunman, sir. Tall, dark."

"The proverbial bogeyman. Interesting."

"What I say is true. They are all dead."

"How would you know?"

Now the youth showed the first sign of fear. "Sir?"

"Let me spell it out for you. A team of gunmen descended on a camp that I am responsible for protecting. You tell me a story of one lone shooter, razing the entire grounds. That you are here tells me you tucked your tail between your legs and ran at the first sign of shooting—"

"But!"

"Silence! Is this what I am out here in the middle of this wasteland to protect? This is the future of the mighty jihad? At the first hint of engaging an undetermined enemy, you run away like a frightened old hag?"

"It was not quite like that."

"Then tell me, what was it like?"

"I...I..."

"Precisely."

He pinned the youth with a dark gaze for a moment, then asked his radioman, "Well?"

"Nothing, sir."

"Take this one outside and shoot him."

He didn't look at the shock and horror veiling the young man's face, but waved a hand, dismissing the pleas for mercy as the soldiers came and hauled him out of the command hut. He had problems of his own, no doubt. The situation called for him to ride out to the camp—or what was left of it. Little doubt the gunman—gunmen—were long gone. They would have left no clues behind as to their identity. And with what the Iranian paymasters shelled out for ownership of this province, someone higher up the chain of command would want answers.

Solid answers. And action, in the form of retaliation.

He was thinking of the mystery and the mess he now had on his hands, when the brief stutter of autofire rang out beyond the hut. If what the youth had said was true...

Impossible. No one gunman could lay waste to an entire camp, slaughter thirty men, even if most of them were inexperienced youth.

Then again, what if the Iranian had been telling the truth? What, then, was he facing? A madman? A crusader?

Ghaziz rose to go check out this mother of all slaughters.

BOLAN UNDERSTOOD the necessity to ditch the vehicle, claim new wheels. There was a strong possibility, if nothing else, the first patrol they encountered could have radioed back a description of the van, and Nhoubaff agreed. Apparently the man had made prior arrangements to stave off just such a problem.

They arrived at a small village of clustered block-shaped huts, the sun up and baking the surrounding desert, promising a day of furnacelike heat. It was going to be hot, all right, Bolan knew, the only question was who would know the fires of hell before the day was out.

The soldier gave Nhoubaff credit for having foresight enough to keep a backup vehicle nearby and waiting. The dark man in the white turban greeted them as they stepped out of the van. Bolan didn't care for the sudden appearance of any more unknown human factors than necessary, but Nhoubaff assured him the man could be trusted. As usual, the soldier knew that remained to be seen. AK-47 in hand, he kept himself braced for any sudden difficulties.

The backup vehicle was an old pickup with a covered bed. They stowed the weapons under false floorboards in the back, then Bolan told Nhoubaff, "Things are just getting heated up."

"I can believe that."

"From here on, it goes to the mat. No turning back."

"I understand. I am with you."

"I need a large black tool bag, some coveralls."

Nhoubaff said he knew another contact who could get him those things on the way to Port Sudan.

"Ahmed will want a little something for his trouble."

Bolan nodded, pulled out his war funds, peeled off enough Sudanese pounds to bring a smile to Ahmed's face.

When they were rolling in the truck, Bolan laid out his game plan. Nhoubaff grew more grim by the minute.

"This kind of action, understand they will marshal all their resources to find us."

"We'll work it out as we go along."

"The radio station, you say?"

"Our next stop."

"Sounds like you had this, uh, shopping list worked out in accordance to movement toward the waterfront."

"Careful planning's always a plus in my line of work."

"And having plenty of bullets likewise."

"That, and seizing the initiative."

"Well, let us go seize some more of that initiative."

"Sounds like a plan. At some point I'm going to need a secured line."

"A satlink. I can arrange that through the contact who sent me to you."

Bolan needed an intro to that contact anyway. Assuming he saw the other side of this mission here in Sudan, he would need to nail down arrangements to get him out of the country.

Now, though, was the time to crank it up, and bring down a few houses of the unholy.

GHAZIZ FELT his anger mounting to a dangerous boiling point. First they had ridden up on the remains of Captain Hassan and his squad, the bodies already taking a savaging from the vultures. Someone had hit the APC with most likely an RPG-7, he deduced, blowing the troops out of their seats before they knew what hit them. Then another roving patrol had reported they had come across Sergeant al-Waddah and his soldiers, stretched out for yet more vultures, his men apparently shot down where they stood in front of their Hummer.

How could this have happened? he wondered. Who was responsible for this obscenity?

Now Ghaziz was inspecting the carnage of the Iranian camp, his rage deepening, questions with no obvious answers churning in his head. All of them—thirty plus—dead, likewise the vultures here hard at work plucking out eyes, gorging themselves on exposed flesh, greedy beaks digging out innards. In a moment of blind fury, Ghaziz unleashed a stream of lead from his AK-74, drilling a few of the more determined scavenger birds into crimson mist and bloody feathers as the other vultures took the clue to vacate and hit the air, squawking away in flight.

Ghaziz moved up to the smoldering remains of where the tents were nearly burning out. He could see what happened here, and found it even more incredible to believe that one man could have done this. Figure some planted charges on the ammo depot, the motor pool, whatever sentries supposed to be watching the grounds probably nodding off as some silent shadows moved in. The initial blasts then taking out a large portion of the tent housing the recruits. Then in some heightened sense of panic whoever survived came running out, the gunmen waiting to cut them down.

However it was spelled out, Ghaziz knew the leader of the NIF wouldn't be happy. Some madmen were on the loose inside Sudan, running amok, killing his soldiers, some twisted scheme to scrap the plans for the training of future Iranian freedom fighters.

Or was there more to it than that?

He didn't look forward to making the first of several calls to report a triple disaster, rife with mystery, no less, no identity on the gunmen. Colonel Issad Bhoutami might be a lower-ranking officer, but he carried more clout with the Iranians, not to mention he had ingratiated himself to the Khartoum government with his grim work on the black rebels in the south.

One last look at the carnage, and Ghaziz headed back for his jeep. He knew one thing right then, and feared the coming hours would bear witness to more such slaughter.

He had problems, no doubt about it, and someone would be held accountable for what was somewhere in the neighborhood of forty-plus dead men. Unless he sounded the alarm, relayed what the Iranian had told him to Bhoutami, that a storm of unknown, faceless gunmen were headed his way, Ghaziz knew it would be his neck firmly placed inside the noose.

Colonel Issad Bhoutami was enjoying a cup of Turkish coffee when the call came through. He was at his desk early in his office headquarters of the National Islamic Front, expecting good news that the promised shipment of high-tech merchandise had arrived at his warehouse on the waterfront. Instead he nearly choked on the steaming black brew as he listened to what amounted to a horror story from Major Ghaziz of the al-Wad post. What he heard defied reality, and he asked the major to repeat himself.

"How could this be?" Bhoutami barked into the phone. "You are telling me you have a bunch of bodies, nearly fifty men all over the desert out there and no witnesses other than one Iranian recruit who claims one gunman did all this? Why am I suspicious, Major?"

"I am calling—"

"As what? A courtesy to warn me some mysterious killers may be headed in my direction?"

"I thought you should know."

"I know the CIA, the DIA are like cockroaches swarming all over the country."

"Perhaps," the major informed him, "they have mounted a covert operation against us. Perhaps, as we suspect, they know you are waiting on that shipment. Perhaps, they suspect you are making inroads and progress toward seeing the return—"

"Enough speculation." The line was secured, he knew, but the CIA were devious enough, with all their high-tech surveillance, to tap into his line just the same.

"I need to make some calls myself now. I need to think. Get back to me within the hour."

He hung up, staring at nothing, the walls of his office seeming to close in, crushing him with paranoia and anxiety. The first call he decided to make was to his head of security. If some undetermined threat was headed his way, he needed all the help he could muster.

Someone had just declared war.

CHAPTER SIXTEEN

Bolan was going in, prepared to leave behind a strong message for the fires of hate. Up to then, Sudan's rising star of morning radio had been pumping out the hate over the state-controlled airwaves, the fanatic spewing out the contaminating poison for as far as he could shout it out from the black depths of his soul. But when the warrior left there the man would no longer be sitting at the mike to trumpet the message of death to the West to consume those Muslims who straddled the fence, those undecided masses who might be influenced by the diatribe to turn into killers.

There was nothing like fighting fire with his own brand of dispensing the cleansing conflagration.

According to his intel, there was also a small force of NIF gunmen on hand, hunkered inside the radio station, guarding their star disk jockey from stalkers, angry listeners who might come there to take the law into their hands out of rational disagreement with the man's message. No clear fix on numbers on the hardforce, but either way it would be a bonus, shaving down some of the troops, a few loose mad dogs he wouldn't need to deal with in the future.

And then there was his own message, Bolan's own personal touch to signal his revulsion and angry disagreement with the message of hate broadcast all over Sudan from here.

Nhoubaff was parked three blocks over, where the souks began in this northern edge before the jumbled blocks of apartment buildings began blending into the city proper.

As luck would have it, an access ladder led to the roof. The giant satellite dish would be the soldier's last victim, but first up to receive a destructive waiting nudge on the way in. The large tool bag with the necessities he needed slung over his shoulder, he scaled the ladder after giving the alley a search and finding it clear of watchers. The problem would come later when he was vacating the premises, retracing his steps back to the truck. The last thing he needed was to find a waiting convoy of authorities and soldiers scrambled to the scene.

The AK-47 fit snug inside the bag, with the Beretta 93-R, sound suppressor already threaded on the muzzle, stowed beneath his white coveralls. A few Russian grenades were stuffed in the pockets of his coveralls, one of them an incendiary bomb, meant to burn the building to the ground.

He hit the roof running, made the satellite dish and fixed a block of C-4, set the timer to give himself ample time to get in and out.

It was going to get hairy, he knew, from there on. No doubt the alarm had been sounded by at least one runner he knew about. He had made it this far, but there was a long way to go. The laser weapons or their component parts were somewhere in the city. Once he started kicking down key doors and grilling guys under the threat of death, he would find those weapons, one way or another, and send them up in smoke.

First to douse the fires of hate.

The Executioner made the door at the edge of the roof. He didn't know the layout, but a running blitz below was in the cards either way.

Bolan found the door open, slid free the Beretta, the AK-47 resting near the top of the bag, ready for a quick pull. Combat senses on full alert, the Executioner ventured down the steps, going for the bulldoze approach to set loose a raging fire of his own.

OMAR GIRGIS HAD a good life as the morning host for Radio Free Islam of Sudan, and he intended to keep both the trappings of his celebrity status and to make sure, on a daily basis, the message of "us" and "them"— Islam versus non-Islam—went on ringing loud and angry to call the faithful to service.

It hadn't always been so grand a life. There was a time, not long ago, when he climbed the ranks of the army the hard way, up the ladder all the way to colonel because of his war against the black rebels of the south. His service to his country had been rewarded by the minister of finance and the leader of the National Islamic Front. They were both personal friends, had pulled a few strings to land him this job as a glorified mouthpiece to spread the word of Islam across Sudan, and as far north, thanks to a tie-in to a Chinese satellite, to Cairo. A Mercedes, an expense account, paid vacations to Europe and a villa on the Red Sea were a few of the more noticeable perks for Sudan's most popular disk jockey. The gaggle of prostitutes he wiled away the nights with was another fringe benefit, long orgies after a hard day at the radio station, which kept him looking forward to going to work the next morning. Not necessarily something, he knew, he wanted broadcasted to his listeners.

Yes, he had a large following, pushing near seven hundred thousand strong, a possible talk show in the near future, and he didn't think the Muslim faithful would appreciate knowing their hero indulged long hours of wallowing in a tangle of limbs with common whores.

He always waited until his listening audience across Sudan was finished with morning prayers before he greeted them. "In the name of God, the compassionate and the merciful, this is Omar Girgis, his humble servant who has been sent in his name to encourage our holy war against the West."

Each morning he began with issuing the fatwa, hoping to incite his countrymen, believing, if nothing else, he could march them out to kill black Christians wherever they were found. This morning he railed against the latest uprising by black rebels in the south, the SPLA fighting to hold on to land that was believed to be awash with oil, a potential gold mine for all Muslims if the area could be returned into the rightful possession of Arabs. Black rebel blood for black gold, was his favorite mantra.

He went on with the usual spewing of venom toward renewed American efforts to use commandos in the Middle East. He said the Americans had unleashed mad dogs after the attack on the USS *Cole,* devils in human skin who were hunting down holy Islamic warriors around the Middle East and north Africa. There was yet to be any evidence of that allegation, but it never hurt to inflame passion and righteous indignation with the right dose of paranoia and fear. Wherever a Westerner was to be found in Sudan, it was the sacred duty of all Muslims to expunge even a single walking blight of infidel presence in the country.

He looked through the open doorway to his studio, face close to the mike, feeling the heat of his passion burning inside. These were hard times for Muslims, he proclaimed, but they had to rise up, stand strong against the infidels. Of course, he knew, not everyone in Sudan agreed with him. Anyone opposed to his views, well, that was the reason he kept an armed security detail of NIF loyalists at the station, close by in the hallway, close enough where he could call out and have them refill his coffee cup. Just in case some lunatic made it past the six loyalists—a long shot, since all of his guards had earned their reputations in the killing fields of southern Sudan—he kept the Makarov pistol on the console.

He was calling for Arab unity, the usual spiel, when he thought he heard a chugging sound, the thud of a body out in the hall. Alarm bells went off, and a moment later he heard the stutter of an automatic weapon, voices raised in fear, the pounding of feet, followed by the scream of a secretary. This couldn't be happening, he thought, frozen at his console, wondering why he couldn't find his tongue, a man who could talk loud and angry volumes for hours on end.

Radio Free Islam of Sudan was under siege, and he knew he'd better get it together quick.

THERE WAS NEVER any time like the present to burn down the enemy. Bolan came through the door, found himself in a narrow hallway when he hit the first two NIF gunmen who came into sight. It was a rapid one-two punch, catching them from behind, the Beretta 93-R sneezing out death, the 9 mm Parabellum manglers coring through brains.

Two out of play, but how many left?

The AK-47 was out next, Beretta stowed, and Bolan was rolling down the hall, ready to let the Kalashnikov do all the talking for him from that point on, homing in on the angry voices of men in that direction.

They nearly had their act together by the time he

reached the archway of some sitting room. Four NIF goons, leaping to their feet, cigarettes falling from gaping mouths, hands clawing for AKs, when Bolan hit the trigger and began hosing them down with a long burst. By now whoever did the paperwork, probably performed the real chores around the station, was pounding out the screams.

Time was running out.

A final sweep of the AK-47, right to left, and Bolan turned the room into an abattoir, limbs twitching out as lifeless bodies folded up, sliding down walls streaked with dark red smears.

It was dumb luck, surging on, finding the secretary reaching for the phone, when he shot the instrument into a hundred flying pieces.

Now for the studio, where the fanatic superstar of Islam radio sold his message of hate.

And the Executioner found the guy, going for a pistol on his console. Two steps into the studio and Bolan hit the glass partition, hoping it wasn't bulletproof. The burst dropped the glass shield in a rain of shards, and Bolan spared a millisecond to thank these thugs for being more brazen than they were cautious. Adjusting his aim a little, the soldier hit Omar Girgis in the chest with a 3-round burst. The boneless sack of Islam's voice of hate hammered down on the console.

So much for free speech, he thought.

The soldier palmed the incendiary grenade, pulled the pin and dumped the bomb in the studio.

The few employees were running for the lobby, he saw, an unarmed stampede that didn't look back. He left them to their evac.

Time to bolt himself.

Racing against his own personal clock, Bolan made the rooftop in seconds flat, hit the ladder and descended in rapid succession. A quick check of his watch, and with any luck he'd be on his way before Radio Free Islam of Sudan cried out its death knell for anyone in the neighborhood to see.

"WHERE TO?"

Bolan was back in the shotgun seat, searching behind them when he told Nhoubaff, "The quickest way to Gamil Abu Said. Tell me what I can expect in terms of resistance when I hit the man's home."

Nhoubaff wheeled the truck around, falling into the heavy congestion. They were just another set of wheels, as far as Bolan could tell, clogging up the narrow streets. Nothing out of the ordinary, or so he hoped.

The rumble of his final touches to the radio station hit the air, jolting Nhoubaff.

Bolan showed the man a grim smile. "Omar Girgis just went off the air. For good."

Stony Man Farm, Virginia

"YES, SIR, I understand. In that case, I'll simply have to wait to hear from you. Yes, sir, good night."

Brognola felt a new round of weariness settle deep into his bones as he put the receiver back on the red phone to the President. He worked on a fresh cigar, checked the clock, piecing together the time zones between the Stony Man warriors. Phoenix on the way to Saudi. Able having landed in Idaho. Striker—God only knew where. He felt the eyes of Kurtzman and Price on him, sensed the anxiety reaching new levels in the War Room.

"There's good news and there's bad news, folks," Brognola finally told them. "The President sends along a job well done as far the Phoenix situation is concerned. He says he would have liked for them to have brought a few more of the heavies back in one piece. But they may get the chance to have another go at it."

"And the bad news?" Price prodded.

"Able is on hold for the moment. Yes, before you say anything, we know DYSAT is dirty. I sense he's ready to cut Able loose on the complex, but he says he needs to think about it."

"What's there to think about?" Kurtzman growled. "They're already in Idaho. Beefed up on hardware, Gadgets has his hang glider to take him over the fence around the perimeter."

"That's just one problem," Brognola said. "Say Gadgets can't get the gate open to let them in, or gets shot down in midair. Say he's stuck inside, they're forced to blast their way in, no stealth, all blood and guts. We don't know how many mad-dog blacksuits Lake has on-site. We're not even sure Lake is even on the premises. The Man's concerned about, well, civilian casualties. You have legitimate researchers, engineers, like that on the compound."

"I know what Lyons would say," Kurtzman offered with a tight smile.

"I'm almost afraid to ask. But, what?"

"He'd tell them to duck."

"Well, they're on hold. For the moment. I think with some amount of prodding I can finagle a green light."

"If, say, those laser weapons, a final shipment of Ramrod Intercept technology," Price posed, "is set to fly out, there's not a minute to wait."

"I understand the urgency. Let's give it a few hours. Then we have a situation regarding Phoenix, phase two. Here's the deal. Okay, we know they are en route for the American air base near al-Jubayl. What McCarter found out was that Arakkhan and Fhalid were funneling some of the DYSAT technology to Khalid Ruballah on the island of Qeshm in the Strait of Hormuz."

"Ruballah," Kurtzman rasped. "A known fanatic, believed to have had a hand in some recent suicide bombings. A known lackey of bin Laden's."

"Couple that," Brognola said, "with the fact Iranian gunboats have been making threatening passes at American tankers in the past week, well, the President is very concerned about another suicide bomb attack on one of our ships."

"And he's prepared to do what?" Price asked.

"Go the distance on this one. He's informed me a U.S. Special Forces black-ops team is set to hit Qeshm. The CIA has apparently seen the same renewed military buildup on this island, and they're finally feeling their nerves. What I'm told by the Man is that an all-out saturation bombing will hit specific targets on the island. The black-ops team will be air-dropped to mop up on the ground."

"And where does Phoenix come in?" Kurtzman asked.

"They will be attached to the team, but acting as an independent arm on the attack. The President seems to want to give them, in light of their success on Madagascar, a chance to hunt down and bring this Ruballah to justice. Only now I'm hearing how he wants Phoenix to turn them over to some spooks from the Company once they land in Saudi."

"Sounds like Fhalid and the man who would be king of all Sudan," Kurtzman said, "were probably never meant to go to trial from the beginning. He's changing the goal on us in midstream."

"Politics, I'm sure," Brognola groused. "At any rate, David got what we needed out of the two big fish. We know where Ruballah is. We know DYSAT has been shipping the merchandise to Sudan—for money, bottom-line greed, I have to believe. We know now that some of that technology has already found its way into Ruballah's hands."

"Which could explain why the Iranians are suddenly acting as brazen as they are in the Gulf," Price said.

"This kind of operation could have serious impact on the world oil market for some time to come," Kurtzman pointed out. "It could even prove disastrous, inflame the fanatics even more."

"The Man understands all that, but the operation has apparently been on the drawing board for some time,"

Brognola said. "His advisers are telling him a preemptive strike is, quote, 'the best redeemable course of action in light of what we know about the Iranian military buildup.' In other words no one wants to see another USS *Cole,* and a few people around Washington want the chance to strike back. Question is, does Phoenix want in or do they want to come home?"

"I can be sure they'd like their shot at Ruballah," Price said.

Brognola nodded. "I concur. Run it past David, see what he thinks." He fell into a heavy pause, then asked, "Any guesses when we might hear from Striker?"

Price told him that a secured satlink was somewhere in Port Sudan with the CIA agent, ready for Bolan's use.

If, the big Fed thought, Bolan even got that far.

"How do we plan on getting him out of Sudan?"

"Again, arrangements will be made through the CIA man," Price said. "I don't have the particulars, but my source at Langley informs me he can pull it off."

"Okay," Brognola said, "why don't we all try and get some rest. There's nothing we can do at this point but ride out the waiting game."

They received that advice, he saw, with grim reluctance. He could well understand their nerves, and suspected no one would be closing his or her eyes until the Stony Man warriors were on the way home, safe and sound.

CHAPTER SEVENTEEN

Gamil Abu Said considered himself something of a man of leisure, had long since figured he'd been through enough in his life to enjoy the hard-earned rewards from his trade. Normally he didn't get out of bed until close to noon for the start of a long day of pleasure mixed with business. He spent his days in the city, getting there midafternoon, feasting on a hearty lunch of lamb or curry in the company of cronies, moving on next to try his luck in a local gambling parlor. He would kill an hour or two, grooming new contacts, hopefully picking up a little extra pocket change from a card game in the process. Then he would work his reliable contacts before dinner around the city, finding out when and where the next arms deal was holding steady in the wings, thereby getting the jump on competitors to try to cut himself a slice of the action. He was also an information broker, a veritable walking encyclopedia on the who's who and what was what in Sudan.

Which meant he was also mired in the business of deceit and double-dealing. Often working both sides of the fence between rival groups of Muslims, he wasn't above selling out anyone he suspected meant to do him bodily harm. Especially if one group or another had placed a bounty on some unfortunate troublemaker's head. Paranoia, and watching his own back, had kept him alive through the early lean years, and he wasn't about to go down in flames from lack of vigilance as he neared fifty.

Which was why he was suspicious when one of his clients, Colonel Issad Bhoutami, began railing at him about a crisis out in the desert, one involving the slaughter of thirty-plus Iranian freedom fighters, with another two kills in the vicinity of the camp where vultures had been found gorging themselves on the remains of Arab soldiers.

Not even two minutes out of bed, barking at his security detail to get him coffee, and he was beginning to think this had all the earmarks of a bad day, one full of treachery and backstabbing. The colonel was making it sound as if an army of mass-murdering invaders was running berserk all over Sudan, some tone of voice, as if he were responsible, flaring on Said's radar for a setup.

"Slow down, Colonel. What, precisely, are you asking me?"

The good colonel didn't answer right off, a noise between a snort and a grunt sounding on the other end. It seemed he just received a report about an attack on the radio station where Radio Free Islam of Sudan had been burned to the ground. Eyewitnesses, the colonel said, claimed one gunman had gone into the station, blasting NIF loyalists where they stood, before killing Omar Girgis, using some sort of incendiary device to raze the building. Gone, too, without a trace. The very same gunman, the colonel suspected, who was responsible for the massacre in the desert. A tall dark man, as if that vague description alone was enough to hunt him down.

Said found his head reeling with questions, spinning, in fact, from overindulgence in too much wine well into the night.

A lone gunman had gone berserk during the night, while he slept the sleep of the newborn? Impossible, he thought. The colonel was either hungover, or suffering from some paranoid delusion that simply came hand in hand with his relationship with the exiled Arakkhan.

"If you are asking me if I have heard from my own contacts about say, a CIA covert operation being mounted against the camps, I have not. However, we both suspect the Muslim brothers have absconded with a recent shipment of merchandise that was destined to fall into your hands, which in turn was meant to go to our Iranian counterparts. Perhaps you should look to them to vent your rage on."

"I will deal with the Iqwhan soon enough. And where did you hear this?"

"It would seem that is unimportant for the moment, considering the gravity of what I am hearing from you."

"Yes, we'll discuss what is and what isn't important

later. Right now I want you to make some calls to every rival dealer, every source of information you have and find out something! Do not forget! I pay you handsomely for information on my enemies. And, if they are my enemies…"

The dial tone buzzed in Said's ear like an angry insect, the implied threat echoing in his head.

"Thoubek!"

A moment later the head of his security detail swept into the bedroom, a steaming mug in hand. Natural paranoia got the better of Said. It was time to have every man on full alert, and God pity the fool who let him down. Say what the colonel relayed to him was true? If some gunman was running around, wasting Iranians and Sudanese soldiers, what was to keep him safe from this maniac? Say the maniac knew about him as one of the biggest arms dealers in Sudan, the eyes and ears of the underworld? Say the maniac was armed with a scorecard, looking to wipe him off this sheet of his music of death? And why hadn't anyone been able to identify this lunatic with more description than might fit three dozen men walking around the city? Sure, it made sense enough that he wasn't leaving any eyewitnesses behind. But, still, someone, especially from the radio station, should be able to give a solid description.

He wasn't sure why, but Gamil Abu Said suddenly felt very much afraid.

"Beef up security by calling in three more of your people from the city," he told Thoubek. "For the moment have your men here on full alert. Let me know of anything unusual, if any strangers approach the gate."

This wasn't going to be a good day, his gut churning with some foreboding of dire circumstance. Said drank the coffee, grimaced as the hot liquid scalded his mouth. He decided to get dressed, make some phone calls, and in the meantime arm himself.

THE INFORMATION-ARMS broker's security force appeared to be agitated, if he judged the sound of their voices and tightly wound limbs right. It warned Bolan that bad news was traveling fast around Port Sudan and vicinity.

Which meant it was also time, Bolan decided, to pick up his own pace. Not even midmorning, and he could feel the heat stirring all around him.

Counting up six gunmen lugging AK-47s, and the soldier intended to stoke the flames of the hellfire even more before he was finished here.

He used the coveralls, draping them over the razor wire, before he scaled the six-foot fence, then dropped down on the other side, sliding off for concealment behind a wall of shrubs. He perched, got his bearings, watched as a group of four separated themselves and marched around the front of the building.

It wasn't quite a mansion, but it was big enough, Bolan guessing ten bedrooms on the second floor, as he counted windows. Seven guns, ten on the outside, according to Nhoubaff's own sources. Apparently Said wasn't an early riser, a big shot in the underworld game who came and went when he pleased, but someone had sounded the alarm from the city, possibly alerting the man trouble of the killing kind could find its way to him.

Bolan had three spare clips for the AK-47, one frag and one incendiary grenade in his pants pocket, hoping it would be enough to bring down the house. According to Nhoubaff, there were no sensors, with only two cameras near the front gate. It seemed Said the arms dealer believed the best security came from the barrel of a gun.

That suited Bolan just fine, making his penetration that much easier, while knowing the score going in.

Two major pluses were now working for the soldier to keep him running and gunning. One, Said had planted his French colonial-style white-scrubbed compound far enough away from the nearest locals that the shooting from the hit should go undetected. It was an hour's drive alone to get there, but Nhoubaff turned up another bonus prize, a much needed pleasant surprise for Bolan, in fact, as they were pulling away from the funeral pyre of the radio station. Seemed Nhoubaff's buddy had handed over the Sudanese version of a police scanner, capable of tapping into local frequencies of military authorities. It certainly aided Bolan's campaign, the scanner able to steer them clear of roadblocks, rolling search convoys and the like.

Getting better all the time.

Bolan needed this wrapped up, pronto. A house full

of known terrorist recruiters working for the NIF was up next, on the way back to the city.

First an arms broker, who was likewise plugged into the darker machinations and movements of the Sudanese underworld.

The soldier opted for the straightforward approach. Nhoubaff was waiting a quarter mile to the north, just over a low hill, parked in what passed as an oasis. Once again, Nhoubaff would have to fend for himself, a dicey proposition, at best, if some roving police car or military patrol pulled up and starting to question him.

No choice. From the beginning, Bolan knew the whole campaign was one of the biggest risks he'd ever undertaken. Here, in Sudan, they recruited, trained and shipped out future mass murderers, kidnappers, suicide bombers. And now they were apparently accepting shipments of high-tech weapons from American traitors. It was a choice hunt, targets all over the map, and it was Bolan's way and his want to do some righteous terrorist headhunting. Especially in light of recent events in the Middle East.

The Executioner selected the French doors, somewhat cloaked by transplanted jungle vegetation as his point of entry into Said's not so humble abode.

Judging the distance to the two standing hardmen, Bolan drew the sound-suppressed Beretta from beneath his tunic, sighted down. In the neighborhood of forty yards, give or take. The twin kill wasn't the problem.

No, it was getting to the side doors, cutting a hard run across the no-man's-land before…

Do it.

And he did.

They never knew what hit them, a look of shock outlining the second hardman's face in freeze frame at the sight of his comrade's brains getting splashed on his shirtfront. Before he bellowed the alarm, Bolan nailed him, one 9 mm Parabellum shocker coring through his vented mouth, driving whatever he was going to shout back down his throat.

Another moment, searching the grounds, the curtained windows for watchers, and Bolan found he was in the clear, moved out, hard and fast.

So far, so good, charging in, shaving it down to ten yards when—

The sentry appeared like a ghost, rolling out from the shadows. He might have tagged Bolan, but he froze at the sight of the human bulldozer coming straight at him. As it stood, the hardman never got the AK-47 quite lined up. Bolan tapped the Beretta's trigger, painted a ragged red hole between the hardman's eyes.

The problem was the hardman's nerves, frying out in death spasms, and holding back on the trigger as he toppled into the brush.

SAID WAS a jumble of electric nerves as he paced around his living room, cell phone pressed to his ear. He listened as Ahmed Shalidah, a reliable counterpart with whom he had worked several deals in the past, relayed the line on the coming events. Shalidah told him he was the middleman in the deal with a strange American he was to meet that night on the waterfront. He had, in fact, negotiated, in league with the AWOL Arakkhan, the original deal with American arms dealers.

"So, you are telling me the colonel has the merchandise?"

Shalidah's tone was cautious for a moment, as he played it smooth. "My good friend, Gamil, we go back a long ways, you and I. We have done business together with honor. I begin to fill in all the details on this transaction, well, from what I've already heard is happening in Sudan, it would seem several dominoes in our chosen occupation are already falling, or are being hunted."

"I need information, Ahmed. The colonel seems to think some massive CIA or DIA conspiracy is storming across the Sudan."

"We are dealing with Westerners. Who knows? Perhaps the colonel is being set up, because of his ties to Arakkhan, but I do not think so."

"There is a madman on the loose, that much I have heard."

"I have heard different. I have heard it was a small group of commandos. Fear not, this is what I have been telling several of our associates. This large a group, they cannot possibly expect to move about freely, gunning down every- and anyone even remotely connected to the colonel's deal. Since we are old friends, I will tell you this much. The colonel is sitting on the weapons in his waterfront warehouse, with more on the way. I tell you this, because I know the colonel can be treacherous."

"Meaning should something happen to you…"

"Precisely. I see we can still trust each other. Now, call me later in the afternoon. We can do lunch, perhaps by then I'll have a better line on these madmen killing our people all over Sudan. I know the colonel is anxious for good news. The truth is, he grilled me right before I called you. We'll speak later."

Said tossed the cell phone on the divan, disgusted that he really didn't know much more than when he woke up to Bhoutami's railing. There were other calls to make, to be sure, but he wasn't expecting any great revelation to shine through on who was behind all the killing.

He took his mug, was sipping the strong Turkish coffee when he heard the familiar stutter of an AK-47. That was no accidental discharge, his gut warned him.

Before he was aware of it, he was slapping at the hot coffee he'd splashed on his shirt, yelping at the fiery touch seeping through. Then he was racing on for the assault rifle leaned up against the divan, checking the load on his Makarov pistol on the way.

His mind was racing with questions, wondering how this could be happening, how many gunmen were on the premise, when he heard a full-scale battle erupting from somewhere to the north.

CHAPTER EIGHTEEN

Bhoutami was more baffled at the moment than he was angry. Venting of any rage would come in due time, likewise vengeance, once the mysterious gunman—or gunmen—was identified, cornered and caught, and strung up by his thumbs.

Flayed and dipped in burning oil, he hoped.

It was something of a crapshoot, though, determining just who was the lunatic wreaking all the havoc, killing Arab soldiers under his command, the Iranian freedom fighters he had brought into Sudan. The list of his potential enemies, he knew, was long, not to mention somewhat murky since the faces changed all the time depending on who was the day's casualty. The shortlist of who might want his head in a trophy case comprised three, maybe four rival Muslim groups who wheeled and dealed in arms, some minor drug trafficking or an infrequent dabbling in the white-slavery mar-

ket which was extremely lucrative by itself if the right
sheikh from Saudi or Oman came calling. The shortlist,
on the one hand, was known to him, even as those jealous rivals were always lurking about, sharpening the
blade, ready to stick it to him and claim his, the biggest
piece of action in town as their spoils of war.

The longer list gave him a headache just to consider,
since it was deeply submerged in the shadow world of
espionage, faceless saboteurs and assassins who could
move about undetected, ghosts in human form who could
murder and vanish without a trace. There was the CIA.
The DIA. The NSA. Even agents of Interpol were rumored to be crawling about Sudan, looking for clues as
to the whereabouts of the AWOL Arakkhan, the so-called
Butcher of Southern Sudan, the favorite whipping boy,
he thought, of the mighty Western intelligence agencies.

His personal friend and mentor he intended to bring
to power with an eventual coup in Khartoum.

And there was yet another mystery to ponder.

No one, not even his contacts in the capital city of
Madagascar, was returning his phone calls. And the di-
rect line to the French garrison, where Arakkhan had
staked out his temporary home, was dead.

Events, he thought, were becoming more and more
strange with each round of violence, to the point of
unnerving.

He shifted his beefy bulk on feet already sore from
standing, turning next away from his office window, the
sunlight suddenly hurting his eyes as it glared off the

Red Sea, which was choked by now with dhow boat traffic and the sluggish crawl of the large freighter ships coming into or leaving port.

There was some good news, he reflected, but it seemed to come to him at the most inconvenient of times. The American contact had called earlier, informing him the next shipment would be pulling into his Pier 9 in roughly eight or nine hours. A coincidence, then, that a madman was shooting up Sudan, still at large, when the shipment was slated to be handed off that night? Treachery on the part of the American arms dealer? What, did he want more money, and was now marching out some message of doom that if he didn't receive additional funds the deal would go down in some blaze of twisted glory?

All the work, just to get the original cargo boated to Qeshm.

Now Bhoutami saw the world suddenly going up in flames around him. He wouldn't admit it to anybody, but he was nearly afraid to leave his office headquarters, venture out into the streets, where some faceless, nameless hunter could strike him down, out of nowhere.

He turned to Habib, his head of security. "How many men are in the building?"

"Fifteen, sir."

"Make it twenty-five. Call them in, I don't care what you have to do or how much you have to pay them. Go."

When he was alone, Bhoutami went and collapsed in the deep cushioning of the swivel chair behind his desk. Sudan, he thought, was a thriving hornet's nest, ever expanding with arms brokers, Iranian agents, information brokers, a land abuzz with murder and treachery at every corner. In short, all manner of cutthroats who might then be counting down his life by the hours.

As in that night when the shipment arrived.

There was really very little he could do, he realized, other than wait out the day and hope the madman didn't find him. The thought alone depressed him, forced to ride it out, not go beyond the bastion of his headquarter walls and make himself a walking target for some lunatic.

He then told himself it was better to be safe than sorry. Sorry in this case, he knew, would be dead.

THE EXECUTIONER expected them to come running from the front, and they fulfilled his grim expectations. On the fly, he nailed one more hardman, then a beehive of lead was swarming above and behind him, chasing him deeper across the patio. They were hasty shots, and the soldier had to believe their trigger fingers were pulling in either blind panic or erratic anger over seeing a few of their comrades in the jihad checked out for their reward.

He meant to bulldoze his way through the flimsy glass panes of the French doors, when zinging lead aided him before he was airborne. Several panes were punched out, the wood slats eaten up, as he felt the scorching heat whipping dangerously close to his scalp.

Bolan launched himself through the doorway and beat a hard run for the first cover he spotted. It was some kind of sprawling game room, complete with regulation-size pool table, a row of pinball machines, dartboards, skeeball lanes. For whatever the man of the house's ranting and ravings about Western materialism might be, he sure didn't seem to mind the finer playthings, imported, of course, from a culture so despised by Islamic fundamentalism.

Go figure the mind of a fanatic, Bolan thought.

Bolan had tallied up four on the fly, about to make the battered doorway. He was over the pool table, rolling off and landing on his feet, when he spied the portly, goateed figure on the landing leading to the living room.

Nhoubaff's description of Gamil Abu Said was right on the money.

The man also looked hell-bent on guarding the palace, if all else failed.

Bolan swung up the AK-47, tapped off a short, precise burst that lopped off a piece of flesh on Said's upper arm. The arms dealer and information broker was spinning, the assault rifle flying from his hands, when Bolan focused full and angry attention toward the shooters filling up the doorway. They milked short bursts from their AK-74s, strafing the room, as if hoping some spray and pray would prove them winners.

It wasn't in Bolan's game plan to get bogged down.

The soldier armed the frag grenade, ticked off the doomsday numbers, popped up and hit the doorway jamb with a burst of autofire, hosing it down one-handed, sending four grim faces lurching back, then pitched the steel egg.

All gunners came back, blazing away with automatic-weapons fire.

The lethal bomb bounced, rolled up nearly at their feet, and blew them into ragged shreds when the smoky thunderclap went off in their faces.

The soldier found Said grabbing for his weapon. Marching on, a glance to the smoking maw behind, and Bolan said, "I wouldn't. You'll never make it."

Said lifted his hands, replied, "Very well. We can make a deal."

It almost sounded too easy, Bolan's radar tracking for the next flying squad kicking in. He held his ground, swiveling, listening for any approach from the direction of the living room.

"I counted eight," the soldier told Said. "I'll know if you're lying. Well?"

"That is all of them. Like I said, we can deal, but what do I get in return?"

Bolan kept the muzzle aimed square on Said's chest. "A little more time."

"May I stand?"

"Slow and easy, hands up."

That done, Said launched into his spiel, clearly hoping that if he played Judas he could save his neck. "Ahmed Shalidah," he said, and rattled off an address where the man could be found. "There is a major deal involving high-tech weapons from America. Pier 9. Tonight, I believe."

"Who's taking delivery?"

"Colonel Issad Bhoutami. He is the man, I hear, who is setting the stage for a revolution to return Arakkhan to Sudan, to overthrow the government of Khartoum."

"I keep hearing that. How about something new?"

"Very well. This shipment, I believe it is not the first. The real purchasers are Iranian, specifically one Khalid Ruballah, a man, I understand, who has personal ties to bin Laden. The weapons, this supertechnology, go, I believe, by boat to an island in the Strait of Hormuz. My sources also tell me they hear Ruballah is looking to launch several suicide boats against either American warships or oil tankers in the Persian Gulf in the coming days. How am I doing so far?"

"You're still buying some time."

"There is an American contact, I do not know his name, but Shalidah is the middleman between Bhoutami and some high-tech American arms manufacturer called DYSAT. You don't look surprised."

"I've been here before."

"How so?"

"Traitors. Selling out their own. Going for the big bucks. Everyone, guys like you, scrambling around to carve themselves a piece of the action. While innocent people, living hand-to-mouth perhaps, families scraping by but sticking it out, get ground up in your death schemes. You have two seconds to say your prayers."

"But you said—"

"I said you bought a little time. Time's up."

"You lying—"

Bolan had seen the way in which the arms dealer had almost reached behind his back when he issued the warning. He knew it was coming, and it made it that much easier to seal in blood the end here for the house of Said.

They were dropping fast, hard and final, down for the count. But the Executioner knew his work was far from finished. Figure the fifty-yard line, and driving.

As the body count climbed, it wouldn't get any easier from there on to the goal line, which was Pier 9 on the waterfront.

Bolan gave it a full minute, walking through the living room, checking the stairs, waiting to see if any more savages reared up.

All clear.

One last glance at the bizarre decor, a mix of African and French colonial art and trimmings, and Bolan armed the incendiary grenade. The soldier was beating a fast exit when the cleansing blast erupted to put the finishing touches on the house of Said.

THE DAY SEEMED to shoot on at an accelerated pace by the time Bolan reached his next target. It usually worked that way, he knew, when any second the end could come crashing down on his head.

So far the gods of war were smiling, but at the next turn they could just as easily, he knew from grim experience, look away and leave him hung out there, no way out.

No way back.

Sticking to the original game plan, the soldier had his routes mapped out according to the shopping list, en route to the waterfront, where he suspected, before landing in Sudan, the final showdown would take place. He let Nhoubaff do the driving, and so far all the monitored police or military frenzy, roadblocks and searches, was confined to the north end of the city as Bolan's accomplice took the long route around for his next stop, coming back in from the southwest edge of the city by the Red Sea.

It was a dingy apartment building, going to seed, with a rusty fire escape leading up six stories to the top floor. Fortunately Bolan wasn't going to the top.

The targeted apartment here belonged to a rival group of the NIF. They did a fair amount of recruiting of young, impressionable minds in Sudan on their own, often linking them up with Iranian terrorist training camps out in the desert. The leader of the Iqwhan, Jamal Abadab, was well-known in the U.S. intelligence community.

He should have been, Bolan reflected, since he was linked to more than a dozen suicide bombings, from Egypt to Jerusalem. He never quite made the effort to lay the killing touch on the innocent himself, since he pumped full and shaped the minds of disillusioned, rebellious youth like putty in his hands, leaving the dirty work and the dying to somebody else while he raked in the fistfuls of dollars.

Youth, no older than twenty, just as he'd seen out in the desert, fixed up and fueled with the fires of hate, shipped off to foreign lands to go out as martyrs for the jihad.

Bolan could have bypassed this stop, moving on in search of bigger game, but, as fate would have it, this den of murderers and saboteurs was on the way.

Why mess with fate, when it was still smiling?

Once again, Nhoubaff came through, just when Bolan figured the man had to have run out of surprises. The flash-stun grenade was Russian made, but it was equal, something like a million candlepower, with noise to match its American counterpart.

Perfect.

While Nhoubaff held down the rolling fort, waiting it out in an alley one block north in this congested area of apartment buildings, Bolan toted his tool bag up the stone steps, eased into a narrow hallway rotten with the universal smells of deprivation and desperation known only to the poor. Of course, Abadad had posher accommodations somewhere near the waterfront, but Nhoubaff confirmed the terrorist puppeteer held down his recruitment center here, could almost certainly be found every day, all day mapping out the future with as many as six to eight flunkies.

The soldier didn't make eye contact with two turbaned men as he climbed the steps to the second floor, checking the numbers in Arabic, marching on until he came to the appointed den.

The fire escape was a lucky twist for this hit, would allow him to clear the smoke, bolt out the den to make a hasty descent to the street. It had to be quick, nailed down within seconds before the neighbors called in the local cavalry.

This was straight slaughter detail, and the Executioner got busy.

A glob of plastique, the size of his thumb, was stuck to the doorknob. Detonator applied, he stepped back, palmed the flash-stun, while holding the radio hellbox in the other hand. It was somewhat awkward, but it was show time, and Bolan juggled the items with deft ease, pulling the pin, letting the spoon drop.

He thumbed the red button and blew the door off its hinges. They were shouting up a storm in a flash, bullets already eating up the jamb, tattooing the wall across the hallway when the soldier hunched low and sent the steel egg whiplashing around the corner. Pulling back, hearing someone holler "Grenade" in Arabic, he hugged the wall, eyes shut and hands clamped over his ears. The wall rocked, felt as if it would come tumbling down, but it was merely an illusion of the moment as the flash-stun rocked their world beyond and cleaved their senses.

The Executioner hauled out the AK-47, slipping an arm through the straps of the tool bag. A spare clip was already wrapped with duct tape around the banana magazine in place, allowing him to pour it back on in one eye blink if he was forced to burn up the first set of thirty rounds.

The Executioner bulled in, firing. They were reeling about in the smoke, as expected, grabbing at blinded eyes, crimson trickles worming out of ears punctured all to hell by the deafening blast.

Four were chopped down before they even took up arms for an attempt at blind spray and pray. Bolan surged on into the roiling smoke, caught a staggering form just as it appeared in the doorway of an adjacent bedroom with a zipping march of 7.62 mm slugs across the chest, caving in sternum, punching the heart to mush. Two rounds from the French FAMAS assault rifle smacked the wall in the area Bolan had just vacated, but any near miss only urged him to nail it down.

A groaner was rising up from behind the splintered matchstick rubble of a coffee table when Bolan ended his misery with a 3-round stitching to the throat.

That made six.

And the Iqwhan recruitment looked out of business. Fax machines, some sort of phone bank were nothing but shattered debris, crushed to sparking shells by the concussive force of the blast.

Bolan made the ragged hole marking the spot of the former window. There, he looked through the shredded strands of curtain, found the alley below clear. One last look over his shoulder, and he was ready to put behind another massacre, only this time a little confusion would be thrown into the fire. The Iqwhan terrorists were rivals of the NIF, after all, but Bolan didn't plan on sticking around Sudan long enough to see who eventually came out the winner in some gangland-style street war.

All finished here, and the Executioner hit the fire escape, stowing the AK-47.

Sudan was smoking, he thought, no doubt about it, but he was merely getting warmed up for the real holocaust.

CHAPTER NINETEEN

Stony Man Farm, Virginia

"The Man just gave Able the green light."

Brognola made the announcement, marching into the Computer Room. It had to have come out, without much enthusiasm, since there was a moment of what he sensed was skeptical silence.

"I'm thinking there's the proverbial catch-22 coming up next," Kurtzman said from his workstation.

Brognola fished out his antacid tablets, helped himself to some of Kurtzman's heavy-duty brew, washed them down and answered, "There is. Able has to first make a positive eyeball ID that Lake is on the compound in Idaho."

"That's not the only glitch Able's looking at," Tokaido chimed in.

"Plan A was just scrapped by Mother Nature," Kurtzman told Brognola as he marched toward their work cubicles.

"A front has moved in, settled dead center over most

of the state," Price added. "Gusting winds, swirling up to forty miles an hour. They seem to shift according to our weather readout, every other hour or so."

"Meaning," Brognola said, already aware of where this was headed, "Gadgets has to eighty-six his hang-glider entry."

"Too risky," Wethers said. "There's the chance he catches a sudden gust and overshoots the entire compound."

"Or he could ride the wind for the mother of all crash landings into the side of a mountain," Kurtzman finished. "Or slam into the fence, or maybe find himself crucified in the razor wire."

"Okay, I've got the picture. So they do it the hard way."

"Blood and guts," Tokaido said, sporting a grim smile. "Storm the palace. I'm sure Ironman will approve."

"He'll figure something out," Kurtzman said. "At least our sat reads are showing the fence isn't electrified. Figure some wire cutters, get in…"

"But only, I repeat, only if they're one hundred percent certain Lake is there."

"Not only that, but we can't scope out the installation from space," Kurtzman said. "This front is apparently going to hold for two, three days, according to the National Weather Service."

"Lay it on them," Brognola said. "It's a go."

"If," Price emphasized. "I'll pass it on to Carl. We've turned up a very unsettling development," she added, "less than an hour ago."

"I'm hearing that bad news and very bad news you folks mention," Brognola said.

"Our worst fear would appear to be in the works," Price stated, and took the remote, snapping on the satellite monitor. "These we just 'borrowed' from the CIA. They came via an SR-71 reconnaissance flyover of the islands in the strait in question."

Brognola chomped on his cigar, raised an eyebrow. "An SR-71? I thought the Air Force retired all SR-71s more than a decade ago."

"They did," Wethers offered. "The Japanese got one for their museum, the British another one for display. Congress ordered three of them reactivated a few years after the Gulf War."

"Moving on," Price said, "these were taken with the SR-71's famed long-focal-length 'technical objective cameras' from eighty thousand feet up. No cloud cover to obscure our view, as you can see. Picture perfect. So good, we have identified several major terrorist players with lengthy track records of bombings, kidnappings, murder and so on."

Brognola watched as Price worked the remote, and he found himself looking at soldiers in buff-colored camous doing what looked like welding on a gunboat. Then it hit him, like a punch to the gut, what they were doing.

"Folks, don't tell me—"

"Very much afraid so, Hal," Price said, tight-lipped, as grim as death. "Those are blocks of C-4 they're bringing onto the gunboats. From what we can tell, they are welding explosives into what we've determined are three gunboats in the port of Qeshm."

"Which, if little else, takes care of the President," Kurtzman said, "having to worry about the one pulling the trigger on an international incident."

"Also," Price said, clicking on another frame, bringing into view three soldiers hauling out a long cylindrical tube. "There's your chemical laser weapons."

"Doesn't look like much," Brognola commented, "but I guess the bomb that fell on Hiroshima didn't, either."

"They have the laser weapons," Kurtzman said. "More to the point, the fanatic of the hour, Ruballah, has them. The SR-71 got a clear shot of his mug."

The enormity of what could happen was sinking in. "If they make a mass run with those gunboats at an American warship or a tanker," Brognola said, "and sink them…"

"Then we're talking about a possible full-scale war with Iran," Price said. "As it stands, with what's in the wings, Phoenix will be on board for a major preemptive surgical strike."

"I'll pass this on to the Man," Brognola said. "I'm sure he already knows…anybody hear from Striker while I was gone?"

"Not yet," Kurtzman answered.

"If Port Sudan and vicinity is going up in flames, thanks to Striker," Price said, "well, we don't know. Not even a whisper of a rumor from our collective sources in the intelligence community."

"And Sudan," Tokaido said, "isn't exactly CNN friendly, as I'm sure everyone knows."

"Get Able moving, at least, closing in, surveying the compound, something," Brognola ordered. "I'll be in the War Room with the Man. If you hear from Striker—"

"You'll be the first to know," Price assured the big Fed.

Brognola was already out the door, barely heard the mission controller's words. In just a few short minutes he felt as if he'd aged another ten years.

Life on the edge, he mused in deep grim thought. Peace on Earth. One was always guaranteed, and the other?

Not in this world, not today, tomorrow.

Sadly enough, he thought, not ever, as long as there were Ruballahs and Arakkhans preying on the world at large.

Sudan

"YOU CAN CALL me Taylor."

"Cooper."

The Executioner gave the dingy apartment hallway one last look. Clear. Then, trusty tool bag in hand, stuffed with the AK-47, just in case all wasn't what it appeared, Bolan followed Nhoubaff into the agent's living room.

"I've been expecting you."

Bolan nearly lifted an eyebrow at that, but gave the Spartanly furnished apartment a look instead, noting the small kitchen, the doorway to an adjoining bedroom.

As if reading his mind, or to let Bolan know he understood and appreciated his suspicions or paranoia under the circumstances, Taylor said, "I live alone. You're safe here. And when I said I was expecting you, I meant you would be stopping by most likely to contact whoever it is sent you."

It all remained to be seen, Bolan knew, who was who, and what was what. In a country as treacherous, volatile and violent as Sudan, no CIA safehouse could be guaranteed. So far, so good, but that could change any second, he knew. Nhoubaff had placed the call here some ninety minutes earlier from a pay phone. They had crawled along the teeming, congested streets of Port Sudan at less than a snail's pace, it had seemed, before finally reaching the designated apartment building. The curtain, Bolan noticed, was drawn, but he heard the faithful being called to prayer for the mosque he'd seen on the way in from somewhere in the distance.

The soldier ran a quick look over the Company man who had sent Nhoubaff to the DZ. He was short, wiry, swarthy. A nest of curly hair, as black as a raven's wing, with matching beard and mustache, and Bolan knew the man could at least blend in with the local scenery, one of the natives, since no intelligence agency ever infiltrated one of their own unless the agent could speak the tongue fluently.

Bolan then noticed the police scanner on the table next to the phone.

"You've been a very busy man, Cooper," Taylor said, moving toward the kitchen. "Congratulations are in

order. You've taken a nice little bite out of the local terror trade here. The radio station was a nice little coup
by itself."

"We've had some luck. And my partner here has
proved himself an invaluable asset. You couldn't have
sent a better man."

Nhoubaff showed Taylor a big smile. "He's mod-
est, too. I will tell you, had I known beforehand what
I was getting into, well, I wouldn't have it missed it
for all the dirty Iranian oil money to ever come
through this bloody country. The man has put on quite
the show."

"Simply taking care of business," Bolan said.

"Taking out the garbage, you mean," Nhoubaff said
with a mean grin.

"You could say that."

"And," Taylor said, stepping back into the living
room with two mugs of coffee, holding them out for
Bolan and Nhoubaff, "there is still much to be done—
this is what you're thinking."

"Barely scratched the surface."

Taylor sipped his coffee, giving Bolan a cool measuring look. "Still a long way to go before you get to the
scum at the bottom of the barrel?"

"That's one way of putting it."

Bolan sipped his coffee, set down the tool bag.

"It's hot out there in the streets," Taylor said. "The police and the military authorities are everywhere. They're
calling you a 'lunatic,' 'madman,' but I look at you and

I know better. Yes, you're taking care of business. Sudan is a country with many dangerous men who need to be taken out. However, may I make a suggestion?"

Bolan nodded. "I'm listening."

"The deal is set to go down in a few hours. Pier 9. My sources inform the *Thai Princess* will be docking, with, I'm certain, one Colonel Issad Bhoutami on hand, with his contingent of Iranians who have already paid for the merchandise in question."

"So I've heard. And your suggestion?"

"Make your call. Wait it out. I have a man watching the NIF headquarters, likewise the waterfront. It seems Bhoutami is a very nervous man, hearing constant reports about all this strange violence blowing all about Sudan, wringing his hands, I imagine, wondering when his ticket will get punched. In short, he's so scared, he hasn't left his office. He's marshaled up a force of twenty-five thugs to guard him. When he leaves for the waterfront, we'll be there, waiting for him to, uh, finish his deal. Over here."

Bolan followed Taylor a few feet to the divan. There, Taylor pushed it several feet away from the wall. He took a small jimmy device, wedged it into the base of the wall and slid back a section of the floor. The Executioner found himself staring down into an arsenal.

"You'll have to abandon your truck, too risky to go back, all the heat that is out there," Taylor said. "There's a chance an eyewitness saw you leave the Iqwhan headquarters, who can say? Why jeopardize finishing your mission if it's your intention to go lop off a few more terrorist heads in the neighborhood? I have everything you need to finish the job on the waterfront. M-16s with M-203 grenade launchers. Uzis. Satchels of grenades, in frag, incendiary, flash-stun, forty mils likewise for the M-203. I have harnesses and webbing. I have combat blacksuits," he said, judging Bolan's size, "even one I believe that will fit you."

"Santa Claus," Bolan said, and saw Taylor frown, the note of skepticism not lost on the man.

"This has taken years to assemble. I have been in the Sudan for nearly half a decade, grooming my own contacts, learning how to do things here. They think I'm a simple shopowner, Persian rugs. At any rate, if I was ever found out to be a CIA agent, and they came through my door…" A grim smile. "It would take a small army, you understand."

"I've got something of the picture."

Bolan watched as Taylor bent and hauled out a small aluminum case.

"Your satlink. There is no monitor in place to home in on the signal to wherever you're calling. I'll have no idea to whom or to where you are speaking. But I'm sure whoever sent you has a firewall already built into their own transmitter-receiver."

That was true enough, Bolan knew. Stony Man Farm was the most sophisticated high-tech covert operation on the planet. If their satellite transmission was monitored, Bear would throw up enough firewalls, the eavesdropper would find himself listening to little more than dead air in outer space.

"Make your call," Taylor said, and handed Bolan the satlink, "then, I'll lay out a plan of attack. I've also arranged evacuation for you. I only hope it's not a fighting withdrawal."

Bolan read a fire of determination in Taylor's eyes, before the CIA man added, "It's a long swim across the Red Sea to Saudi Arabia."

Stony Man Farm, Virginia

"STRIKER."

Brognola lurched up in his chair in the War Room, tied in on the three-way system to the other team members. His heart was pounding, either from relief or anxiety, he wasn't sure.

"Was there ever any doubt?" Bolan said over the satlink, with a grim chuckle.

"Just the usual frayed nerves," Brognola said. "Bring us some good news. We could use it."

"I've been on a roll, but I'm at a stoplight for the moment. Would you believe I've made quite the mess since I've been here?"

"I couldn't imagine," Kurtzman cut in, matching Bolan's grim mirth. "What's the plan?"

"There's a definite DYSAT connection on my end," Bolan said.

"They're going down," Brognola told the Executioner. "It's just a question of when."

"It's already in the works," Price added. "But we'd like to know where things stand on your end."

"A firestorm is brewing. A freighter called the *Thai Princess* is docking in a few hours. Everyone's going to the show. An NIF thug, Colonel Issad Bhoutami, a contingent of his Iranian purchasers for DYSAT's wonder toys, and I couldn't even begin to tell you who else. The good news is I've got on hand what I'll need to go to the party."

"Do you have an evacuation strategy?" Price asked.

"Looks like I'm boating it out of here. I'll call you back when I get to Jiddah."

Brognola rubbed his face. He knew Bolan, and he knew the warrior was trying to assure his friends it was just another day at the office, no sweat. The mission in Sudan, though, was reaching critical mass. For one thing, Brognola could well imagine the carnage the Executioner had strewed over God only knew how many hell's half acres since he'd landed. That meant serious local heat on the angry prowl from military and police authorities. Bolan had pulled off the impossible before, but there was always a first time the best man for the job wouldn't be enough. And in the Executioner's world, the first time would be the last. Final, since it would prove fatal.

"On the plus side, I've put something of a dent in the local trade. I'm told the heat is on, heavy, so I'm laying low until the appointed hour."

Brognola listened as Bolan filled in a few of the blanks. The big item was that the Iranians had been, and were once more intending to ship the high-tech goods to their island bastions in the Strait of Hormuz, political ammunition for the President, if nothing else, Brognola knew, when the shitstorm hit the Oval Office and Qeshm was bombed back into the Stone Age. When Bolan was informed of the situation in the Gulf his voice lowered some to a new grim depth.

"Then I suppose it's up to me to close down shop on this end."

Brognola could feel Bolan's tension from the other side of the world, Striker all but ready to head out, but forced to hole up, maybe plan the coming killing ground, as far as logistics, enemy head count, and so on. Instead, he inquired about Able and Phoenix.

"All present and accounted for," Kurtzman told him. "One piece and rolling on."

"Then I'm off to wrap it up here. I'll be in touch."

A round of good luck was issued, but Bolan had already signed off. Gone, Brognola thought, in a few short hours to burn down any number of savages and hammer the last nail into the coffin of DYSAT treason in the Sudan.

Brognola sat, alone in the War Room, heard a few questions fired off by the team over the speaker, but he was in a world of his own for a long moment. The big Fed felt as if he had the weight of the world on his shoulders. Truth was, he knew he did.

It was good, he thought, no, it was something of a sweet comfort to have friends close by to share the crisis, and the burden of all the somber weight of living on the edge.

Sudan

BOLAN WORKED on his second cup of coffee, indulged a rare cigarette as Taylor laid it out. The soldier and the CIA man sat on the divan while Nhoubaff was hunched up in a chair he'd pulled from the kitchen. Pen in hand, Taylor sketched a rough layout of the warehouse complex and the pier. Stone structure, two stories. He informed Bolan of the route they would take to what he called an industrial wasteland.

"These men are brazen," Taylor said. "Security is lax. Nothing by way of cameras, sensors, the like. The barrel of the gun, they believe, is all they need to keep away trespassers. Or, in our case, a three-man invading force. Just to the north is where we will park. It's open ground, marshy, with a drainage ditch where we can change into blacksuits, load up and head out."

Bolan listened as Taylor said he and Nhoubaff would climb an access ladder on an office building that rose near the target area. They would cover Bolan from the roof when the soldier stated he intended to go in, and place whatever charges he had left at strategic points around the warehouse. As was Nhoubaff, Bolan discovered Taylor was a man of pleasant surprises.

"In case you're running low on plastique, I have an additional twenty pounds, with timers, I can 'lend' you," he said, a grim smile cutting his mouth. "I also have com links. I think communication between the three of us is vital."

Bolan cut to the heart of the matter. "You understand that when the shooting starts there may be no way out."

They nodded.

"I've come this far with you," Nhoubaff said. "I don't think I could look myself in the mirror tomorrow if I bailed now."

"Now," Taylor went on, "his name is Malahkan. Approximately one and a half kilometers to the north of the drainage ditch, he'll be waiting for you in the ruins of a long dead and forgotten sultanate. In a narrow inlet, he will have an outboard ready to take you five miles out to sea. There, I have arranged for a cigarette speedboat to take you to Jiddah. Once you land in Saudi, my man on the boat will instruct you where you can go to call your people and make whatever necessary arrangements you see fit."

"You're staying behind, then."

It wasn't meant as a question born from suspicion, but Bolan both knew and respected the risk these men were taking to go into the fire beside him. To stay behind might drop a certain death sentence down on their heads.

"I have much work yet to do in the Sudan," Taylor said. "I sense you ask me this question, not because you distrust me, but because you are concerned about my— our—continued well-being in the Sudan. That was, and will never be guaranteed."

Bolan could well understand that much, and dropped it.

"I've gotten you this far," Taylor added. "I'll see you make it out of here."

"That's assuming a lot once the fireworks start," Bolan said.

"Indeed. Two, now three," Taylor said, and flashed Nhoubaff a grin, "can play, or attempt to play the sort of deadly game you do. You'll need our help, no matter how good you've proved yourself to be in this business of killing."

"From the sounds of it," Bolan said, "three guns will most certainly be better than one."

"Then it's settled," Nhoubaff said, as if he were concerned Bolan was set to protest and order them to sit out the curtain call in Port Sudan.

"Any idea on what's stored in the warehouse?" Bolan asked.

"My sources tell me," Taylor said, "it is nothing short of one of the largest armories in the country. So, once those charges go off…"

Bolan matched the man's graveyard smile.

"Okay," the soldier said, "let's go over it one more time. Firepoints, movements, the timing. Just to make sure we're all on the same page."

CHAPTER TWENTY

The phone, he thought, had become his second-worst enemy, almost as lethal as the dreaded madman still on the loose in the city—or wherever. The instrument itself, of course, couldn't kill him. But the comrades and counterparts of the dead men, scattered—some of them nothing more than smoking black mummies—from the city proper all the way to the fiery ruins of Abu Said's home on the outskirts to the desert waste-land of the Nubian beyond, could come hunting for his scalp.

And would, he knew, if he didn't come up with con-crete answers, preferably a mangled body that had seen hours of torture. Preferably the lunatic responsible for the belly full of anxiety that threatened to cut loose his bowels any moment.

And the news was getting worse by the hour. More killing. No firm ID still on the lunatic.

Nothing.

Any minute he expected someone in his own circle would reach out and touch him with more than just an irate phone call. As in kicking through the office door, gunning him down where he sat. Not caring if he was responsible, which he wasn't, for the rampage that had stormed into Sudan.

Right then, the Iranian's man in-country was airing his own suspicions, doubts, anger, a whole diatribe that bellowed on in Bhoutami's ear without relent, leaving him to wonder if Abed Hajmin was superhuman, able to keep ranting without the first sign he was even drawing a breath or blinking.

"How could this happen, Colonel? I had an arrangement with you. I had thirty-some freedom fighters, guaranteed your protection in the desert. All of them dead, slaughtered, as incredible as it sounds, by one lone gunman! And you tell me you have no clue who he is, who this maniac works for?"

It galled Bhoutami, for one thing, to know someone had informed the middleman of the disaster in the desert. That meant someone had spoken out of line, behind his back, when his intention had been to keep the murderous fiasco a secret, not wishing to rattle anyone's already fragile psyche, leaving Iranians scurrying about, threatening, worried the whole deal would blow up in their faces. That left him wondering, naturally, whom he could trust. Not only that, but there were rumblings coming out of Khartoum that very hour, specifically dire words issued from those in power he was working against in the shadows with the suddenly vanished Arakkhan. Important movers and shakers the two of them had plotted to remove who were calling for a face-off, front and center, if the initial rumors were true. That meant explanations, solid answers as to the identity of the mystery attacker. A veritable endless stream of questions fired off, all manner of threats in his face.

"I understand you are holed up in your office, sitting there, doing what? Sweating it out? Fielding phone calls from subordinates who have only more bad news? While some lunatic runs around shooting up recruitment centers, radio stations, training camps. What I am saying is who can I trust at the moment?"

No, Bhoutami thought, clearly reading between the lines on that brusque note. The Iranian wanted to know if the colonel could be trusted.

"All I can tell you," Bhoutami said, hoping he kept the tone of desperation and strain out of his voice, "is I am hard at work on the matter. I have men on the streets, questioning witnesses, roadblocks, searches, grilling informants."

"And still this madman is at large. And what of the transaction? What is to keep us safe?"

"We are. I will have twenty-five soldiers on hand. I am sure you will bring an equal number to the pier."

"You can be absolutely certain that many, and then some. I have been ordered to stick to a timetable. There are certain developments happening, under way, as we speak, that need to see the conclusion of our business this evening."

"And so we shall finish the transaction. Unmolested, I assure you."

"I will meet you at the pier shortly. I understand the ship is two, maybe three hours from docking. Be there."

The click jolted Bhoutami in his chair.

He went to the wet bar, shaking hands somehow pouring a glass of whiskey. It went down the hatch, harsh and fiery, but it seemed to smooth out the knot in his gut.

Temporary relief.

And the phone rang again. He considered not answering, then knew that would only make the messenger of yet more bad news and veiled threats possibly seethe it out to the point where rage and paranoia would get the better of him.

Whoever it was, Bhoutami had just about reached a breaking point. The walls were closing in, and he needed to break out. Somehow. Some way. In some anticipated grim fashion it would be a relief to get out of there, make the pier and nail the deal down. Send the Iranians on their way.

One more shot of whiskey and he went to his desk, snatching up the phone. He heard the note of shrill fury in his voice, didn't care, as he snapped, "Yes!"

"Colonel, perhaps you heard."

Shalibah.

"Said was attacked in his home. He is dead. His house burned to the ground."

"Yes, I heard."

"And?"

"And what?"

"There are many troubling questions, a mounting tidal wave of concern, if you will."

"Are you threatening me?"

"I do not threaten. I, together with your help, arranged this deal. To say I am concerned it may fall through…"

"Be there. The deal is still on."

"If this madman is not soon captured, I think your troubles may have only just begun."

"I am working on it. Goodbye!"

He slammed down the receiver. He went to the far corner of his office, punched a button and the panel slid back, revealing his small arsenal. He took the AKM, grabbed four spare clips. They wouldn't quite squeeze into his waistband, certainly with no degree of comfort, considering his ample belly, so he decided he'd hand them off to one of his security people on the way out. Which he intended to keep close enough to reach out and grab a clip if the need arose.

If that was the case…

He didn't even want to dwell on the possibility, but if the lunatic was still running amok when the deal went down?

Bhoutami decided it was best to stay put in the office, a few more whiskeys under the belt in the meantime to solidify his resolve. Wait it out, until he fielded the call the *Thai Princess* had docked.

All systems go.

He couldn't quite shake the feeling, even as another drink burned down the hatch, but he sensed that Port Sudan had yet to see the worst.

If the deal suddenly came under fire, Colonel Bhoutami knew it would be better if he found the nearest tree, lamppost, whatever, and hung himself.

BOLAN READ the look as Taylor set the phone back in place.

Show time.

"My man says Bhoutami just left his office headquarters. A motorcade, twenty-five gunmen strong. The great colonel has come out of hiding and is on the way to the waterfront."

They took the cue, as Bolan hauled up the war bag, stuffed with every last necessity he would need to nail it down. When they had their own war bags in hand, Taylor loading up the police scanner in a satchel, Bolan ran one last look over their faces. They were good to go, he knew, prepared to finish it out, see it to its conclusion, one way or another.

Even if they went down to a man, they would go out roaring. It was something he could see, like a neon sign, flashing in their eyes. They were with him, all the way to what would surely be a bitter end.

It was simply a question of who would swallow the poisonous fruit from the tree of death.

"Let's go to work," the Executioner said, and led them toward the door.

Three men, warriors, he knew, marching on, into the great and very ugly unknown.

Death was the only game left in Port Sudan.

BHOUTAMI FOUND the Iranian hadn't been joking when he claimed he'd bring as many guns to the gathering as he could round up. Not that the colonel doubted the man at his word, but the show of potential force was more unsettling than he anticipated, especially now in light of the fact his own contingent was outnumbered. A roving head count, and he guessed thirty-five, maybe as many as forty Iranians, scattered around the motor pool, all of them armed with assault rifles, faces etched in stone, watching his approach.

As if he was the biggest SOB the Sudan could ever vomit forth.

Sitting in the back of his Mercedes stretch limo, his luxury vehicle leading the convoy around the corner of his warehouse, rolling in from the south, Bhoutami felt his nerves on fire, burning almost out of control, the closer they drew to the small army. Suddenly he found himself staring out to sea, the vast darkness flaring, here and there, with the lights of a passing ship. It was only a fleeting thought, aware he needed to conclude this serious business, but he found himself longing to be on a boat far out to sea, safe from the madness that had torn up Port Sudan like a cyclone.

Maybe tomorrow, he thought.

On his order, since he was in charge of the military in the city, the waterfront was shut down, smothering the transaction with the kind of secrecy and privacy required to conclude this business away from any curious eyes of dock workers, ships' captains, deckhands and whoever else didn't belong here.

Meaning he was all alone with the Iranian force. Not only that, but he caught a view of Shalibah, the Sudanese middleman likewise with an assault rifle slung across a shoulder, a squad of maybe a dozen of the man's own goons standing ready in something like a circular phalanx, near the ramp leading up to the *Thai Princess*.

All there, grouped on the sprawling dock, small shadows tucked up against the mammoth bulk of the freighter. The crane had already off-loaded the wooden crates, Bhoutami saw, a steel container that housed what the Iranians had paid for getting lowered to the concrete.

And still, as the hours passed in agonizing anxiety, no word on the nameless gunman. It was almost as if the lunatic had vanished off the face of the earth, gone, vanishing like smoke in the wind.

Which was Bhoutami's most fervent hope at the moment.

For one thing, he clearly read the faces of suspicion and distrust framed in the headlights as his luxury ride closed in, dark looks silently spelling out to him the many questions still uppermost in their thoughts. Perhaps they wondered if he was simply incompetent, that he hadn't brought the madman to rough justice. Or maybe they believed the mystery gunman was part of some conspiracy he had long since engineered, maybe to help seize the merchandise for himself. If they were thinking along those deluded lines, then they were fools, riddled with paranoia to the point of madness. The lunatic had, after all, slain his own soldiers, unless, of course, they believed he wasn't above any amount of treachery.

Bhoutami suddenly felt the weight of the AKM in hands, slick with perspiration. He told himself the fear was understandable, given all the mystery and unanswered questions dogging him here. And most certainly he detested the fact that events of the day had spiraled out of control, beyond all his reach and reason, leaving him hung out there, a scapegoat to be skinned alive in the event anything else went wrong.

He stepped out of the Mercedes, his soldiers falling in, the colonel wondering who would be the first to voice some displeasure or suspicion.

Hajmin volunteered himself to speak for the group. "You're late," the Iranian rasped.

"I assume you've inspected the merchandise."

"Not yet." Hajmin snapped his fingers, the engines on two nearby forklifts rumbling to life, rolling ahead, as if on cue.

Bhoutami sensed some threat in the dark cloak of night beyond the warehouse, as he searched the grounds, if nothing else than to tear his eyes off the glaring daggers of Hajmin's orbs. Or was it simply his nerves talking to him? Who could say? The day had been so troubling already.

The massive warehouse doors were already open, light spilling from the vast interior, as he noted still more armed Iranians in the maw behind him. It galled him for a moment that Hajmin had marched right in, taking charge, issuing orders all over the place, in short, seizing his warehouse.

"I will do that inside."

"I would imagine," Bhoutami said, "that you would be anxious to load them on your own vessel on Pier 1 and be on your way."

The Iranian's smile reminded Bhoutami of a shark before it lunged for the kill. "There's been a sudden change in plans, due to the day's unfortunate events. I will be flying the merchandise out of here from a location only I know. Once we are over the island, I will send the merchandise off by parachute while flying on for Tehran. I assure you, Colonel, someone from my country will be coming to speak to you about what happened in the desert."

And there it was. The threat. Unless he hunted down the human storm responsible for all the mayhem and carnage, came up with answers and showed the blood of the madman on his hands…

Bhoutami started wondering if he had any friends left in Egypt, even Somalia who might grant him shelter, comfort, and, of course, loan him a small army of first-class shooters, for a negotiable, nonrefundable fee.

THE EXECUTIONER WAS cautiously pleased with progress so far, but the biggest moment of danger before the shooting started was getting the three of them in place, situated, set to drop the hammer.

Nhoubaff had navigated the Volvo to the designated no-man's-land of rusted-out pipes, abandoned vehicles, assorted garbage while Taylor monitored the police and military bans on the drive in. It struck Bolan as incredible to the point of idiocy—or perhaps it was plain arrogance on the part of the enemy—but the way in was free and clear of any blockades, guards, the perimeter on the north and west edges of the targeted warehouse all but vacant of sentries.

That didn't mean the enemy's brazen philosophy that all trouble boiling up their face could be settled by the barrel of a gun.

Easy.

The soldier, jacked up on combat juices, told himself to take it one step at a time.

The Volvo rolled on through the sludge, parked, hidden from anything more than a passing scrutiny behind a stack of empty fifty-five-gallon drums. Out the door, overhead lightbulb already disengaged, and the three men descended into the drainage ditch. The stink of raw sewage, oil and other chemical run-off would have been strong enough to turn their stomachs under normal circumstances, buckle the most stalwart of legs. They got lucky as far as dressing room conditions went when they found a sturdy sheet of plywood they could settle over the sludge, change to blacksuit, buckle on the harnesses, lock and load in relative comfort.

Com links in place, Bolan told Taylor and Nhoubaff he would cover them until they made the roof. It was Taylor's claim that the three-story office building had recently been abandoned by Bhoutami. Reasons for the bailout were unknown, but Bolan was aware of the tactical problem of securing the roof. Say a sentry or two was perched up top, scanning the industrial wasteland. Say a sniper was covered by the darkness in any one of two dozen blackened holes up the side of the structure.

The soldier knew better than to let paranoia skew the works with rust. Still, heightened vigilance never hurt.

They were out and running over the marshy no-man's-land, the soldier taking up position behind the rusted-out shell of a bulldozer. He watched the rooftop, the darkened windows, stealing a second to note the glare of lights that marked the gathering of the savages, at some distant point beyond the edge of the ghost structure.

The Executioner rode out the tense moments as his comrades scaled the access ladder, landed on the roof.

Bolan's com link buzzed, and Taylor informed him, "We're clear." A pause as the warrior began his own jaunt, veering for the southern end of their roost, and Taylor patched through again. "The show's started.

Looks like quite the party. First look, I'm counting seventy, maybe eighty enemy guns."

The soldier keyed his com link, his M-16/M-203 combo leading the way through the gloom. "You'll know when it's started. Maintain strict silence until the curtain goes up."

"Copy."

Swiftly the Executioner cut his course down behind the darkened shell, homed in on the light hanging from the side of the warehouse to guide him through the night. His beast of burden included one satchel choked with forty pounds of plastic explosive, another satchel full of explosive payloads for the M-203. Rethinking his strategy before leaving the safehouse, he inquired about a radio remote control box for the C-4. A wink and a grin, and Taylor came through once more, pulling the requested magic act out of his personal armory. It made it more plausible, running in line with his strike plan to use radio remote detonation. Instead of setting timers all over the western back end of the warehouse, one signal would tie in the blocks to the same frequency. The idea was to get the bulk of the hardforce chasing him out some point of entry he needed to secure and clear to the west. Mow down as many enemy soldiers as possible, wing a few 40 mm doomsayers their way, and have them gear it up for a mass stampede his direction. Out the back door next to beat what would look like a fighting retreat, then bring the roof down on as many of the enemy as he could.

In theory, it sounded a winner. Reality, he knew, could throw something altogether different in his face. Part of the unknown factor was what sort of ammunition, weapons were housed inside. Once the blast went off, a whole slew of small-arms fire could be ignited, deadly lead firecrackers capping off everywhere, with chemicals thrown into the deadly mix.

Nothing to do but forge ahead.

The first snag turned up just as Bolan hit the edge of the vacant office complex. Not much of a problem in terms of taking care of one wandering sentry, but if timing was critical for the soldier, the same timing could work to the enemy's advantage.

He watched the sentry grasp the doorknob, maybe forty yards away. He opened the door, stood there, as if wondering why it was open.

The Executioner palmed the sound-suppressed Beretta, steadied his aim, took up the trigger slack and chugged out a 9 mm Parabellum shocker. The wondering man was left wondering what hit him as he folded at the knees, the lights punched out from a clean head shot.

It was an anxious run, the soldier's eyes watching the shadows beyond the east corner, then he made the door. Dragging the body inside, Bolan got his bearings. It was standard warehouse design: crates piled high in rows, steel containers out on the main floor, workbenches, fuel drums, and interlocking catwalks with offices on the second floor. The usual layout, from Los Angeles Harbor clear around the world.

The Executioner went to work lightening his load, sticking shaped charges with detonator plugs activated to a crate here and there, sticking to the shadows as he navigated a swift course down the west end. Voices swirled his way from the main floor, the rumble of fork-lifts coming into view as he crouched behind a pile of tarp-covered pallets.

At first search, the numbers appeared staggering, but Bolan had tackled greater odds before. Plus he had the plan, all that was left to be done was execute, move them down and his way.

Come and get it.

He finished packing the last of the C-4 on the pal-lets, was lifting the M-16, ready to unload the 40 mm frag grenade first when a scuffling noise to his nine o'clock snared his eye.

There were two of them, coming from the direction of the late Wonder Man. They were looking the wrong direction at first, up a row of crates, AK-74s searching around the compass when Bolan made his decision to get it started.

The Executioner boiled up out of the shadows behind the pallets, saw the whites of their eyes framed his way and held back on the trigger of the M-16.

CHAPTER TWENTY-ONE

Mohammed Nhoubaff had no problem whatsoever with the idea he might die that night, perish in a hail of bullets, blown off the rooftop, or whatever else the enemy sent his way. The truth was, a part of him would be glad to be free at last, gone to his maker, hoping against hope there would be some degree of mercy bestowed him for the wretched life he'd led.

Good luck in that department, he grimly mused.

Only now he had been granted—no, blessed with— the opportunity to make some sort of amends for leading what he knew, in his heart of hearts, had been, at best, a tawdry, lonely, selfish existence.

He was a cheat, a thief and a liar, no way around it, he knew. How many men had he set up to take a fall over the years at the hands of a rival arms or drug dealer? How many spies had he set at one another's throats,

greasing each side with inside information while plucking the cash out of both hands?

Too many to count.

In some way, though, that had been different, then as
opposed to now. He had always marched bad men to
their own justice at the killing hands of another bad
man by his scamming, conning, playing both ends, always hedging his bets. He was amazed right then he had
lived as long as he had.

This Cooper was different. To Nhoubaff the big
American was soldier, warrior, crusader, all the things,
he reflected, he wished he could have, should have been.
But he knew his own character, the shabby, empty life
he'd led, revealed now to him at the ultimate moment
of truth. Nhoubaff knew he just hadn't dug deep inside
for the right stuff all those years, opting instead for
some easy way out, the quick dollar, going for himself.
He was sure, too, Cooper had seen this waffling of character, this straddling of the fence. But the man—either
to his credit or plain grim awareness there was no choice
once he landed in the Sudan—had given him the opportunity to prove himself. Something like the stage-
master allowing a final curtain call on the sorry story of
his life, one last chance to get it right.

The American's war, on the other hand, was meant
to cut out the evil in the hearts of bad men wherever they
rose up along his path. No dancing around, no chi-
canery, no con job. Just a clean, straightforward wal-
loping of the slaughter kind.

The simple approach, as clean as it could ever get.

No, Nhoubaff didn't much care if he saw the night out in one piece or not. It was enough he was there, searching out his own redemption, at least in his mind, going the distance while covering Cooper's tracks.

For once in his life, he knew what it was like to be a warrior, ready to accept the ultimate price for his role in the coming battle.

Death didn't seem like such a big deal, after all, if he thought about it.

For one thing, he wasn't married, no children, at least that he knew of. No woman anywhere, in fact, who would wail and gnash her teeth if she woke up and he wasn't there to fill her bed. As for any earthly riches he might miss?—well, as far as money went, he'd always spent it as fast he got his hands on it.

Ah, well, it was simply his destiny, he figured, to be here, poised to give it all, give something back in the name of whatever good and justice could be found by slaying evil men.

He was crouched on a knee, next to the CIA man, near the retaining wall at the southeast edge of the roof. Their M-16s ready to unload, they watched the wave of cutthroats rolling for the warehouse doors. The ship itself looked deserted, but Nhoubaff made out a few deckhands amidships on a second, longer search, shadows, standing there, taking in the action.

What had the big American said? he thought. "You'll know when it starts."

It started with the muffled retort of autofire from the point of entry Nhoubaff had seen Cooper penetrate, pulling the dead man in behind him. As agreed upon, Nhoubaff would work his field of fire from left to right, Taylor sweeping it back the opposite way.

Flying lead and 40 mm scissoring all goons, large and small.

For the opening shot, Nhoubaff had loaded his M-203 with an incendiary round.

Shock effect.

He tapped the launcher's trigger, heard the muffled pop, then watched it zigzag on its way, before impacting near a group of ten Iranians, or maybe they were Bhoutami's lackeys, it didn't matter.

He dumped a frag bomb down the chute, and sent another hellbomb on its way.

THEY CAME RUNNING scared at first, a little shaky on the move, weaving this way and that, ready to lunge for cover at the next show of force. Understandable, since Bolan hit a group of six out of the starting gate with a 40 mm frag grenade that cut the heart of the timid pack.

The Executioner began spraying the warehouse proper with long raking bursts of autofire, clipping two hardmen off their feet here, three there, bodies thrashing across the concrete floor in running crimson, someone near the doorways shouting out the orders to keep moving, nail the bastard.

Just what he needed, Bolan thought, a stand-up, take-charge guy out there on the dock, getting them in gear to come and nail him.

There was thunder and fire aplenty out front, gunmen and motor pool taking big hits, Bolan tipping a mental salute to Nhoubaff and Taylor. They were unloading the whole she-bang, 40 mm blasts upending fancy cars, shredding gunmen like disected insects under the microscope.

The soldier didn't have but two seconds of luxury to indulge the sight, crouching behind some pallets at the end of the aisle. But he bore witness to what he sure as hell hoped was the mother lode take a terrible pounding. Whether it was a fluke or by punishing design, the crates were pulped to flying shards, debris bowling down gunmen in screaming heaps, some poor unfortunate's arm cleaved off at the shoulder, skimming along the dock, trailing greasy smears of blood. The steel container was the big score, however, and somehow an angry fate, the soldier glimpsed, took care of that problem.

Twin sheets of fire ripped through a couple of Towncars, flipping them up in the air on a wall of roaring fire. Both came down, nose first, when fuel tanks lapped up some fire, then ignited. One fiery fist of warped metal came pounding down through the top of the steel container, as if they were joint flaming can openers.

So much for the dreams and schemes of his enemies, Bolan thought, then started making a beeline for an exit door as lead sizzled the air all around him.

He fired his M-16, covering his retreat, winging

one shooter in the hip as they started leapfrogging down the aisle.

It was all rock and roll, big heavy metal thunder out front, and Bolan left Nhoubaff and Taylor to it.

Nice work.

But the three of them, the warrior knew, were hardly in the home stretch.

Things were just getting heated up.

Bolan hit the back door, checked his flanks, found he was clear. No time enough, so far, for the enemy to try to outflank him, since they were just now getting it together, crawling out from under a falling sky.

And bulling his way.

A rough guesstimate, and Bolan figured he was looking at thirty, maybe forty coming for his scalp.

Coming to get a taste of hell.

"IT'S HIM! The lunatic!"

Bhoutami staggered to his feet, the whole dock going up in a firestorm that shattered his senses, the noise and the horror grinding some nausea deep into his gut, shimmying the whole ball of sickness down through quaking bowels.

"Of course, it's him, you stupid fool!"

The colonel found he was clutching his AKM, stared at the rage on Hajmin's face through a daze. The Iranian was bellowing out the orders for his men to go after the lunatic. They were moving in a strange weaving pattern, Bhoutami saw, stumbling ahead, flinching as sporadic bursts of autofire rang out. Beyond his hatred for the lunatic and the Iranian, Bhoutami despised next the sound of his own terrified cry as another luxury vehicle close by erupted in fiery mushroom cap.

This couldn't be happening, he thought, hearing the pitiful moans of men all around him, seeing them crawling through their own blood and spilled innards, a few of them missing an arm or a leg. But he was lucky, or was he? Somehow he'd survived the opening blasts. Somehow he was in one piece.

This wasn't the way it should have been, he thought. Before, while serving the Khartoum government under the command of Arakkhan, the killing had always been one-sided, doled out by the droves, as he led gunship sorties against black villages in southern Sudan, standing tall in the fuselage doorway as women and children were strafed and mowed down by machine-gun fire, putting the torch to whatever was left standing, raping mothers before their children, the wives of the hated SPLA rebels. Old men digging the mass graves before his soldiers lined up the survivors and mowed them down into the hole.

This wasn't right, he thought.

This was…what?

The thunder of hell? Calling out to him, death screaming, or chuckling out his name? He couldn't be sure if the lunatic was thinking along these lines, but Bhoutami was viewing this slaughter as something like reverse genocide.

On him.

"You will pay for this!"

Bhoutami watched the horror show as bullets slashed through darting figures, dropping them in their tracks on spurting lines of scarlet. The colonel also despised the fat jiggling around his waistband as the fear kept shooting down him, head to toe. He saw Hajmin backpedal toward the doors, the Iranian still directing the rage and the threats his way.

"I lost my merchandise! You will answer for your incompetence! You provided no security! Just your thugs by your own side! Tehran will hear! Khartoum will skin you alive! I will see you strung up by your balls!"

All was madness, more explosions peppering the motor pool, torn bodies flying away in all directions, screams of agony trailing out to sea. Somehow, Bhoutami found his voice, as he pinned down the direction from which the missiles were flying. The office building he had abandoned, months back, having seen no need to be so close to the waterfront, paying lackeys, civilian or otherwise, to watch the store.

"Get your men to that rooftop, Bhoutami! The lunatic has comrades up there!"

Bhoutami could tell they didn't like it, shuffling all about, hunching for cover behind a stretch limo.

"Go! To the roof!"

They went, reluctant, moving out but veering on a course for the warehouse front.

Bhoutami was turning, wondering how he was going to get out of there, when he saw the mountain of fire, roiling up from the skeletal remains of two vehicles, leaping from the steel container. He groaned. He was a dead man, indeed. Inside that container were component parts for the Ramrod Intercept satellite tracking station. Plus a sizable cache of laser weapons and more component parts. Something in the neighborhood, he knew, of fifty million U.S. dollars, getting melted down to silver goo.

Oh, yes, he was a walking dead man. Better to hold his ground, as bullets tore into the less fortunate and flung them to the dock.

No. Time to bail.

"You will pay for this!"

The Iranian shook his fist, wheeled to follow the point charge into the warehouse, when Bhoutami lifted the AKM, drawing a bead on his back.

The explosion rocked the air, Bhoutami feeling the heat, a furnace belching flames for his face. He was darting off to the side, aware he couldn't outrun the blast in time, when he was bowled down, something heavy slashing off his head.

Flying next, but before Bhoutami hammered down to the dock, he saw the lights wink out.

HAJMIN SAW the charge was losing steam. His own men were mingled in with Shalibah and his goons, plus a half-dozen of the colonel's thugs. They needed someone to lead the charge, to send them after the dreaded lunatic!

"Move ahead! Move!"

He turned, hugging cover behind a forklift, glancing at maybe a dozen sprawled bodies, then decided whatever Bhoutami had sent to the vacant office building might not be enough to take down the rooftop shooters. He barked at a group of ten of his men, firing—at nothing he could see—to fall back outside and storm the office.

The lunatic had stopped winging around grenades and bullets for the moment. Hajmin wondered why, then realized the maniac was retreating. He nearly sobbed, as he thought how cruel fate was, crushing, now burning up the high-tech merchandise Tehran had paid fifty million and change to the Sudanese middle-men, who in turn had paid…

The Great Satan!

It was unthinkable, unbelievable, but someone, namely him, was going to be held accountable for this disaster. Well, if he went down, he would make damn sure he didn't hang alone.

"Move! Go after him!"

He waited until the lines of his men were rolling ahead, picking up some momentum down the aisles now, obviously gathering courage since the lunatic had stopped shooting them up.

Why? he wondered. Where was he?

He was falling in behind two stragglers, AK-74 gripped and ready to fire at the first sight of even a shadow popping out of nowhere, when something caught his eye.

He was edging ahead, his men gathering in crouches

and hunches near the back door when he saw the glob of white-gray…

The red light was on!

"Fall back!" Hajmin shouted.

Then the world exploded in his face.

"HIT THE DECK!"

Bolan made the edge of the office building, the radio remote in hand. Twisting, he triggered off a long burst of autofire, pinning them inside the doorway. The distance to ground zero wasn't much, but Bolan had spread the plastique in areas where he hoped enough crates and steel containers would buffet the blast, confine it to the bulk of the hardforce, chew them up from the inside, while taking down only a portion of the warehouse.

Bolan found a hole, about six feet deep, where, he guessed, some roving band of thieves had helped themselves to the air-conditioning unit.

The soldier jumped down into the trench provided by fate, hit the doomsday button, and rocked their world all the way to oblivion.

CHAPTER TWENTY-TWO

He didn't see the start of the conflagration, eyes shut, stretched out on the roof and hugging the low wall, but Nhoubaff heard it. To him it sounded as if the sky had opened up, the wrath of God coming down in one endless peal of thunder, one gigantic bolt of lightning striking half of the city, shaking the whole works to the core of the earth. The next thing he knew the sky was, in fact, falling. He flinched, covering his head, holding on as rubble hammered the roof, grateful when only a few chunks went pelting off his shoulders.

A little discomfort he could live with right then, since they were dying hard and ugly inside the warehouse. They were screaming from some distant point beyond the ringing in his ears, and Nhoubaff shuddered, taking in the destruction, braving the falling storm, now petering out to a jagged sprinkle of rubble.

A few bodies came sailing out the gaping wound in

the warehouse, then he glimpsed the pummeled shells of what looked like fifty-five-gallon drums, riding a forked serpent's tongue of fire through the massive smoking hole. Pools of airborne chemicals, fuel for boats, he guessed, were ignited in midair, turned into flying bats of fire.

Doomsday on the waterfront.

He was about to go back to his butcher's work, when he saw the last of maybe ten shadows charging the office from below.

"They're coming up!"

He didn't need Taylor to urge him to get it in gear. He was dropping a 40 mm frag bomb down the M-203's snout when they burst out the stairwell housing, screaming devils with automatic weapons already blazing. Nhoubaff hit the M-203's trigger, the frag missile streaking on and true, impacting to vaporize the stairwell housing, launching the pointmen off the roof in screams and missing body parts.

Still they came, more howling demons, crazed with fear, pumped on murderous rage.

This was it, Nhoubaff knew. The end.

So be it.

He was up and rolling ahead, holding back on the trigger of his assault rifle, the stutter of his weapon joining Taylor's blazing line. They marched ahead, side by side as dark shadows, flaming tongues leading their surge out of the smoke, charged across the roof.

Nhoubaff felt the first of several fires racing down his body as bullets tore into his upper chest, spraying his lips with the bitter salty taste of his life's juices. The lead wall nearly stopped him in his tracks, bowling him over, but his own war cry ripped the air, the sound of his death knell urging him onward.

He figured he dropped two, maybe three, with Taylor churning up the flesh, matching him, body for body, when he felt himself lurching, shoved back.

He was falling next, floating down, it felt like, saw the sky going fuzzy. For some reason he thought of the big American, wished Cooper well, and hoped the stranger who had come to this bloody unholy land would make an accounting for the deaths of his comrades.

And finish the job they helped start.

Then Mohammed Nhoubaff said, "God have mercy on my soul."

And the lights dimmed, faded to black.

BOLAN NEARLY ATE the dirt when it happened. He rode out the firestorm, slabs of giant shrapnel flying by, dangerously close, a few of the larger hunks skidding past, clawing out whole tracts of earth. He'd cut it close, no doubt. But judging the billowing mushroom clouds of fire shooting from where half the side wall was missing, a nick proved far easier to accept and manage than a full slice across the old jugular.

He found a flaming demon thrashing all over the noman's-land between the buildings. The Executioner spared the guy a burst of lead compassion, kicking him down, his screams still hovering in the air a full second after he was dropped, as if the shrieking call were some sort of goodbye tune for his sudden funeral.

Then the soldier made out the rattle of autofire, above, from the roof, cracking in stuttering waves through the ringing in his ears.

Nhoubaff and Taylor, under fire.

He was out of the hole, fresh clip up the M-16, a 40 mm bomb down the hatch, and peering around the corner. Nothing but jagged fangs there, the side of the structure having been pounded by the blast, but he caught sight enough of the action downrange to know his comrades were in a world of hurt. The last of the armed shadows poured into the building when he un-leashed a quick burst, tagging the rear hardman, and sent him flopping to the ground.

Bolan knew he had to act quickly, spare no moves. The stock of his assault rifle took out a window several paces back, beyond the ditch. If he could cut them off…

Three gunmen were framed in the firelight, and Bolan hit them with a scything burst, flinging them away from the stairs. The real grim problem, he believed, was the heart of the charge appeared to have landed on the roof.

Damn!

The soldier squeezed through the window, a shooter lagging behind at the foot of the steps pivoting his way, squeezing off a few rounds. They flew high and wide, peppering stucco behind Bolan, and the soldier didn't miss a beat.

He couldn't afford to.

The sound of weapons fire roared on from above, mingled with men screaming out their rage, giving it up, knowing they were going down but hell-bent on taking as many of the opposing side as they could on their ride to oblivion.

Bolan chopped the straggler down in the next heartbeat.

Surging ahead, he saw two shadows toppling through the boiling smoke where one of his partners had blown the stairwell housing off the roof.

The Executioner gave the sheen of firelight washing the grounds beyond the door a quick search, found it clear of invaders at the moment and hit them from behind, holding back on the trigger. He aimed the stream of lead upward, sticking on a straight line of flesh-eaters pounding them through the smoke, his rounds stitching up the staggered line of hardmen on a rising burst. Rubber limbs led the tumble back down the steps, bloody dominoes rolling up at his feet. It burned up another clip, but if he helped turn the tide, saved...

Cracking home another 30-round mag, the soldier bounded up the stairs, stepping over sprawled forms on the way up. He hit the roof, M-16 fanning the whole area, and he spotted them, stretched out, midway across.

Already gone.

Three strides along, and their empty stares sought him out, eyes shining still in the umbrella of the firestorm.

He knew it was pointless, but he crouched beside them, felt and found no pulse.

The faintest bleat of a distant siren told Bolan the time to grieve, offer up a prayer for Nhoubaff and Taylor, had to be dumped on the back burner.

Even still, the Executioner intended to steal a few minutes below, tidy up the mess if any survivors, wounded or otherwise, were meandering about or looking to exit.

BHOUTAMI ALMOST CHOKED on the sob. He couldn't believe he was still in the land of the living, if he could call what he found when coming to anything other than a vision of hell on earth.

He staggered about, checking his limbs. All there. Now the sob rang in his ears, loud and clear, at once chastising him for his cowardice and urging him to get moving. Now what?

He looked around, stunned still, nearly vomited as the full force of every stench imaginable, the scorching heat from any number of swirling firestorms slammed his senses.

He stole another second to gather his thoughts, searching the carnage, sucking wind. Nothing but bodies, strewed all over the dock, heaped in the warehouse doors, with a few charred corpses, some of the dead burning to black mummies where they fried near flames lapping from overturned or pulverized shells of vehicles.

Next, the sight of the *Thai Princess* moving out to sea, gathering steam as it headed on a southerly course, further urged him to seek his own avenue of flight, his limbs oiled and loose now, motivated by fear to flee.

Beyond this, he told himself he'd find a way out of Sudan. There was cash, numbered accounts spread around Khartoum. Get to those, clean them out, and someone, anyone with a hunger for quick money would take him in.

Money talked.

First get the hell out of there. Bribes later.

He couldn't believe his good fortune, viewed it as a miracle, in fact. But there it was! His Mercedes, unscathed, sitting there, just beyond a ring of fire, calling out to him.

Sweet mother of freedom!

He nearly ran to the vehicle, ignoring the searing flames dancing at him as he made his way to his Mercedes, reached it, threw open the door. Another stroke of good fortune greeted him, finding the keys were in the ignition. He fired up the vehicle. Back it up, he told himself, reverse it from the graveyard of wreckage, the sea of bodies, the joining bands of fire that would block, even threaten his escape. It had been some time, years, in fact, since he'd driven himself, always relegating those menial chores to lackeys who were paid to obey and to serve. Thus it took a full few seconds, and ten yards shooting ahead, before he realized his blunder. He was hitting the brakes, slamming the gearshift in reverse, when a tall figure emerged, stepping out from behind the fiery hulls of pulped machinery.

He couldn't be absolutely positive, but it was something in the eyes of the big shadow, as if the figure were judging him, the shape dressed in some sort of black-suit. He was jolted by fresh currents of fear coursing through every limb.

The lunatic was still alive!

Bhoutami heard himself croaking out the terror, flooring it, swiveling his head, back and forth, as he screeched it in reverse, clipping a burning wreck on the way to desperately craved freedom. He felt compelled to look back, hoping the horror of the night was merely creating illusions of some bogeyman. But he was still there, marching ahead, slow and in command of himself, some demon clearing the fires, eyes burning at him through the windshield. Then Bhoutami heard his squawk coming out in a shrill scream.

The lunatic had raised an assault rifle, what looked like an attached grenade launcher already spitting smoke and flames.

Bhoutami stomped on the gas, gathering speed, but the missile seemed locked on, homing in, streaking for his face. In a nanosecond a cloud of fire was in his face, incinerating him where he sat.

"I AM Malahkan."

"Cooper."

The Executioner held his ground on the bank, not sure of the moment, since the dark, bearded man in the turban didn't seem certain himself whether to lift his AK-47 at a point any higher than his hip. Any more rise with the weapon, and Bolan would just as soon gun him

down, leave him floating in the water. How many cigarette boats could there possibly be five miles out in the
Red Sea?

Malahkan settled the assault rifle in the outboard,
tugged on the starting cord, the engine grumbling to life.

"We must hurry!"

Bolan didn't need any more urging, as he stepped
into the outboard. South, he saw the grim handiwork,
climbing for the sky in licking mountain peaks.

All done down there.

A few mercy rounds for the wounded, and the growing sirens had chased him north, to the crumbling ruins
of that forgotten sultanate Taylor mentioned.

As his driver headed the outboard from the inlet,
pumping up the knots and moving them out at rapid
surge to sea, Bolan felt his heart grow heavy. He couldn't
be sure, but Malahkan had to have read his thoughts.

"Taylor?"

"He didn't make it," the Executioner replied as he
settled on a narrow bench, finding nothing but a maw
of blackness ready to swallow them up the deeper they
shoved out to sea.

"Nhoubaff?"

"He didn't make it, either."

The silence weighed down on Bolan, as Malahkan
seemed to consider something, then said, "They were
my friends."

The Executioner nodded, looked away from the man.
"They were mine, too."

Saudi Arabia

"LET ME BE crystal clear on something, gentlemen. I am from the old school of combat. I prefer eyeball confirmation of an enemy kill. I prefer the up-close-and-personal touch. I am warmed to my bones by the sight of enemy blood spilled by my own hands. I am no fan of smart bombs, cruise missiles, Tomahawks, all that high-tech, long-distance, Ma Bell reach-out-and-touch-someone chickenshittery. I do not read Tom Clancy. Thou shalt not even mention the name of the used-car salesman in my presence. Thou shalt not even utter the idea of using Ma Bell high-tech, that is if you wish to ride with me into battle. That said, let us move on. The hour of doom for our enemies is at hand."

David McCarter wasn't quite sure whom the good Major Sabol was addressing, but gathered from the gist of it some sort of personal battle line was being drawn between the Special Forces black ops and Phoenix Force, tagged, going in by the Farm, as the X Squad.

Whether the major resented their presence, their attachment to this, what he knew would be the mother of all surgical strikes...

Well, they were there, and that came straight from the President of the United States, who had been briefed by Brognola on how they would maintain both their cover as covert commandos and define their own role in the mission.

Phoenix Force took up the last row of metal chairs

in the massive tent at the Saudi air base near the shores
of the Persian Gulf, a few klicks northwest of Bahrain.
Down the line they were known only to the major and
his troops—platoon strength, times three, as McCarter
took a head count of the Special Forces warriors, all of
whom were togged in blacksuit and sitting rigged at attention—as follows: McCarter, Commander Mac; Encizo, Mr. R.; Manning, Mr. M.; James, Mr. J.; Hawkins,
Mr. H.; Grimaldi, also taking up the last row, accom-
panied for the final briefing with the blacksuit crew of
the Spectre, was tagged as Mr. G., with crew being
numbered two and on.

According to both the Farm and the major's initial
earlier brief, McCarter understood the extreme urgency
of this strike against the Iranian island strongholds in the
Strait of Hormuz. Once again, the major, using his remote to click through the slide show, pointed out the
gunboats, docked in a small harbor of Qeshm, that were
packed with explosives. All ship traffic had ceased to
exist in the Persian Gulf in the past twenty-four hours.
Gunboats in question were under constant satellite surveillance. If they had moved out before then, the mission would have already been under way.

McCarter and company listened as the major laid it
out. The man was cut from the old blood-and-guts
school of warriors, and McCarter, despite initial reservations about linking up Phoenix with unknowns, liked
what he heard and saw. The major was all iron and
sinew packed into a broad-shouldered six feet, with a

lean face that looked carved from a razor's edge, his shaved head seeming to shine in the overhead lights powered by the generator outside the tent. One look in the man's eyes, and McCarter knew he had both the talent and the experience to back up the tough talk.

When the major explained the program's onslaught, detailing the mass air saturation of the islands, pointing out the antiaircraft batteries, the gunboats, the airfields, the radar and tracking stations, McCarter started having visions of Armageddon.

Air saturation, times the Apocalypse, he thought. He could damn well believe it was going to go down just like a glimpse of the end of the world. Outside, the air base seemed to go on forever, cutting runways and tarmacs and hangars clear out into the Saudi desert. When landing and handing off their terrorist cargo to what he assumed was a team of spooks, he had seen more F-15Es, more Apaches, more Stealth fighter F-117s...

Add on two B-52 Stratofortress winged monsters, leaving him to wonder if they were nuke ready, throw in their AC-130 ride, now refueled and rearmed to the gills...

The mother of all air saturations, he knew, Armageddon from above, and then some. He had to wonder if there would be any leftovers when they dropped in by parachute to mop up.

Well, McCarter was a Stony Man warrior, first and last. Even still he had to wonder about the political fallout when the smoke of the coming conflagration died and the fanatics of the Islam world were screaming for revenge. The bottom line was that the fundamentalist world had called the shots here. They were arming suicide boats to send out to sink American warships, oil tankers in the Gulf. If that happened, the entire oil market around the world could bottom out, creating anarchy, wholesale panic in the West; oil prices off the scale; lines of motorists, stacked twenty blocks deep at the pump, or stampeding ahead to grab up what little fuel was left.

The collapse, he believed, of Western civilization.

Preemptive strike, right, McCarter then concluded, with more than a few of the notable terrorist garbage on hand for the show to come.

The only option he could see.

He was proud to be there, no matter what, even if he was playing second fiddle to the major. No problem. Duty called. There was a job to do.

The lineup for the flying armada, McCarter heard the major state, was as followed. The F-117s were leading off, a few of them designated to drop laser-guided two-thousand-pound bombs with incendiary payloads. He said Qeshm and four other targeted islands would be nothing more than a giant bonfire, for the most part, and if there were any queasy stomachs over whiffing toasted human flesh, they were to either speak up now or forever hold their peace.

No hands shot up for objection or dismissal.

Moving on.

The F-15Es would come in behind the stealth

bombers, two full flying squads in all, hit them again. Then the B-52s, just to let any survivors left reeling about to understand they were serious.

Last, in the cleanup spot, the major and his troops would drop from their C-130, hitting Qeshm on the far eastern edge. The timing, he said, had been worked out to tick off to the second when X Squad would hit the ramp of the Spectre, a thousand-foot combat jump, their drop site, McCarter saw, circled at some point near the harbor of Qeshm to the far west.

All things considered, McCarter couldn't find any flaws in the strategy. Whatever was left alive would have its senses so cleaved to mush it could prove a rolling turkey shoot.

Then he mentioned there were underground bunkers, how big and how deep, he couldn't say.

The catch.

If they had to, they would go in, go down and root out the bastards, a few of his troops toting flamethrowers to the show to light up anything that wanted to resist.

McCarter listened as the major wrapped it up, going through it again, then he announced, "Dismissed. Let's saddle up, gentlemen. We're wheels up in sixty minutes sharp."

McCarter and Phoenix Force were rising when the major called out, "X Squad remain seated."

Phoenix Force, Grimaldi and crew took McCarter's cue, easing back into their chairs, passing a few looks between themselves. Whatever the major was about to lay on them, he took his time, rolling his shoulder, doing some kind of massage therapy on his neck, cracking bones. Then he slid a fat cigar out of his shirt pocket, torched it up with a Zippo lighter, the gold gleaming for a moment in the firelight.

X Squad waited.

The major took the long slow walk until he stopped at a point beside the next-to-last row.

He spoke slowly, nodding at each of the Stony Man warriors in turn. "Congratulations are in order for a job well done in Madagascar."

McCarter felt the noose being slipped over his head, but felt compelled to fill in the silence. "We had some luck, sir."

"Uh-huh." The major worked on his cigar. "Well, this won't be Madagascar. And luck won't have a damn thing to do with the outcome of this mission. Now, I see you, sitting there, thinking this is where I call you a bunch of hot dogs, prima donnas getting attached to my thunder, like that. Wondering who the hell you really are, who the hell you really work for. Don't care. Not my style anyway. We have a job to do. And part of that job falls square on your shoulders. Because this Khalid Ruballah is some hot shit terrorist with known ties to bin Laden, my orders are to take him alive. Our intelligence, coupled with the fact his mug has been framed by sat imagery, shows him hunkered down in your neck of the woods where you will be inserted and moving in. Alive."

McCarter cleared his throat, the leader of Phoenix Force not about to guarantee bagging a trophy if it meant endangering the lives of his men. "We will take him alive, sir…if at all possible."

Major Sabol grinned around his cigar. "'If at all possible.' Understood."

"Are we dismissed, sir?"

"You are."

The Stony Man warriors rose, ready to file out the same path the major's troops had taken out the tent, when the major said, "One more thing, Commander Mac."

McCarter turned, looked the major dead in the eye, braced for some punchline.

"Say you don't bring in Ruballah, all body parts intact, for the Company spooks to grill from now till kingdom come. Say he…meets that bullet with his name on it, and one of you did the deed." The major wasn't grinning any longer, puffing away on his cigar, smoke funneling out his nose like some living gargoyle. "Well, if it goes down that way, you won't hear any squawking from me." The grin came back, two rows of pearly whites bared for all to see. "Like they say—shit happens."

CHAPTER TWENTY-THREE

Khalid Ruballah had a dream. In it, he saw himself at the helm of the control panel, his divine gift from God, punching in the strings of access codes, setting loose the ICBMs.

Letting fly the nuclear arrows, he envisioned, annihilation in flight, over the poles, en route to signal eternal triumph for the jihad.

Standing by then, monitoring the sat imagery as New York, Chicago, Washington, Israel vanished off the screen in a radioactive—no, he corrected, a holy cosmic wink.

The blinding smile of God.

Since it was only a dream, at least for the present, he would settle for reality. And that involved the three gunboats roped to their individual piers. Six hundred pounds of C-4, welded into the boats, stem to stern, shaped so they would blow forward for a maximum lethal punch. Further, the pot of reality had been sweetened in the past few months, beyond the suicide boats he intended to send out as soon as he decided on the target. No, he wasn't in charge of the island—that was left to Major General Qad—but he had helped usher his brother Iranians into the new age of Western wonder technology. He was respected here.

Beyond seeing himself as something of a genius, master strategist, he knew he was something of a celebrity in the world of Islamic jihad, the ayatollah, so to speak, with the master plan to bring the infidels to their knees. Or, at worst, slay a large number of them.

Hundreds, he hoped. Thousands, if he was truly blessed with the kind of judgment day he craved to drop on his hated enemies.

Perhaps sink an American warship, he thought, or a tanker, spilling so much oil in the Gulf it would become a vast ecological wasteland. Beyond that mother of all disasters, OPEC would crawl into a hole, threatening to put the price tag on a barrel of oil in the two- or three-hundred-dollar range.

Bringing the fuel-starved West to its knees.

Part of the problem was he didn't have all the right component parts to the wonder toys.

That was merely, though, one of several matters troubling Ruballah at the moment, as he stood on the beach, staring out across the black glassy surface of the Strait of Hormuz. One, there was no word on progress of delivery for the satellite-disruption system out of Sudan, no idea of when he would likewise receive the next set of chemical lasers. Delivery of the bulk merchandise, though, didn't necessarily guarantee some quantum leap into the future of high tech. Without the technical manuals, the necessary microchips, without expert hands on board to assemble...

Number-two concern was the fact no boat traffic was showing up, seen either by the naked eye or as a blip on the radar screen in the command central on the island.

Strange, to say the least.

He needed answers, and he needed action to prove his mettle to his imams. He was Tehran's man on the islands, sent there to ratchet up the heat, send the jihad soaring for new heights to burn down as many hordes of Western devils as he possibly could.

His reflections were interrupted, as the jeep rolled up over the dune. Hakin Ashud materialized out of the murk, a slight figure outlined in the headlights, a flickering shadow as he moved past the lamps hung from the corrugated iron workstation where the last of the explosives were being packed and fused. Earlier, Ruballah had ordered the gunboats beefed up to one thousand pounds each.

"Bring me good news, or turn around and leave me this instant."

Ashud cast his eyes down, shamefaced, looked poised to wheel in an about-face when Ruballah snapped, "Speak!"

"The major general says it is not a good idea."

Ruballah sounded off a grim chuckle that seemed to float out across the black waters. "And why not?"

"He says it is wrong. He says God would be greatly displeased. He says God would bring his wrath down upon us if—"

"Enough! I will speak to him personally." He studied Ashud's bearded face for a moment. "What? You feel it would be an evil thing also?"

"They are simple bedouin."

"They are our shield against an attack by the Americans! I cannot believe this! Two days you've had to go to the north end of the island and convince them. I told you to promise them food, drink, gold, anything to bring them here!"

"The major general—"

"He may be in charge of this island, but I am in charge of operations! I say we need a human shield, then we get a human shield! I want to make certain the Americans, should they attack, know they have slaughtered hordes of innocent women and children and old men!"

"The major general—"

"I will go speak to him now! I will make him see reason! Come!"

It could have been simple anger that the major general was making some personal statement, sticking a dagger into his plans, but Ruballah felt his senses heightened right then, like the exposed ends of severed nerves. He was three steps up the dune when he balked, began searching the endless heavenly velvet ceiling winking with stars, a scimitar moon hanging almost directly over the island. Something felt strange to Ruballah, as if the world were set to spin off its axis. Call it paranoia, he thought, an urgency to get his strike launched against something, anything, but he...

"Did you hear that?"

"What?" Ashud asked.

"I thought I heard a jet. West. Over the water. The Gulf, that is. From the direction of Saudi."

Ashud followed his stare skyward, shook his head. "No. I hear nothing but the water breaking against the beach."

Ruballah looked back toward the dock. Eight gunboats, with three of them packed with his own vision of a smile from God, almost set to head out for a glorious blow against the infidels.

"Ashud," he said, stare fixed on the sky over the Gulf, "there is a narrow inlet, just over that dune."

"Yes, I know of it."

"Meet me there."

"What are you going to do?"

"Just meet me there," Ruballah snapped over his shoulder, already striding toward the piers.

The Americans, he thought, weren't above any manner of treachery. It had been too quiet, too still, too desolate for the past day. Something felt strange to near unnerving.

Ruballah decided he needed to move at least one of the gunboats. Out in full view like that...

Well, the Great Satan had eyes in the sky, fleets of

ships, armadas of attack planes. Better to be paranoid, Ruballah decided, than to see his dream become a nightmare.

Stony Man Farm, Virginia

BROGNOLA WAS on his feet, juggling the coffee and his cigar, ticking off the doomsday numbers in his head. Heart pounding, briefly thinking his blood pressure was off the monitor, the big Fed stood next to Price, with every pair of eyes in the Computer Room wide and rapt, focused on the sat imagery on the monitors.

This was it, Brognola thought, as he watched the flying armada winging over the Gulf, the F-117s breaking into the airspace over the Strait of Hormuz.

Bearing down. All systems were go, the enemy radar and tracking screens, he knew, nothing but blanks, leaving them scratching their heads, but likewise aware something was terribly wrong.

"I'm going to say two minutes, and counting down," Price announced.

Kurtzman pointed out X Squad's ride on the monitor, the Spectre holding at one thousand feet, picking up the number-five slot. Major Sabol and his black-ops team were in the C-130, the Hercules already banking to the south, prepared to come up to drop the team at their insertion point on the far eastern edge of Qeshm. On the screen, the island struck Brognola as little more than a giant sandspit. But it was the largest of the five

targeted islands. The bulk of the enemy soldiers and
matériel was housed on Qeshm, but there were plenty
of sitting targets spread across the smaller sandy bastions of Larak, Henqin, Sirri and the Greater Tunb. No
problem watching the action, he knew, since three separate American satellites were now parked in space.

The word was the Russians were also watching.

Brognola knew he could have dropped from a massive
migraine alone if he dwelled on the political fallout when
the smoke cleared and the fires of the coming Apocalypse
finally died down. Not really his problem, but at least the
President was armed with verifiable and undeniable proof
the islands were being used to stage massive terrorist
strikes in the Gulf. He could only imagine where it all
headed from here, after the fact, but the Man would
march out his advisers, Pentagon brass, a White House
spokesman with more satellite and aerial proof….

Forget about it.

The covert war to end all covert wars was about to
begin.

"I just thought of something," Brognola said, all eyes
rolling his way, the collective stare-down telling him
they were braced for him to play the messenger of bad
news. "That island is going to go up in flames. A sea of
fire, folks. We're talking a firestorm in a relatively small
and confined area, two-thousand-pound bombs…well,
what I'm saying is when Phoenix jumps what's to keep
the firestorm, which, I can be sure, will create super-

heated winds…gale force. A swirling cyclone, reaching out, like a giant magnet. You see where I'm headed?"

"Jack's due to check in before they jump," Price said. "The last thing any of us wants to see is Phoenix getting sucked into the inferno."

"If it goes off like we think," Brognola said, "they'd be like dust balls getting sucked up by a vacuum. A fire-breathing Hoover."

"When Grimaldi calls, we'll figure something out," Price said.

Brognola took two nervous chomps on the cigar, then the monitor pinned on Qeshm began to light up.

Qeshm

RUBALLAH WAS RUNNING the mental dialogue through his head, working out the details, shaping up the finer points of his viewpoint to use simple bedouin as a human shield against infidel attack for the coming argument with Major General Qad, when the world nearly blew up in his face. A giant white mushroom blast roiled for the sky, spearing a blinding flash into his eyes, digging invisible needles deep into his brain.

He bolted up in the passenger seat, opened his eyes and saw the end of the world.

Or at least the end of Qeshm. And if Qeshm went up in flames, his dreams died along with it.

They were clearing the dune, on the last leg of the two-klick ride from shore, when command central was vaporized before his eyes. The airfield, choked with MiGs and Soviet Mi-24s, went up next in one exploding march of white fire. Ashud was shouting now, throwing the wheel to the left, as if that would save them from the concussive shock wave that came roaring their way.

Ruballah ducked beneath the dashboard, not a second too soon, he discovered, as the windshield came apart and wind like the fires of hell blew into the jeep, scorching his feet, leaving him wondering for the briefest of moments if the skin had melted off the bones. They were airborne next, tumbling back down the slope of the dune, the winds of hell lifting the vehicle as if it were nothing more than a bicycle blown asunder in a hurricane. Ruballah rode it out, best he could under the circumstances, his grunts and curses lost to the cacophony of explosions beyond the dune. His head slammed off the roof, smacking the dashboard as metal groaned, and he lay utterly still when the vehicle came to rest on the driver's side. Ruballah felt a terror like he'd never known, a hot dagger slicing through his belly. He found himself pressed up against Ashud and shoved himself away. Looking down, he saw the whites of Ashud's eyes staring him back, brimmed with what struck him as either wonder or accusation, he wasn't sure. He shook Ashud, terror taking over reason, before he realized the man was gone, his neck broken during the hard tumble.

Ruballah knew what was happening, even as he hauled himself out the jeep. The first of several screams, a volcano of rage, erupted from his lungs. The sky above was lit up in blinding wavering sheets of white and orange, the sand actually trembling beneath his boots. He strained his vision, staring skyward, barely able to make out the batwing shapes of Stealth fighters, but they were up there, cutting loose with their laser-guided payloads. He heard the pounding beyond the dune of the antiaircraft batteries, the thunder of the Russian ZSU-23-4. The sky above was peppered with shells going off in jagged blankets of thundering explosions.

In the next moment, Ruballah knew all hope was lost, when the earth once again rumbled beyond the dune, and the antiaircraft batteries were silenced by a series of explosions that threw up such a glowing umbrella of firelight he thought it could have been noon instead of full-blown night.

Khalid Ruballah trudged ahead, fighting down the bitter sob that burned in his throat.

MCCARTER CAUGHT the grim note, nearly a tone of sudden urgency as the Briton heard Grimaldi announce over the intercom, "David, come in!"

They were gathered near the ramp, ready to jump, chute packs on, each Phoenix Force warrior having packed and double-checked his ride down, with weapons in nylon housing, attached to trailing bootstraps.

Ready to fly, and now McCarter sensed a major glitch about to get dumped in his lap.

McCarter punched the intercom button. "What?"

"Looks like I've got to change the plan a little."

"How come I don't like the sound of that, Jack? Why?"

"If you were up here, looking at what I'm looking at, my friend...I'm seeing the end of the world below, David. Half the island is on fire already. That B-52 alone could have cleaned their clocks. What I'm telling you is I'm dropping down to five hundred feet. Firestorms, David. Whirlwinds."

"Understood. Last thing I want is for us to get sucked into an inferno before we even hit the ground. Drop it down."

"I've got a spot, a little farther out than the major's original insertion point, but it's clear of any fiery vacuums reaching out to suck you in. Besides, a shorter fall, you'll be what—fifty, sixty yards apart when you land?"

"Do it! Then get your arse up and away from the island. I don't care how many tons we've already dropped, there's still a chance some soldier's crawling toward that one antiaircraft battery that was missed."

"Copy. Start counting...let's see..."

Grimaldi, he knew, was checking his instruments, McCarter already feeling the big warbird dipping.

"Ninety seconds, then hit the ramp."

McCARTER SHUFFLED up to the ramp, bootstrap dragging his weapons housing. He forged into the wind gust right behind Manning as the big Canadian sailed away from the ramp. Even though they were flying in from the west, coming in on the blind side of the conflagration, the Briton could see the lay of the land glowing from the raging firestorms to the east.

Time to go.

Time to hunt down whatever fanatics were left standing, crawling or staggering about in the ruins of their terrorist bastion, and blast them back into the inferno.

McCarter shuffled up the last two steps, and jumped.

CHAPTER TWENTY-FOUR

Qeshm

Ruballah took it as a sign, a divine blessing indeed, that he was still alive, untouched, in fact, when so much death was strewed for as far as he could see.

It was nothing short, he found, of a sea of bodies, graveyards of burning wreckage where a sprawling military installation once stood proud.

Everything in flames, ruins, the roar of hungry fire all around a hateful reminder that his dreams were in jeopardy, poised at the edge of extinction. The stink of roasting flesh assaulted his nostrils, an invisible force that nearly knocked him off his feet. Severed limbs, he saw next, panning on the carnage, his heart racing with fury, spying then the scattering of burning mummies jutting up from the sand in frozen postures of death.

Nothing short of vengeance was called for.

"You must go! Into the bunker!"

One of the soldiers was barking at him, but Ruballah didn't budge at first, nursing the fires of his hatred for this cowardly attack on the Iranian military complex. Every last aircraft was nothing but a flaming shell, if it hadn't been blown to obliterated pieces of scrap. Craters, the size of half a city block, coughed up clouds of black smoke from all over the compound and airfield. Whatever troops were left alive came running up the dune, most of them now barreling through maws of concrete housings that led to the underground bunker.

Some of the living, he next discovered, might have been better off if they'd been incinerated outright, or blown into countless bits and pieces of raw meat. He froze at the sound of all the wailing of horribly wounded soldiers, bansheelike cries that echoed from the inferno, the call of the damned. They reeled about, framed like broken mannequins in the raging bands of fire, a few charred stubs for hands stretching out, beseeching. Their pitiful moans for help fell on deaf ears. Other shadows, stumbling forth from the outer reaches of the screaming fires, were missing arms, while a few of them appeared completely limbless as they crawled on their bellies through the sand, great streams of dark red pumping from where their legs had been sheared off at the hip or the knee.

Then there was the dreadful steady soughing of wind, a superheated gale lashing his face, born from and blowing out in all directions from any number of the firestorms. He almost couldn't believe what he witnessed next, but two soldiers near the inferno that was the airfield were stumbling away from the fire, somehow spared, a miracle of sorts.

Or so it first appeared to Ruballah.

They plodded ahead, desperate puppets, being tugged back by what struck Ruballah as an invisible vacuum, the firestorm like some great sucking machine.

Or a magnet.

He watched, a morbid fascination mixed with fury rising in his chest, as they screamed out, dragged next by the winds, foot by foot, until they swirled, lifted off their bellies actually, and were swallowed into the inferno.

"Go!"

Ruballah went, but he was coming back out, he determined, as soon as they believed the air bombardment had ceased.

And what would be left?

He prayed that at least the gunboat he had hidden had been spared. Yes, he would crawl back out of this hole, he told himself, and if that boat was still in one piece, he would take the helm, ride out, full throttle, and fine the first ship that came into view.

There was no choice. "They" had left him nothing but the fire of his hatred, something that could only be expunged by vengeance.

It would come, in time, very soon, he vowed, even if that meant he would become a martyr in the next few hours. Anything, he thought, was better than burrowing himself like some rat in a hole, quaking in fear, waiting for the next round of bombs to shake and eat up more of Qeshm. Ruballah plunged through the doorway, descending into the bowels of the bunker, to stay put, wait it out until he was sure the immediate danger had passed.

When it did, he would find a target, even if that meant running from the devils in the sky, under fire.

McCarter believed a soldier made his own luck, but he took it as a stroke of good fortune, believing the gods of covert war were smiling on all of them, when he found Grimaldi had made the right call. It meant a little longer hike, but anything was preferable to landing in a mass furnace, torched alive, nothing left to do but let the fire eat them to the bones. The sand, a bonus, however he looked at it, cushioned what would have normally been a hard landing, the risk of hitting solid earth always involving the potential for a sprained or broken ankle.

Well, Phoenix Force had landed, square, on its feet, and good to go, as Manning had patched through.

On the way.

And the sky was burning in the distance, calling them to move in and clean up whatever was left moving.

McCarter was out of his chute pack, weapons claimed from the nylon housing, when the four shadows of Phoenix Force came loping over the dune. They were keeping the weapons basic this go-a-round. M-16/ M-203 combos to a man, ten pounds of plastic explosive in satchels, just in case someone chose to circle whatever wagon might be left standing. Encizo would pull double duty with the multiround projectile launcher. Harnesses then, pouches in combat blacksuits hung and stuffed with a mixed bag of frag, incendiary and flash-stun grenades, spare clips for any protracted engagement or the need to burn down a small army. Holstered Beretta 93-Rs as side arms, all around, finished up the killing goods.

McCarter heard his com link buzz with Major Sabol's gravel voice. "Alpha One to X Squad commander, come in."

"Commander Mac, here."

"Sitrep."

"All present and accounted for, sir. We're assembling now."

"We're under heavy fire on this end," Sabol informed McCarter, shouting over the racket of automatic-weapons fire coming over the com link. "Small arms, but we're bogged down for the time being. Linkup schedule off! Confirm!"

"I copy."

"Touching base to make sure you and your people landed in one piece."

"Affirmative."

"Then move out! I'll be in touch."

"Let's roll, mates."

McCarter led the way up the dune. Topping the rise, he figured they were maybe a two-klick jaunt until they ventured up to the foot of the great firestorm.

And went to work.

Even at that distance, he could feel a heat so intense

it stung his face, singed his eyes. Almost, he thought, as if the firestorm itself were alive and kicking, angry at the living and looking to devour.

Stony Man Farm, Virginia

"I COUNTED eight."

Brognola found Wethers pinning him with a strange look as the former professor's fingers flew over the key boards, using the satellite to scan the Gulf.

"What?" Brognola nearly choked on his cigar stub, aware already of what Wethers was trying to tell him.

"I counted eight gunboats before the strike."

"You're telling me one's missing," Brognola growled, rolling toward the man's workstation, peering so hard at the monitor, nerves so jangled it took him a full few seconds to get his eyes refocused. "Or moving out into the Gulf?"

"There it is. It's tucked away in an inlet," Wethers said.

"How did we miss that?" Brognola wanted to know.

"In the confusion of the moment," Kurtzman offered. "It happens."

"It damn well better not happen," Brognola growled. "Raise David and let him know about our missing suicide ship. Keep an eye on it. If it moves out, raise Jack and have him fly back and blow the damn thing clear to Saudi Arabia!"

Qeshm

"I COPY. Just let us know if any hostiles are moving for it," McCarter told the Farm over his satlink tie-in. "Me and the troops are sort of busy at the moment. Later."

The Briton didn't have time to ponder any horrifying scenario of a suicide boat racing out to the Gulf.

There was horror and problems enough greeting the men of Phoenix Force as they came over the dune and marched closer to the firestorm.

Phoenix Force crouched at the rise of the dune, spread out in a skirmish line. McCarter heard the voices shouting in Farsi, two soldiers pounding on the steel door leading to the bunker, eleven o'clock, thirty meters out.

They wanted in.

They were taken out.

A stream of five converging leadstorms nearly obliterated the two Iranians, blowing them open, gutted like fish, from head to crotch.

McCarter was counting up another dozen or so shadows, seeking shelter behind the concrete housing, firing off bursts from their AK-47s and AKMs, when he gave the order, "Blow it!"

It was overkill, to be sure, but McCarter didn't care to get stymied by some standoff, wasting bullets while some larger force, he suspected, was dug in below.

Which meant Phoenix Force would have to blow the door down and descend to root the enemy out.

Five 40 mm hellbombs chugged away, then merged into one mushroom cloud downrange, impacting as nearly one blast. Moving out, leading the charge, McCarter peered into the thick wall of smoke, found nothing left of the housing but a few jagged concrete teeth at its base.

He reached the pile of bodies and severed body parts, the air choked with toasted human flesh, burning fuel, emptied bowels.

The smells of war and death, he knew.

He was searching for any straggling wounded—no takers he could find out there in the lake of fire and wreckage—when he spotted the two fifty-five-gallon drums. It was nothing short of a fluke that both barrels had been launched from some point near the inferno, riding it out, before they landed, impaled into the sand at a near forty-five-degree angle.

McCarter told Encizo, "Move it out, Rafe! Find the openings to the ventilation shafts! Gary, go with him! Let me know the minute you find them and stand by! Cal, T.J., give me a hand with these drums!"

It was pure muscle work, but they had the drums rolled up moments later, resting on the broken lip leading down a short flight of steps to yet another steel door.

"Let's get these uncapped and dump them!"

James bared a grim smile, but there was nothing other than a steely edge in his voice as he said, "If we're about to do what I think we are, didn't I see this somewhere before?"

"You did at that," McCarter grunted back, twisting the cap off the first drum, the stink of high-grade aircraft fuel squeezing into his nose as he sloshed the flammable liquid down the steps. "And it worked for Lee Marvin, didn't it?"

THEY WOULD HAVE MISSED the first ventilation pipe altogether if it hadn't been for the fact the sky was on fire above them, lighting the way as clear as if a dozen klieg lights were beaming through the night.

Encizo crouched beside the pipe, which was sticking no more than six inches out of the sand. He swiveled his head, watching as Manning scurried up a long rise in a dune so high it appeared to touch the umbrella of firelight. Manning was little more than a flickering shadow, but Encizo clearly saw the thumbs-up as the big Canadian found another air pipe.

Encizo had some idea what McCarter was set to unleash. If they didn't burn them all down in the bunker, then it stood to reason there was an exit, some back-door escape hatch. Probably, he figured, over on the other side of the dune. The terror of being burned alive or buried under tons of rubble and steel might flush out anyone quick enough to make the dash for freedom, but that left Encizo wondering just how many Iranian fanatics were down there, and how many would come out shooting.

And where.

He patched through to McCarter. "We've found two. Running, so far, in a straight northerly line."

"Meaning there's more. On my count. Start dropping a mix of incendiary and frag down the chute. Three to a hole. Find the other ventilator shafts, on the run, and both of you use every last egg."

Encizo felt the tight smile stretch his lips. "Didn't I see this in the—"

"Get busy!"

"Aye, aye!"

Encizo relayed the word to Manning, then started plucking grenades off his webbing.

RUBALLAH SNATCHED UP the first AK-47 he saw when he heard the screams, the shooting, followed by the massive explosion. Sounds of more death, he thought, aware some invading force of infidels was right then ready to blast its way into the bunker.

He was sick of what he had seen anyway. All around in the chamber the wounded were gasping for help, some of them with punctured lungs, wheezing for air, while others clutched at the free-spouting blood from a missing arm or hand before toppling over, left unattended where they fell. In the few minutes he'd been holed up with maybe twenty-five or so survivors from the bombing, the less seriously mangled who had a slim chance at survival had been given shots of black-market heroin.

Just to keep them quiet and still, he thought, allow

him, at the very least, to clear out that awful pathetic moaning from memory, let him think straight.

It was time to rally the survivors. "Listen to me!" he shouted at the soldiers, and those few left alive who were part of the Islamic Free Movement of Iran. "Out the back! Go out shooting! I am going to the harbor! God willing, one boat is left."

A tinny clang from above, and he looked up, wondering what new horror was next. Two more grenades bounced up, he saw, rattling around the screen before they settled in next to the first motionless egg.

Ruballah broke into a sprint, fleeing the chamber. It was something like another forty meters or so before he made the back door. A stampede sounded behind him, and he knew they needed no further encouragement to leave the bunker.

Exit first, if they got that far, he feared. And how many enemy gunman were lying in wait outside?

He would find out soon enough, and gathered speed before the crush of his charging brothers in jihad on his heels beat him to the exit, trampling him on the way out.

There was too much left to be done, he thought. He wouldn't be cheated of his glory, and prayed, on the run, to be delivered from the infidels outside.

CHAPTER TWENTY-FIVE

McCarter keyed the bottom com-link button, told Encizo and Manning, "Go!"

The Phoenix Force leader, James and Hawkins, stepped back as a trio, about fifteen paces and began to lob a combination of frag and incendiary grenades down the well. Three apiece, McCarter figured, should not only bring the door down, but with the fuel he'd seen damming up against the entrance, a firestorm would ignite. With any luck a lake of fire, touched off by the blast, would go washing into the bunker, setting off the panic, driving them out whatever the exit hatch. A further blessing in the wings could be ammo, explosives stored up, rows of crates maybe, piled high in the rat's nest below.

The whole works, uprooted, if it was a ten-strike, skybound.

They were hauling it triple-time up the dune when the deafening mesh of detonating grenades rocked the air. The fireballs screamed out of the hole, rising as one into the air, a giant devil's tongue, driving the scorching heat up behind them, hurling the stink of burning fuel and more cooked flesh up their noses.

M-16's swinging around, they searched the upswing of the sandy knoll. North, grim satisfaction settling into his bones, McCarter spotted the fingers of fire jetting up, squeezed out the ventilation pipes, shrieking up and onward from what he hoped was one long message of doom for the rats below.

It should have become a fiery tomb down there, but McCarter and the other commandos weren't about to lolligag around and leave the rest of it to chance.

McCarter ventured back a few yards toward the latest inferno, inspecting their latest effort. No point in going down that way, he knew. And only the most desperate of their enemies would dare attempt a crazed rush out of that burning hole.

Which told McCarter if there was any way out it would be someplace else. North, east, or west, but he figured if the ventilation shafts were running due north, then whatever charge they made would come from that direction.

There would be survivors, runners; he was certain of that, those lucky few, either galvanized to act, bail, save themselves, whether out of cowardice, terror or desperation. No matter what drove them out into the stinking air of death and destruction, the Briton wanted to be on hand, set to crank it up, when the human vipers slithered out of the hole.

"Let's go find our good mates, Mr. R. and Mr. M.," McCarter said, and headed off for another showdown with the enemy.

With their world burning down around them, something warned the Phoenix Force leader the Iranians were saving the worst for last.

MANNING FLOPPED to his belly, and held back on the trigger of his M-16 A-4, cranking out the streams of 5.56 mm lead in long chattering sweeps, taking them down as fast as they popped out of the hole.

They found exit, a good eighty-yard run from the first ventilation shaft, barely beat the Iranians to the starting line. The grenades were going off, Manning feeling the ground tremble beneath him, but the Iranians were streaming out the back door by the fours and fives, beating the rumble and the blasts by mere heartbeats, if the big Canadian gauged the distances between the shafts and the rear exit right.

Targets were certainly swarming all over the place, but the stampede to clear what he could only imagine was a dragon's tongue of fire chasing them out, sent them pitching to the sand, all tangled heaps of arms and legs, guys squawking in Farsi, bleating out the pleas for God's divine intervention.

Encizo slid into the periphery of his vision, his M-16 joining the full-auto shooting match.

A few fanatics rose right away, but wheeled straight into the faces of doom, their AK-47s flaming skyward in death grips as Manning and Encizo dropped the double lead hammer down.

The sheer crush of numbers saved maybe six or seven out of the gate. Long enough for a few AK-47s to seek out the enemy, a human shield of sorts, able to launch a few rabbits on the run.

Return fire started snapping the lead over Manning's scalp, divots of sand spitting in the face. Realizing that Encizo was likewise catching hell, Manning decided tactical good sense called for a wide split.

The problem was, by the time he had sidled a good ten yards from Encizo, back in position, two rabbits were almost out of range. One of them turned back, capping off a burst of autofire for effect, or maybe hoping to get lucky. For a second, the face shone against the inferno. Manning bit down the curse, as the Iranian he memorized from the photo lineup vanished into a deep cut between two dunes.

"Rafe! That was Ruballah!"

Manning burned through a clip, after nailing a few more trying to escape his reach. Then he slapped home another 30-round mag just as the cavalry hit the dune. Five M-16s chattered on, drilling runners, any fanatic reckless or foolish enough to hold his ground. Ten-strike, and perhaps then some, as gunmen toppled, this way and that, piling up below.

McCarter gave the word, and the other Phoenix Force commandos headed down, the smoking muzzles of assault rifles raking the carnage, ready to nail any wounded or Iranians looking to play Lazarus.

Clear.

Until they reached the maw of the back exit.

It was a distant rumble, at first, as Manning crouched beside the concrete well, finding the exit burrowed into the side of the dune. James and Hawkins bounded over the top, flanked the other side as shouting echoed from somewhere deep in the bunker. McCarter took a perch above the concrete housing, M-16 pointed down, ready to add fury to what would prove devastating interlocking fields of fire. Sporadic bursts of autofire peppered the stone housing, voices now hollering in Farsi, before the real, and bone-chilling waiting erupted in decibels that assaulted Manning's eardrums.

The way the explosions came thundering from the bowels of the bunker, Manning had to figure some fuel depot or ammo housing was touched off by any gush of fire blown around by the incendiary grenades. He lurched back as a gust of air, hot as burning coals, surged out the exit hatch, the devil's breath.

They were cooking down there, Manning knew, the screams of men burning alive fading, muted altogether in the next few moments as more explosions rumbled out the well.

"They're toast," James said.

"What the hell is Rafe doing?" .

They followed Hawkins, who was gesturing up the dune ahead where Encizo was crouched at the top, milking short bursts at some phantom target.

"Rafe!" McCarter shouted. "What in bloody hell is going on?"

"Ruballah," Manning told the es-SAS commando. "He made it out."

"He's gone," Encizo hollered back. "He's heading for the harbor. He's got a two-, maybe three-hundred-yard jump!"

McCarter keyed the button on the com link that patched him through to Grimaldi. "X Squad to Mr. G., come in!"

"Mr. G. here! Problems?"

"You could damn well say that. What's your position?"

"Island hopping, one door down."

"Turn it around!"

RUBALLAH PRAISED God on the run, the AK-47 seeming to add momentum to his sprint, like a baton in hand. He was alive, when so many lives had been sacrificed in the cowardly attack, he thought, by the infidels. He needed to exact retribution, right away, even if that meant sailing clear across the Gulf until he found a thriving port, ram whatever was available, maybe drive it up into a city block by the sea.

Two kilometers at least, since he'd cleared the site where his brothers in jihad had offered up their lives to get him this far, and he could see the gunboat, intact, anchored in the inlet.

He was going to make it, fulfill his destiny, even if that meant riding out the great ball of fire, all the way to the sky.

To paradise.

Once he was in the boat, at the helm, he figured full speed was somewhere in the neighborhood of thirty knots. It could be a little less than that now, factoring in six hundred pounds of explosives, six or seven fifty-five-gallon fuel drums for longer seagoing patrols. It was foresight, or simple master planning, he thought, that the whole package was already wired up, tied in to a remote switch beside the wheel. When moving the boat, he'd checked the box, to be certain the package was ready. A flick of a switch, and he was in the red-light zone.

He turned, saw them, the five commandos, rolling up over a dune, far away. Too far to hope they could cut him down with a lucky bullet. Figure he'd gained five hundred yards before they fell in for the chase.

Whoever they were—American commandos, most likely—he hoped they caught the show. The first boat, ship, and Ruballah would ram it, right down the center line, amidships.

BITTER FRUSTRATION would have seen Phoenix Force firing off shots and grenades as they hit the beach, nothing more than a hope and a prayer. A sorry waste of ammunition, without a doubt, since the gunboat was already cutting across the water, a quarter mile out, and surging along at top speed.

As it stood, McCarter had turned the show over to Grimaldi. All they had to do was stand by, and wait for the Spectre's hammer to come down.

Ruballah, McCarter knew, was minutes away from getting the ride of his life, on the way to hell.

McCarter judged Ruballah's course due southwest, figuring the architect of the mass suicide-boat scheme would straighten it out once he hit the Gulf waters. The gunboat, like the great fish of Madagascar, would then go hunting for the first available prey.

James and Encizo were searching the skies to the east, wavering in bands of multicolored light, a rainbow of firelight cast out across the Strait of Hormuz from the furnace that was Qeshm.

"Come on, Jack, come on!" Manning urged the skies.

They didn't have much longer to wait. The familiar rumble first, then a collective sense of relief dropped over the five commandos.

Curtain call, with the Spectre the encore performance.

And the Spectre, maybe three hundred feet up, swooped down for the water a little more, straightened, then flew on. Grimaldi and crew, McCarter envisioned, manning the guns, lining up Ruballah off to port. The Briton stifled the chuckle, wishing, just the same, he could see the fanatic's face when the aircraft unloaded the works. Combo howitzer, Vulcans and Bofors opened up, with a sound and fury, McCarter had to believe, they might have heard all the way to Bahrain. The end result, the light show, was spectacular.

"Whoa." Encizo whooped as a volcano flashed out to sea, cleaving part of the sky, it appeared, with a mushroom cap that went on and up, taking whatever was left of Ruballah with it.

Finished.

They listened to the thunder, rolling in from a great distance, the Spectre aglow in the fire wash as the war bird sailed on.

McCarter heard Sabol patching through. "Yes, Major."

"What the hell is going on? You want to tell me why you pulled your ace out?"

"A little problem involving a suicide boat that all of us somehow missed."

"How's that?"

"Ruballah."

"What about him?"

McCarter turned away from the firestorm out to sea. "Shit happened."

Stony Man Farm, Virginia

THE EARLY RETURNS WERE in from what was simply tagged, "the strike," from the White House all the way to Langley. On the surface, the strike was a winner.

As for the future, well, Brognola knew, like the song said, it was always in doubt. In the world where he, the Farm and the Stony Man warriors lived, it was simply always in jeopardy.

Brognola was taking a time out from the Computer Room, wishing, for reasons he couldn't quite fathom, to sit alone.

Reflecting.

Worried still about Striker's safe passage home.

It looked as if the strike was all it was intended to be, and then some. Ruballah was out of the picture, all suicide boats accounted for, nothing more than some wreckage floating out to sea. Phoenix Force was in one piece, nothing left but a walk-through of the island in fire, waiting for a chopper ride out and back to the Saudi air base. Major Sabol's people had sustained a few minor casualties, having gone head-to-head with a contingent of Iranian soldiers bunkered on the east end of the island before burning them down.

A clean wrap, for the most part.

So, why didn't he feel like tap dancing, throwing a party? Brognola wondered.

One item of concern was the fallout, all those consequences and repercussions from the strike. Sure, the United States had launched some smart bombs into terrorist camps in Afghanistan in the past, hoping, but failing to nail bin Laden. Sure, there was that obliterating strike against the so-called "pharmaceutical" company in Sudan, which, every American intelligence agency knew, had been creating and housing chemical and biological weapons. And now, a clear and present danger in the Gulf had been eliminated.

So, what the hell was bugging him?

He knew, and as soon as Barbara Price walked into the War Room, she read the look.

"Striker called from Jiddah. He's at a CIA safehouse."

Brognola showed the lady a tired smile. Good news, for a change.

"DYSAT's smuggling operation was burned down. A clean sweep. Striker came through."

There was never any doubt, just a few of the usual anxiety attacks along the way."

"I'm arranging for him to fly to JFK on the next flight out of Jiddah."

Brognola smiled as the lady took a chair. "First class, I hope."

"Nothing but."

She paused, Brognola feeling the weight of her probing stare.

"What's wrong, Hal?"

Brognola gave that some thought, heaved a breath and said, "I was just wondering, Barbara."

"About what?"

"If what just happened over there…if we cleaned up a mess or opened the door for a future round of horror."

"That's always a possibility. That's why we're here."

"Indeed. Where does it all end? Does the madness ever stop?"

She smiled, and Brognola could read the grim weight on her own shoulders, in the momentary downcast stare. "It doesn't. But we both know that. The President made the right, the only call. What can I say? Evil doesn't sleep."

"I hear you."

And they sat in silence for a moment, sharing the relief, as temporary as it was, of a job well done.

"When was the last time you ate?"

Brognola shook his head. "I can't remember."

"Well, let's go see what's in the kitchen, shall we?"

It sounded like a plan to Brognola, the best one he'd heard in days. There would always be another war on the horizon, more Ruballahs out there, ready to rise up and savage whomever and whatever they could.

And Stony Man, he knew, rising from his chair, would be there, ready to slay the next dragon.

It was what they did.

"We still have Able's situation," Brognola said.

"I know. Let's eat first. There's been a development."

"I look at you, and I see Carl straining at the chain."

"Let's just say Carl's making some headway."

"Oh, God," Brognola muttered, but couldn't suppress one last weary smile as he followed Price out of the War Room.

CHAPTER TWENTY-SIX

Idaho

"These guys are really starting to piss me off."

Jim Lake couldn't decide if it felt like hours or days since he'd flown from Los Angeles. Time felt strangely frozen in place, since he'd circled the wagons once he'd landed at the DYSAT research-and-production facility in Idaho.

He supposed time didn't matter in the final analysis, other than the few hours he'd need to fly away from the States, the classified military flight already paved for his next destination.

Now three human monkey wrenches thrown into his plans, threatening to grind it down before he was wheels up.

He sure didn't much feel like laughing, either, since all the callers from overseas, from his man in Sudan, and the captain of the *Thai Princess* were sounding off the SOS every time they called in.

And his bulldogs had landed, in his face.

"Look at that guy," Lake growled, gripping his uzi subgun so tight he heard a knuckle pop.

It was damn sure time to move on, he knew, but three loose ends had suddenly reared up out of the woods. One of them, the so-called G-man passing off his alias as Lemmon, was standing at the south gate. Smiling into the cameras, waving, then showing two middle fingers, mouthing, "Hi, Jim. Will you come out and play?"

Yes, he'd thrown out the challenge back in L.A., but he didn't think they had the stones or the smarts to get this far.

Life was full of surprises lately, he thought.

Well, the walls were closing in, Lake knew, swiveling some in his chair, checking the other monitors for some phantom force in the nearby wooded foothills. Clear on all points, he found, no one out there, except to the south. Lemmon's buddies, he saw, were hunched shadows, thinking they were concealed in the fir, pine and ponderosa, watching their pal play games.

Lake had already called in the security force, scrambling sixteen black ops from Nevada while in the air for Idaho. They were on hand when he landed, loaded down with weapons, with orders to shoot to kill the first individual who walked up to the gate, and he didn't give a damn if it was some rancher looking for his wayward steer.

About an hour earlier, though, he changed the plan, ordering all personnel into the compound. Give the whole complex a desolate look, leave the three bulldogs out there wondering if anyone was home, freezing in their sheepskin or bomber jackets.

Psywar.

Mr. Cheerful was now pulling back his sheepskin, showing off the .357 Colt Python in shoulder rigging. Mouthing more challenges, everything but pulling down his fly, but Lake figured with the wind shipping the way it was, the guy didn't want to risk pissing on his foot.

"Monroe," Lake said over his shoulder, "how much C-4 did you say we have?"

"Two hundred and twenty-five pounds."

"And the Herc?"

"Loaded up with fifty barrels of the laser guns, plus component parts, tech manuals."

"And the microchips for the Ramrod Intercept?"

"Just delivered to me, about an hour ago."

"Okay, here's the plan. All work personnel is to be ordered to their quarters. Cite some, I don't know, leak in a seal on the uranium reprocessor. Once that's done, begin spreading the plastique around."

"Detonators?"

"I have the box. The radio frequency will be tuned in to my personal touch."

"And those three?"

"Send Marshal out to have a chat with Mr. Cheerful. A little mind probe, feel him out. I've got something in mind, but I want to see if he has some backup."

"Word is he's been hanging around the local watering hole, asking all kinds of questions about the complex. Throwing your name around."

Lake chuckled now. He could see the showdown coming. Hell, he was looking forward to it. "Have Marshal take his handheld, leave the line open. I want to hear the exchange."

"The general still hasn't returned your calls from the Pentagon."

"I know. Problems. Sudan went to hell. I don't know what happened, but we need to bail. I've made arrangements to get us as far as Thailand. I figure something like twenty million in high-tech toys, someone will cough up with the cash. Let me know when you're finished mining the store."

Monroe left to plant the farewell touch. Time to fly soon, Lake thought, but not before he nailed three pieces of unfinished business to the wall of the compound.

"Okay, Lemmon, you want to play games, I'm up for a little more fun."

"THIS IS NOT GOING to be good, Gadgets."

Blancanales repeated that two more times, turned to see if Schwarz was even still with him. Since taking the military flight from L.A. to Boise, then rounding up their SUV rental ride, delivered courtesy of the Farm, Blancanales had seen the strange look in his friend's eyes. It was troublesome, he decided, to the point of spooky, that thousand-yard stare never leaving his friend's face. He wasn't sure what was bugging Gadgets, but guessed it could have been any number of items. Such as the weather, the wind gusts hurtling down from the mountains, eighty-sixing Gadget's hang-gliding plans. If there was something else, he couldn't say, but Blancanales sensed his comrade was nursing a time bomb in his belly.

And it was cold out there, no mistake, as they crouched in the trees. The thermal underwear went a long way in keeping the shiver out of their bones, as did the black turtlenecks, matching corduroys and bomber jackets. But the way Gadgets was cradling the HK MP-5 SD-3 subgun…eyes shining now, a human wolf sizing up the prey.

Then there was Lyons. The local tavern, the Moosehead Inn, had become the Able Team commander's personal interrogation central. The idea was to make some noise, inquiries about the installation, spook the locals into revealing what they knew or believed about the DYSAT complex. No luck. Just the cold shoulder. That alone, Blancanales hoped, could work. Say Lake had a pair of eyes and ears, tuned in for any paranoid talk, running back to the crazy colonel, describing Lyons. Get the bad guys nervous, have them come gunning.

Not the best-laid plan, but Lyons was a live grenade himself, looking for a place to go off.

"Gadgets?" Blancanales said, his M-16/M-203 combo watching Lyons back. "Can I ask you something?"

A grunt, Schwarz keeping that wolf's stare locked on the gate.

"You've been acting kind of strange since L.A. You want to talk about it?"

For a few moments, Blancanales was looking at a piece of stone, then Gadgets showed some life. The mean slash, passed off as a grin, didn't stir much confidence in Blancanales over his friend's state of mind.

"It's not the hang-glider thing, if that's what you're wondering."

"Okay," Blancanales gently prodded. "Then what?"

"Lake. He's bad news."

"No question."

"I feel…I don't like letting myself down. I don't like having been laughed at by that bastard. I want him. He's mine."

Blancanales drew a deep breath of cold air, a move that only gave the raw chill tapping down his spine an extra bit of walking freeze. No, he thought, this wasn't going to be good.

He couldn't think of any appropriate response, so went back to watching Lyons. This mission had ground them all down, pushing them out there into some shadowy borderland of boiling rage and frustration. Catching, then losing Lake all over L.A. Borderline but not entirely innocent folks getting gunned down in the process. And still the psychopath was somewhere, on the grounds, Blancanales was certain.

If something didn't break soon, he knew both Ironman

and Gadgets were set to go over the fence, all but flinging the presidential directive back at the Oval Office.

Suddenly, even Blancanales found himself getting antsy, some hot blood lust stirring in his belly.

Not good at all.

"HI, BUZZ, how the hell you doing? Jimbo around? You're looking kind of mean today. Problems with your bowels? Maybe the little woman's on you about rethinking your objections to Viagra? Or maybe you have a boyfriend?"

Lyons was baring his teeth, holding the shark's smile as the hardman walked toward the gate. He felt both his anger and the cold working hard to cut loose his temper. He knew he was being watched by the two cameras mounted over the gate, but that was part of the ploy. Two big main buildings, made of some kind of steel, were all that made up the DYSAT complex. Lyons could well imagine they ran belowground, intersecting hallways, work areas, and somewhere in one of those buildings he knew Lake was hunkered down. He could almost see the guy, somewhere in a room, chuckling even then.

"Something I can do for you, pal?"

Lyons laughed. "You sure can." He looked into the camera. "Tell Jimbolina I'll be down at the Moosehead. Happy hour's still in swing. Tell Jimbolina I'd like him to make it. I'll even buy the beer, seeing as his C-130 looks set to fly. A farewell toast, wishing him good luck, all that good-buddy jazz."

Lyons looked at the stone face on the other side of the gate. "Hello? Anybody home, Buzz?"

"I'm listening."

"So, you're telling me Jimbo's around?"

"I'll go have a look."

"And that beer?"

"I'll see if he's available."

"Make it happen, asshole."

And that nearly tripped the switch. The hardman's hand twitched a couple inches toward the holstered side arm, Lyons ready to grab his .357, blast it out right there. Buzz thought better of it, his chuckle making Lyons wonder if there was some special Jim Lake course they took to sound like that.

"I'm done—'we're' done playing games," Lyons said, putting an edge to his voice. "If he doesn't show, I'll assume he's either a coward, hiding in some hole underground. Or he's plain old rude. I don't like rude people. I don't like cowards, either. One hour. I'll be back. And if he has good sense he'll try and run. If that Herc is still grounded, as sure as I'm standing here, I'll blow that plane into the next state."

"I'll pass it on."

There it was. Lake was home. But Lyons was already walking away, braced, just in case Lake passed on the order to shoot him in the back. He didn't think that was the man's style, but he wasn't about to put anything beneath the crazy colonel.

Now, all he had to do, Lyons thought, was wait a little while longer. Lake had an ego the size of the Rocky Mountains, and Lyons had to believe he'd pushed the right psychotic buttons.

If not, well, when he came back with his Able Team comrades in tow his mind was made up.

They were going to storm the fort.

Lake was going down for the count, one way or another, whether it was the tavern or here at the compound.

Lyons had reached his limits. It was time to kick ass.

End of discussion.

"OH, I KIND of like you guys, I really do. I'm going to miss you even."

Lake chuckled, pacing around the command-and-control room, enjoying, as he usually did, the sound of his own voice. It sounded especially sweet to him when he was all alone.

"Damn shame to waste talent like that. Almost breaks my heart."

He grabbed up the handheld radio, patched through to Monroe. "Mr. Monroe."

"Sir?"

"Everything in order?"

"Another thirty minutes."

"Leave that particular task to someone else. Round up eight men. We're going out for a beer."

FEELING THE BOMB ticking in his gut, Lyons occupied the last booth, nursing a draft beer. Gadgets and Pol were outside, watching the tavern, covering his back. He checked his watch. Forty-six minutes, and still waiting.

It was a cowboy crowd, he noted, packed pretty much wall to wall with locals, sawdust floor to soak up any spilled swill, or vomit.

Maybe even the blood, if some rancher tied one on, maybe a sore loser erupting at the pool table where Lyons saw them shooting eight ball, rumpled bills on the railing.

Blood, he thought. If or when Lake arrived, he couldn't help but wonder just how crazy the man really was, if he would go berserk, start shooting up the place, innocent bystanders and all. He didn't think so, Lake's ride to wherever ready to fly, the man believing he had a future, all light and sweetness, as he sailed off for the horizon. Meaning the crazy colonel couldn't afford to start gunning down local heat.

Or so Lyons hoped.

And what was with Gadgets, anyway? he wondered. Schwarz had lapsed into some state of silent, simmering anger since Los Angeles, chewing on whatever his thoughts, looking ready to rip the head off the first guy who even gave him a chance.

It was going to blow, Lyons knew. He and his men were at a breaking point. It was unprofessional, to some extent, letting emotions filter into cold, rational judgment, but Lake had pushed them to a point of no return, where the only way back was to wax the bastard.

Thus Lyons could allow Gadgets his silent rage. He understood it all too well. Since he felt the same exact way.

The handheld radio crackled with Blancanales's voice. "Yeah."

"The colonel just arrived, Carl. Two vans. I'm counting eight goons."

Now Lyons wished he'd brought the Uzi subgun. Six rounds, two speedloaders for the Colt Python, well, it would have to do the job, if Lake went ballistic. Of course, at the first sound of an opening shot, his teammates would come barreling through the door, weapons blazing.

The cowbell jingled, the door going wide. It was uncanny almost, Lyons thought, how Lake met his stare right away, as soon as he marched in, pinning him down. Grinning, no less, the arrogance of the man infuriating Lyons even more.

The locals went quiet, all heads turning toward Lake and his goon squad as they filed in.

"You're obviously not the toast of the town," Lyons said as Lake pulled up and slid into the booth, his hard-force taking up posts around the tavern. Three made some elbow room at the bar, a glower from one of the goons turning a cowboy into a mute statue as he looked ready to pursue a protest.

Three more slid over to the gaming area, hands folding at the crotch. The last two flanked the door. It was a bad setup, all things considered, Lyons knew, the goon squad split up, in position to both block any flying charge from Pol and Gadgets, while creating interlocking fields of fire on his roost.

"Who wants to be popular anyway?" Lake said, giving Lyons the full treatment of his ghoul's chuckle. "I'd rather be rich than famous. Fame is overrated. Hey, I've been living in Hollywood. They can have it. The revolving door of rehabs, or whether it's gross or net. The hangers-on. The lawyers, the snippy little no-talent film execs, shoveling shit up their noses around the clock, wondering why they haven't seen a hard-on since Christ was a carpenter…well, you have the picture."

"Is that what this has all been about, Lake? Money?"

"I'm a little deeper than that, but, essentially, yes."

"It's over, Lake. Sudan's finished. The *Thai Princess*, I understand, is going to be boarded and seized by the FBI. The Iranian end users for your toys went up in flames under a major U.S. surgical strike."

"So I heard."

"You don't sound too concerned that you're next on the list."

"We're looking at the end times, good buddy, my human freight train, my bulldog. You might as well get it while the getting is still good. The pie's getting smaller by the day. Me? I'm bailing before the whole roof comes crashing down. Now, whoever did whatever over there? They think maybe it was revenge for recent events in the Middle East, or some preemptive strike to show the Muslims Uncle Sam didn't come to that particular dance to sit in the corner. A quick fix. All they did was make the fanatic Islam world even more angry, more determined. I've seen it coming for years. They're going to be here soon, lots of them, whole armies, hell, they're here already."

"I'll play along. Who?"

"The terrorists. Come on, crawl out from under your rock."

"My eyes are wide open, and I'm looking at nothing more than a traitor, no more, no less."

"The hell you say." He chuckled. "This country hasn't even begun to know what horror is yet. Yes, I see them on *60 Minutes,* telling the civilian masses not to fear, they've got all this super counterterrorism intelligence that will save the day, their tidy little suburban enclaves, their shopping malls. No one is safe. You know, a part of me considered offering you a job."

"You're serious, aren't you?"

"Deadly. Then I thought, nah, you can't be bought."

"First rational thing I've heard you say yet."

"You know, I sit here, looking at you looking at me, I'm reminded of Al Pacino in *Scarface.* I'm the bad guy. But, you know, the guy was right about something. You people need me to feel alive, to validate some naïve notion that you're the good guys."

"We can do this the hard way."

"Yeah, yeah, or the easy way. I throw my hands up, hit my knees, grovel for mercy and forgiveness, all will be right again in heaven. Come on, Bulldog, you know better."

"I'm afraid I do."

"Where's this beer you were going to buy me? No, forget it. I don't accept generosity from fools. I see you. You want to pull that piece and just blow me away. Go ahead. I've got eight men here. We'll clean this place out before you cap off the first round, before your girl-friends get two steps away from their SUV. I know you don't want that, all that innocent blood on your head."

Lyons screwed his eyes shut, his anger building in the face of this evil, blood pressure pulsing in his ears. He put his hands in his lap, trying to will away the trembling in his arms. It was all he could do to keep from pulling out the Colt Python, go for broke.

"Suck it up, Bulldog. What have you lost? A few soft bastards who were nothing more than scapegoats, marched right into the trap by me from the beginning. This was a done deal, long ago."

"I guess so."

"Goodbye, Bulldog."

Lyons waited for Lake to go for it, but the man was all chuckles and loose limbs as he rose from the booth. Slowly backing up, he tossed a wink at Lyons.

The guy appeared like some wraith, floating on air, and illusion, of course, Lyons knew, owing the moment to his own extremely heightened combat juices. Lake chuckled on as he backed away, folding into his phalanx of goons.

"See you soon, honey," he called back, then was gone.

"You can count on it," Lyons muttered, and drained his beer.

"Carl! Carl!"

Lyons thumbed the button on his handheld radio. "I'm here."

"What's the story?"

Lyons simply told Blancanales, "Lock and load, gentlemen."

CHAPTER TWENTY-SEVEN

In some perverse way, Lyons decided the setup fit the crazy colonel's style.

Nuts, all the way, a high-noon touch waiting for the three of them.

It wasn't the best approach for Able Team, by any stretch, but the gates were wide open, lights beaming down over the bare stretch between the two buildings.

Calling them. Daring.

Before moving in, Able Team had given the entire complex and perimeter a lengthy scoping. The Herc was still parked on the runway to the north. From a high surveillance point, they spotted no snipers on the rooftops. Lake was home, burrowed inside, Lyons knew. He hadn't expected less.

The challenge, after all, was issued back at the Moosehead, the colonel defying them to all but come on and try their damnedest to take him out.

Three men, at least, were more than willing to oblige.

Two problems they discussed before moving in on foot, weapons ready, harnessed up, with webbing, each man loaded down with frag and incendiary grenades, half-dozen spare clips for their respective weapons.

One—Lyons and company had no firm read on enemy numbers. Two—the civilian workforce. Knowing Lake wouldn't pull any punches now, Lyons figured the guy to keep either human body armor close at hand or have the guns aimed at the heads of hostages.

They hashed it over, and the end result—the grim reward of dropping Lake and his goons—outweighed the risks. Any hostages or innocents snapped up as shields would be dealt with, as it happened. If it happened.

Uzi leading the way, his satchel with five pounds of C-4 hanging down his back, Lyons led the slow walk past the gate. They were tied in via com link, if they were split up, forced to go their own ways.

Communications wasn't the issue, Lyons guessed, since he knew all three of them were steeled in a mindset to run and gun, take their chances.

They knew the drill, from long, hard and sometimes even painful experience.

Problem number three, however, was complete ignorance of the layout in either building. They were hunting Lake and goons on their home turf, where any number of hidden chambers, passageways, coves and cubbyholes gave the enemy a definite edge.

Nothing to do but go in blind, shoot it down if it showed up, armed and dangerous.

There was no trouble in the motivation department, since Lyons could feel the heat, easily read the looks in the eyes of Pol and Gadgets for what they signaled.

Time to rock.

A cold wind slashed Lyons in the face, howling down from the mountains at nearly the same instant the enemy gunners showed and got the rock and roll under way.

Midway down both buildings, a door flew open on each structure. Subgun fire stuttered from each opening, chasing Lyons and Blancanales for cover at the edge of the west-side building. Lyons sent a long burst of autofire at the shadows in the doorway, but Blancanales, even as the lead snapped the air around them like crazed bees, triggered his M-203 on the fly. Lyons didn't see the explosion, but heard the thunder, the earth trembling under his feet.

And the brief screams, of course, told him Blancanales scored a big one. Guys wailing out the pain one second, then going silent, toppling down, out of play.

They were directing subgun fire at Gadgets, Lyons saw, chasing him to cover, but Schwarz was hosing down the doorway with his HK MP-5, sparking the jamb, lead shrieking in their faces, driving them back into their hole. But not before he tagged another, as a scream ripped from inside that opening, guns going silent, as if the surviving shooters were reconsidering their options.

The men of Able Team hadn't forseen such a brazen show of force, weren't necessarily surprised, but thought when they found the gate open and the grounds cleared that Lake was lying in wait until they breached one entrance or another.

No matter. It was game time, and none of them was about to slow it down for any oversight.

Lyons keyed his com link, told Schwarz, "Up the side. Hug the wall tight. We're moving out, same thing."

It made Lyons nervous for a moment, when Schwarz simply grunted, not even looking his way. No thumbs-up, nothing but him hauling out from cover, sprinting up the side of the wall.

Charging the shooters!

"Let's move, Pol!"

They were nearly in sync, Schwarz taking the lead when a shooter kicked open the door, subgun poking out, loosing a short burst that sent bullets skidding off the wall over Schwarz's head. It was one of the most anxious moments Lyons had swallowed down in some time, certain they had his teammate dead to rights, an eye blink away from chopping him down in his bulldozing path.

In the heat of the moment, Lyons knew he missed the grenade in Schwarz's hand, armed and already flying. It caromed off the open doorway, a perfect bounce slicing off into their murky firepoint.

A crunching detonation, and then there was smoke boiling out the doorway.

And the silence of death.

Lyons ordered Schwarz to link up. They were going through the door, as one, together, or they weren't going at all. Schwarz was hung out there in some twilight zone of killing hunger, and not even Lyons wanted to touch it.

Lake, he figured, contaminated even the best of men.

On cue, as Schwarz sprinted across open ground, Lyons sighted down on the smoky maw ahead, while Blancanales covered the death hole on the opposite side for any peepers.

Schwarz picked up the rear, falling in on a crouch behind Blancanales. Lyons mouthed, "Three count," held up the same number of fingers and dropped them down, one by one.

Lyons went through the door first, and found bad company waiting on the other side.

"NO RESPONSE from either team one or two, sir."

That meant seven shooters, out of the picture, Lake knew.

He wouldn't second-guess himself now, even if the thought tugged at him that he'd underestimated the tenacity and martial skill of the three bulldozers.

They were on the way.

Lake slipped three spare magazines into his waistband, took up the Uzi. He patched back to Monroe. "Take maybe a dozen or so of the civilians. Put them in the hospital ward. In case of injuries," he said, and chuckled. "Let them come to you, make some noise about waxing the civs, then unload on our friends."

"Sir?"

He didn't like the questioning tone in Monroe's voice. "Mr. Monroe, you have your orders, you will kindly carry them out."

"Aye, aye, sir."

"Now, gentlemen," Lake said, palming the remote radio detonator, "come to daddy."

LYONS FLUNG himself to the side as he glimpsed at least four subguns, one shooter stacked over the other to either side, blazing from what appeared a doorway beyond some sort of chamber-foyer. He wasn't about to pat himself on the back for catlike reflexes, since they were tracking on, and he couldn't find the first bit of cover.

Blancanales took care of the problem before it became his funeral. The area was fairly tight, maybe fifty feet to the enemy's stand at the next entrance, when Blancanales let fly a 40 mm bomb. The blast hit the edge of the door, gouging out half the wall, leaving Lyons with his bell rung to deaf, dumb and choking on the cordite.

Standing, he met Blancanales and Schwarz at the midway point, allowing Pol to take the point, since his ears were in better shape to home in on any movement beyond the boiling cloud.

The stink of running blood and innards cleared Lyons's senses some as he crouched at the jagged edge. Four more gunners down, shredded to red rag dolls, faces ground up to the bone, like some warning poster on bacteria-infested hamburger.

The next problem sounded off, in clear tones of

panic. Peering around the corner, Lyons strained his senses, his hearing coming back by small degrees, but he made out the frightened voices, rolling down a long hallway, northward. Lyons looked the other way, back again, and found the main hall opened up to another corridor, westbound.

Clear, for the moment, but Lyons feared what they would go charging into next.

He moved out, Blancanales and Schwarz picking up his six. Swift, he led the march, the voices of fear growing, mounting in volume, angry question hurled about. Lyons hugged the wall's edge, spotted the doorway across the hall, empty, at first look, then gestured for Blancanales to take up post there.

Blancanales shot across the hall, when Lyons turned, wondering where...

No Gadgets.

Blancanales was gritting his teeth, shaking his head, shrugging.

Lyons bent at the knees, swung his weapon around the corner and found five gunners had corraled civilian hostages.

"DROP THE WEAPONS and these gentle folks don't get hurt! Now! I've got a room full of civilians."

"Where's your boss?"

Schwarz thought that was the best question posed yet. He had peeled off, when Lyons and Blancanales weren't looking, scurried down the west hall. Homed in now on the terse exchange, he discovered the corridor cut back, north, where the standoff was going down.

He swiveled on his heels, HK MP-5 fanning closed doors. Empty.

So, where was the colonel?

Schwarz didn't think he'd leave the killing, or the dying, he hoped, to the troops, but he couldn't be certain. On the way, bearing down on the far edge, the unfamiliar voices rose in angry decibels.

He slid up against the edge, HK subgun up and poised, a full clip up the snout. Inching his face around the corner, he took in the scene. Five gunners, fanned out across the way. One of them, the talker, had an elderly man in white lab coat by the hair, held out, shaking him like a wet dog.

One last look down the other way, finding a series of closed doors, and Schwarz sucked in a long, quiet breath.

He let it out and whipped around the corner.

Schwarz took out the talker first, a burst of 9 mm manglers zipping up the spine, paralysis first, followed by a crimson fall of rubber limbs. The whitecoat cried out, but had good sense and speed enough to hit the deck.

Four gunners remained, caught in a cross fire, chewed up to jitterbugging sieves as Lyons and Blancanales opened up with double streams of autofire. Smoke, blood and disintegrating fabric rained the hall before they danced out, dropping one by one.

Schwarz had a fresh magazine in place, cocked and locked when the chuckle hit him from behind.

"Gadgets!"

Lyons had to have seen the remote radio box first, before Lake showed it off. Some narrow tunnel vision squeezed Lake into Schwarz's focus, a red film of rage hitting his sight, there, then gone. Lake had come out of hiding, his ever present Uzi up and aimed.

"Not so fast, honey!"

Schwarz ventured a few paces down the hall.

"One more step."

He pulled up, as Lake waved the box around.

"Nice work, fellas. Caught the whole show on my screens. Sixteen down, the best that black ops out of the Pentagon could buy. Or so I thought. Hey, you want a job?"

That infuriating chuckle, Schwarz daring to cut the gap by two more steps.

"I didn't think so. No problem. I'm flying out of here. You know why? I've got this place wired to go. I've got enough U-235 below, primed to splash up the mountainside, well, you see your problem? If I don't walk, nobody does. I'll Chernobylize the whole state for the next thousand years."

Schwarz saw some flicker of uncertainty dance through the crazy eyes, Lake moving his thumb, up and down the box, playing games.

"One flick of the switch…"

And Schwarz dived through the narrowest window of opportunity, the subgun leaping up, spitting out a burst. There was a stretched moment, a freeze from

Lake as he stared at the stump where his hand had been amputated at the wrist.

The curse, or whatever insanity Lake was on the verge of bellowing out, never came.

Schwarz hit the trigger.

LYONS WAITED until the clip was burned out, smoke curling out the muzzle, Schwarz looking strangely whacked, as if he wished he could bring Lake's diced frame back to life and shoot him again.

"Gadgets?" He nodded at Blancanales to cover his rear, just in case Lake had spun out some con job about his hardforce's numbers. "Schwarz!"

Easing closer, Lyons wasn't sure how to take the moment, as the thousand-yard stare slowly melted out of Schwarz's eyes.

"Yeah."

"You all right, Gadgets?"

Lyons sensed it next, the man coming back, whole again, as if some monster of burden, shackled on his shoulders, had just been unchained and set free.

"Better now."

"I can imagine. With you there."

Lyons stood by his friend, gave Lake a look, felt some inflation of relief himself. He recalled Lake's performance in the tavern, that devil's chuckle still echoing in his memory.

"I keep thinking he's going to get up."

Lyons shook his head, looked back and saw Blancanales moving in to check on the hostages. "It's over, Gadgets. I can guarantee the guy's gonna stay down. Let's get out of here."

James Axler
Outlanders®

SUN LORD

In a fabled city of the ancient world, the neo-gods of Mexico are locked in a battle for domination. Harnessing the immutable power of alien technology and Earth's pre-Dark secrets, the high priests and whitecoats have hijacked Kane into the resurrected world of the Aztecs. Invested with the power of the great sun god, Kane is a pawn in the brutal struggle and must restore the legendary Quetzalcoatl to his rightful place—or become a human sacrifice....

Available May 2004 at your favorite retail outlet.